HAUNTINGS IN NEW ENGLAND

HAUNTINGS IN
NEW
ENGLAND

Richard Rezendes

HAUNTINGS IN
NEW ENGLAND

CONTENTS

ONE

HAUNTINGS IN NEWPORT

The Salve Cliff House used to belong to Salve Regina University. The property had been vacant for more than 20 years near the Cliff Walk, on the Salve Regina campus. The building was sold because many students had complained of ghosts attacking them there. Paranormal investigators and priests had visited the property many times before a buyer bought the million-dollar mansion.

This mansion was closed off, surrounded by fences, gates, and no trespassing signs to keep people out. Once in a while, students on campus jumped the fences late at night to enter the property, and they got a rude awakening.

One night before Halloween, about five Salve students jumped the fence and broke into the mansion on a stormy night looking for ghosts—three women and two men. One girl threw a rock through a window to get in. The doors around the mansion were chain-locked. One of the students was picking the chain locks while the others went in through the broken window. A bolt of lightning struck the chain-picker and killed him.

The three girls were inside the mansion when suddenly part of the second floor collapsed on top of them, trapping all three under the rubble, and they screamed for help. The other man saw the floor coming down when the lightning flashed outside and yelled, "Watch out!" He escaped in time, or he would have been trapped himself.

A bright flash of lightning was followed by a loud bang. Suddenly, he heard his other buddy screaming outside when he was struck by lightning. He ran out of the broken window and saw his buddy lying dead on the ground. He quickly got on his phone and called 911. Lightning bolts were flying around him, and he was in a panic. The girls trapped were still screaming for help.

Newport Police, campus police, rescues, and a fire truck arrived. A wrecking crew cut a hole in the fence to get to the girls trapped in the mansion. Rescue workers tried doing CPR on the lightning victim but were unsuccessful.

"The man is dead. Put him in the rescue and take him to the hospital and see what they can do there," one rescue worker said to another.

Meanwhile, the caller had questions to answer.

"What's your name?" asked the police.

"My name is Erick Andrews."

"Come to the police car out of the rain. What were you doing here?"

"My friends and I climbed the fence to look for ghosts in the vacant mansion," he said.

"You saw signs all over the place—no trespassing and yellow police tape dominating the property—but you kids broke the law, and now you have a man dead and three girls trapped by falling debris. You are under arrest, and the other three girls will be too after they get medical treatment or after getting out of the hospital. You are to remain silent. Any words can be used against you in a court of law. You may hire a lawyer, and if you don't have one, we will get one for you. Do you understand these rights?"

"Yes, officer."

While Erick was being questioned by the police, the rescue team was working to free the girls in the mansion. The fire department and wrecking crew were moving the debris the girls were trapped under. One girl suffered a broken leg, the second girl broke her arm, and the third girl had a rusty nail driven between her ribs and a big shiner across her face and head.

A white shadow of a woman passed by, but no one saw it. Orb lights floated around the mansion after everyone left. The building had multiple ghosts inside.

The next day, a new fence with barbed wire was installed. The rescue workers identified the dead man. His name was Jimmy Pulaski. He had played basketball at Salve Regina.

The next day, papers read: *October 20th, 2020. One man dead and three hurt, breaking into mansion in Newport.*

The campus was quiet during the pandemic year, and students were looking for fun things to do. Days later, a meeting was held at the Salve Regina Gym.

"Good morning. My name is Sister Marie Martha Mayo, the Head of Students here at Salve Regina. On Tuesday evening, October 20th, 2020, five students broke into the old Salve Mansion, a vacant building under construction. I am sorry to say, Jimmy Pulaski was struck and killed by lightning, and three girls were hurt by falling debris. Erick Andrews reported the tragedy before being arrested by police.

"There had been several break-ins on this property, which no longer belonged to the university. As of right now, anyone caught breaking into the mansion again will be expelled from Salve Regina. Years ago, students were haunted by ghosts when the mansion was a dorm, a women's sorority—'Phi Kappa Sigma.' The White Lady was a mean entity that would get into your body to stop you from breathing and throw things at you, affecting people's ability to sleep at night.

"The rest of the campus will get emails from me. Thank you,

and enjoy your day. And don't forget to wear your mask while on campus."

A year later a buyer had bought the property at the old Salve Mansion, planning to make a bed & breakfast out of the facility. Olympic Builders had purchased the property. The mansion was still fenced in, now with barbed wire tops like at a jail and chain-locked gates. The mansion was heavily guarded by police 24/7 since the break-ins the previous year.

The campus police met with the new buyers outside the main gate.

"Good morning. Officer Glenn Joel, campus police, Salve Regina."

"Hi, my name is Leo Davies, and this is my partner, Jennifer Strings, from Olympic Builders."

"Pleased to meet you. Before I open these gates, I want to warn you that this mansion is haunted by multiple ghosts. I have a priest coming to bless the property. In the future, before the grand opening, I would suggest you hire a paranormal investigator. They have been here before with Catholic priests. When the priest gets here, I will open the main gate and let him in first to say prayers inside the mansion and around the closed-off areas."

"Officer Joel, has anyone been killed here?" asked Jennifer Strings from Olympic Builders.

"One person was killed last year breaking into the mansion. He was struck and killed by lightning. That's the only death we've had here, but many people have suffered injuries and been taken to the hospital. The ghost here is called the White Lady. She gets into your body and stops you from breathing. Other students reported seeing white orbs that looked like the moon flying around the room. Here's Father Harris," said the cop.

"Hi there. Father Richard Harris, the head chaplain priest of Salve Regina."

"Good morning, sir. My name is Leo Davies, and this is my partner, Jennifer Strings, from Olympic Builders."

"Pleased to meet you," said the priest.

The police opened the gate, letting the priest inside. After the priest blessed the property outside, police let him into the mansion. The inside had spider webs everywhere, rats running around, and bats flying from window to window.

"Be careful, Father. This place is very unstable," said the police.

When the priest was done, he came out and said, "I believe you have a lot more than a White Lady and flying orbs. This place is evil. You should be okay. I did a full blessing. If you have any problems, contact me at my email address—richardharris@gmail.com." Then the priest left.

The property owners worked on the property, and the mansion was opened for business in the summer of 2022, with no issues. Priests and paranormal investigators made frequent visits before the grand opening, cleaning out all the ghosts.

Friday, June 10th, 2022, was the grand opening of the Salve Cliff House Hotel. A ribbon-cutting ceremony was held at the main gate entrance. Many tourists visiting the mansions took a tour of the Salve Cliff Hotel. The tour started at 2 p.m.

"Good afternoon. My name is Jennifer Strings. I will be your tour guide showing you our lovely mansion. This area here is the main check-in desk. Go to the right and this is the breakfast and tea party room. A full breakfast was served seven days a week from 7 a.m. until 11 a.m. We had a tea party from 2 p.m. until 4 p.m. in this room. The room on the left side of the check-in desk was the restaurant. Lunch was served from noon till 3 p.m., and dinner was served from 5 p.m. until 9 p.m. We also had music and dancing from 9 p.m. till 1 a.m. The band tonight was the Amish Fish Heads, a heavy metal rock band. The kitchen was located behind the stage where the band played. Let's go through the restaurant and I will show you the kitchen. We have a very big kitchen here! Now let's go back to the lobby. Make a right at the breakfast and tea party room — the main lobby living facility. We have velvet and leather furniture, a six-foot-high fireplace, and a 65-foot flat-screen TV. Let's go up — this spiral staircase led to the rooms. We had bedrooms on the second and third floors with church-stained windows, chandeliers, and mahogany furniture. There were four bedrooms on each floor with two queen-size beds and a pull-out bed in each room, sleeping as many as six people. You have a bathroom in each room with a jacuzzi, shower, sink with gold faucets, and a toilet; shower storage included a pull-over robe. The rate was $175 a night during the week and $295 a night on the weekends. It was not cheap to stay here — we were in Newport in the summertime and it was a weekend. Let's go back downstairs and I will show you the basement. Down here we have the mile-long tunnel laundry room with 20 washers and 20 dryers. We have a meeting room that seated 100 people and a fireplace. Let's go upstairs and I will tell you the history of this mansion. After that I will show you outside and the gardens. Help yourselves to the coolers full of water.

"In 1444 this mansion was built, the second oldest in Newport, and the owner was Dik Suk, a multiple millionaire from Bangkok. In today's money, it would be in the billions. He lived until he was 111 years old and he owned this mansion for 88 years. He bought this property when he was 23 years old for $51,000. This mansion today was sold for $39,000,000. After Suk's passing 223 years later, Salve Regina, loan owner and then the university named after him bought the property and transformed this mansion into a sorority dorm for students at Salve Regina University. This building had been vacant for about 25 years before Olympic Builders bought the property last year and did a complete renovation, rebuilding this mansion and turning it into a bed & breakfast hotel. The name was Salve Cliff Bed & Breakfast Resort Hotel.

"This place had a dark side. We had a ghost here called the White Lady who rose from the ocean and haunted this mansion after being vacant so long since the 15th century. When it was a dorm, the students complained about seeing ghosts choking them in their sleep. Before Olympic Builders bought this property, priests and paranormal investigators came in to remove the ghosts. Since I had been here, I had never seen any ghosts or strange things going on. Let's go outside and I will show you the lush green gardens and property viewings. Out here we had a maze full of flowers and gardens overlooking the ocean and Cliff Walk. We did not have a pool but a shuttle would take you to First Beach/Easton's Beach. We had tennis and basketball courts out here. We had a tiki bar and a snack bar and tall oak trees surrounding the mansion. That concluded our tour. Check in if you may; if not, have a nice day."

Jennifer Strings, the tour guide, went back to the checkout desk.

Before dinner, just before 5 p.m., waitresses and waiters were putting glasses, dinner and salad plates, soup bowls, etc., on tables when suddenly a wine glass flew off a table and smashed against a wall. No one saw it, but someone heard the glass breaking.

A young waitress went into the restaurant/dining room to clean up the mess. Suddenly a dinner plate flew off a table all by itself, crashing into a wall near a window out of her view. Now she had another mess to clean up. She yelled, "Hey! Who's breaking dishes?" Suddenly a table tipped over on its own, throwing glass and dishes everywhere, sliding across the floor and breaking into pieces as she watched in shock, screaming, "AHHH! We have some kind of activity here!" she cried.

Other help came out to assist with the cleanup, and the strange happenings stopped. The time was 5:02 p.m. The young waitress ran out into the lobby crying. "We have a ghost in the dining room — breaking dishes and glasses flying off tables and knocking tables over. I saw it with my own eyes!"

Jennifer Strings at the checkout desk was stunned, standing with her mouth wide open. "Close the restaurant and get out of the kitchen. I'll call the priest," she said.

The priest came and said, "I don't feel there's a ghost here. I will bless the dining room and kitchen. What may have happened is that the activity from the broken glass flying around may have made the entity mad, but because guests were moving in, it chased the entity out. After it happened, it stopped. If a ghost had been here to stay, it would still be here. When I came to bless the dining room, nothing was there. Keep me posted if any more strange things happen."

The other owner, Leo Davies, said, "I don't believe in ghosts; I've heard many ghost stories before. I think the hauntings in the dining room have something to do with the Earth's magnetic field. When air mixes with water by the ocean, it sometimes causes things to move, lift up in the air, and toss things around, and suddenly it stops on a dime. I believe it's air pressure coming off the ocean. There's no such thing as ghosts. Until I see something, I will not believe in ghosts."

"There is such a thing as ghosts!" the priest insisted before he left the mansion. Leo Davies laughed, then went to the bar to get a drink and a sandwich before returning to the front desk. Some people were checking in.

About 8:30 p.m., the band was setting up equipment in the nightclub when a black mass with arms and hands reaching out of it — like it was trying to grab something — crawled on the ceiling and then disappeared. No one saw it. The bartender was a woman getting bottles from the back room to set up the bar. A dark black shadow followed her, but she did not see it. After she was setting up, the black shadow went into the back room, into a heating unit, and vanished.

A customer came in to order a drink just before 9 p.m. "Good evening, miss. Could I have a Hennessy on the rocks?" The bartender poured the drink and the glass moved away from the customer; he had to grab the glass before it fell on the floor. The bottle slid across the bar and the bartender grabbed it before it slid off the bar. "Holy shit! Did you see that?" said the customer. "Yes, sir. We have something going on here!" said the bartender.

The strange happenings stopped, but the customer and the bartender were stunned. Later, more people came in and the Amish Fish Heads began playing. The bartender called the front desk, and Leo Davies answered the phone. "Carla, there's no such thing as ghosts — the Earth's magnetic field is acting up due to water and air pressure blowing off the ocean, causing things to move. Dishes and glass broke in the dining room earlier today. It's like getting a strong thunderstorm or a tornado; we're dealing with a high-pressure clear-weather storm. It comes and goes quickly and it's over! Don't be scared."

Carla was the bartender, and the strange happenings stopped for the rest of the night because the club was crowded. Leo went into his office and then heard a voice behind the check-in desk: "Get out!" Then guests began arriving and he greeted them.

The time was 11:02 p.m. on Friday night. His shift ended at midnight, and the night person at the desk was a Black man whose name tag read Marvels Marvin. It was 12:02 a.m. on Saturday morning. Leo was getting ready for bed and looked at the alarm clock; the time was 12:34 a.m. He went into the bathroom to shave. While looking in the mirror, his eyes started getting bloodshot, his ears moved, and his nose turned black. After he finished shaving, his face expanded up and down, then widened ear to ear, and his salt-and-pepper hair turned black as the ace of spades. His neck seemed to breathe side to side. When he turned his head and looked back at the mirror, his face and hair were back to normal. He said to himself, "Something must be wrong with my eyes. I need to see the eye doctor." Then he stripped down and took a shower. He washed his hair and face, rinsing in the shower. When he started washing his body, blood poured out of the shower head all over him. He quickly turned the shower off and was covered in blood.

"What the fuck is going on with this shower?" he said to himself. The blood on his body began turning blue. He turned the shower back on and it was normal. He finished washing himself and the blue and red color disappeared as soon as he turned the shower back on. It was 1:02 a.m. He dried off, put his PJs on, and went to bed. He looked at the alarm clock; it was 1:12 a.m. He lay down to sleep, but then he heard a faint voice waking him: "Get out!"

He looked at the alarm clock; it was 2:02 a.m. He heard people talking in the lobby. The owner had a private apartment in the back of his office behind the front desk. He looked around his bedroom and then went back to bed. By about 2:30 a.m., the mansion was quiet. Then Leo woke up hearing a loud scream. It was 3:02 a.m.

"I guess I'm not getting any fucking sleep tonight!" he muttered. He went to the front desk and asked the night person, "Marvels, did you just hear that loud scream?"

"No, sir. It's been quiet."

"I must be dreaming," Leo said, and then he went back to bed.

He woke again to what sounded like flowing water. He saw what looked like black mud dripping down the walls and ceiling; the room flooded with this liquid mud and smelled like the dead. He turned on a lamp and the room was normal, the smell gone. He checked the clock; it was 4:02 a.m. He thought, this is not a dream — I am seeing something evil here. He turned the lamp off and waited to see what happened next.

Marvels was playing games on his phone when he suddenly felt breath at the back of his head. When he turned around, no one was there. It was 5:02 a.m. Leo went to the lobby to talk with Marvels.

"Were you just blowing on my neck trying to scare me, Marvels?" Leo asked.

"No — not at all. But something strange was going on here in this mansion. I don't believe in ghosts, but the experience I'd had this evening made me wonder. I once thought the Earth's magnetic field might be acting up. But the strange things that happened to me tonight made me think otherwise. When I was shaving before my shower, my face made strange blurry shapes in the mirror. I thought my eyes were playing tricks on me. Then in the shower, blood came out of the shower head. I turned it off and back on and it went back to normal, and I finished the shower. Later I heard a loud scream, then the sound of water like a river. I saw black mud flowing down the walls and ceiling and spreading across the floor toward my bed. I wasn't dreaming — when I turned the lamp on, it stopped. Then after 5 a.m. we heard glass breaking in the lobby. A large flower vase fell and broke on the floor. We watched the flowers, glass, and water move across the floor and into the fireplace. I was so damn scared I thought I was having a heart attack." Leo said.

A flower vase suddenly jumped off a table and broke on the floor. It was 6:02 a.m. Marvels and Leo went to investigate after hearing the glass break. The vase had broken into pieces. When they went to the lobby, the flowers from the broken vase had slid along the hardwood floor into the fireplace and the water had followed the flowers into the fireplace. The floor dried up as if nothing had happened while Leo and Marvels watched.

"This is fucked up! Do we have a ghost here or is the Earth's magnetic field going crazy? Marvels, I want you to call Fr. Richard Harris to come and do a blessing. Something is happening that I can't understand. I'm going back to bed. Jennifer Strings will be coming in at 8 a.m. for her shift," Leo said. He went back to bed with the lights on.

A few guests came down for breakfast a few minutes before 7. A girl put a muffin in the microwave when suddenly the microwave door flew open and her muffin went flying across the room and landed on the floor. It was 7:02 a.m. The guests screamed. The microwave door closed by itself. The guests grabbed what food they could and ate it cold, then ran out of the breakfast room in a hurry. The girl went to the front desk; Marvels was on the phone with the priest. When he got off the phone, the girl laughed and said, "Sir, we have a ghost or something in the food lounge! I put a muffin in the microwave and the door flung open and my muffin flew out and landed on the floor!"

"Don't worry — a priest is coming to bless the hotel. Some strange things are happening here," Marvels said. The girl went back to her room.

Another woman came to the front desk to check out.

"Good morning," said Marvels.

"Good morning, sir. I'm checking out early because there's a ghost here. I couldn't sleep — I was told to get out and I watched a white mist and bright lights flying over my bed. Please credit my card. I'm out of here!"

"Sure, Miss Colleen Bowls. We do have strange things going on here. A priest is on his way and hopefully he will get rid of the hauntings. Before you leave, there's free continental breakfast in the lounge."

"No, sir — I'm fucking out of here!" she snapped.

"Good morning. Salve Cliff House Bed & Breakfast, Marvels Marvin speaking."

"Good morning, Marvels. I am Fr. Richard Harris. I will be by about 9:30 to bless the mansion."

"Thank you, Father," Marvels replied.

Jennifer Strings arrived for her shift. "Good morning, Marvels. How was your first night?" she asked.

"It was very interesting. The hotel is haunted with ghosts. You were right — this place is spooky. I didn't believe you when you hired me, but I'm a believer now."

"Let me check into my office and I'll go over what happened during the night." Jennifer put her pocketbook down and got ready to start her shift, 8 a.m. to 4 p.m. Then she heard a voice in the office: "Get out!"

"No! You get out — white trash, in Jesus' name!" she answered. It was 8:02 a.m. The voice continued, "Get out!" Jennifer kept shouting, "You get out!" The voice stopped a minute later.

"Jennifer, Father Harris will be here about 9:30 to do a blessing," Marvels said.

"Did you hear the 'get out' screams in my office, Marvels?" Jennifer asked.

"No, but I heard you screaming to tell it to go away. I heard the 'get out' voices during the night, and Leo and I witnessed a vase break in the Salve lobby and watched the flowers and water wash into the fireplace and disappear. Leo was up all night. Marvels, have a good day — sleep well, and hope tonight will be better."

Suddenly Jennifer heard a big crash in the lobby. It was 9:02 a.m. She went to check the loud bang, found nothing, and returned to the office to wait for the priest. The priest arrived at 9:30 a.m.

"Good morning, Fr. Harris."

"Good morning, Jennifer."

"We've been getting strange things happening here," Jennifer said. "I just heard a loud bang and when I went to investigate, nothing was out of place. A woman checked out early this morning complaining she saw a ghost in her room. The night person and I heard voices saying 'Get out!' I told the voice, 'You get out!' but the voice kept telling me to get out!" she said.

"Good morning, Fr. Harris. You're right — something was here that I couldn't explain. I never believed in ghosts. I thought the Earth's magnetic field was acting up, moving things: dishes and glass falling off counters, bottles and drinks sliding off the bar and throwing things against the wall. But last night, before I went to bed, I was shaving and looking in the mirror and the mirror went blurry. My face changed — expanding up and down, side to side — my eyes turned red, my ears moved, my nose went black, and I looked like I was turning into some kind of animal, a wolf or something. I thought my eyes were playing tricks on me because my vision goes off once in a while. I turned my head after finishing shaving and I looked like I had a big head and big ears. When I turned back to the mirror, everything was normal. Then in the shower, blood poured out of the shower head and covered me. The blood turned blue. I turned the shower off and on, the water came back normal and washed the blood off. It all lasted a minute. About an hour later I kept hearing very soft voices telling me to get out. Then about 3 a.m. I heard the loudest definitive scream waking me from sleep. I went to the front desk and asked Marvels if he heard the scream; he said no. These hauntings, or whatever you call them, seem to happen two minutes after the hour. An hour later I woke to the sound of flowing water and saw black mud dripping down the walls and ceiling onto me. The mud covered the floor and worked its way up my bed. I watched in the dark with only a night light on. I turned on a lamp and whatever I saw disappeared. The clock read 4:02 a.m.; when I turned the lamp on the display switched to 4:03. All this lasted one minute, and as soon as I turned the lamp on, it was over. Then after 5 a.m. we heard glass breaking in the lobby. Marvels and I went out and saw a large flower vase full of water fell and broke on the floor. We watched the flowers, glass, and water move across the floor and into the fireplace. I was so goddamn scared I thought I was having a heart attack," Leo said.

"Oh my goodness, sir, you shouldn't use those bad words! Say 'oh my God' without the F-bombs," the priest admonished.

"Oh — I'm so embarrassed. I didn't realize I used bad language in front of a priest. I am so sorry!" Leo said.

"You're forgiven, Mr. Davies. When you bought this property you understood there was some kind of evil here. Catholic priests and paranormal teams have been coming for years trying to remove the evil from this mansion, but it does not want to leave. What I'm going to do is bring the chaplain of Salve Regina in to do a three-day exorcism beginning Thursday through Saturday. You have to close this mansion so we can do the work. If the exorcism does not work, you will have to hire a professional paranormal team. If that doesn't work, you will have to leave before someone gets killed," Fr. Richard Harris said.

"Father, did you just see that? A white mist passed along the ceiling — now it's coming toward us!" Leo exclaimed.

"I see it, Leo, and it's starting to fade. I will bless the mansion in every room and the property outside one more time and I hope the hauntings will slow down. Until the exorcism is done, and unless things get physical or worse, you have to leave. If you see little things — hauntings not threatening at two minutes after every hour — say this prayer: 'Go away in the name of Jesus Christ.' You may have to repeat that prayer several times for one minute," the priest advised. The time of the vision was 10:02 a.m.

"Let me pray and sprinkle holy water in your apartment and at the check-in counter first," the priest said.

After the priest finished, Leo went to his room to get some sleep. He was on the clock from 4 p.m. until midnight. Jennifer was on the day shift.

The priest was going through the mansion saying prayers and throwing holy water in the rooms when suddenly the cross he was wearing started choking him. He was able to pull the cross from his neck until it broke off. The time was 11:02 a.m.

One hour later he saw smoke coming out of the lobby fireplace. He said prayers and threw holy water inside the fireplace until the smoke mist vanished. The time was 12:02 p.m., Saturday afternoon.

At 1:02 p.m. a voice told Jennifer to get out, and a black mist went by the front desk. Jennifer kept telling it to leave until it disappeared one minute later, and the "get out" voice stopped.

Leo was having a nap when suddenly he heard a baby crying in his bedroom. He got up to check it out and found nothing. He went back to lay down. He had the lights on in the apartment in the mansion in case he saw something evil. The time was 2:02 p.m. when Leo, the property owner, heard the baby cries.

A tour group of about twenty people came to tour the mansion. They got off a bus and met in the lobby when suddenly the damper in the fireplace flung open with a noise so loud it scared the shit out of the tourists waiting to view the mansion. Then soot poured out of the fireplace with a roar so evil, covering everyone in the place, and it kept pouring out of the fireplace, filling the room in black. The time was 3:02 p.m.

The tour ran out of the mansion like a bat out of hell, screaming. Jennifer saw the black soot mist flying around the lobby, and the lobby was so dark it looked like nighttime. The soot mist flew back into the fireplace and up the chimney, and the damper shut. It only took a minute for all this to happen. When the tourists ran out of the mansion, the soot mist blew off them. Jennifer went out to see if everyone was all right. The lobby was clean like nothing had happened — in one minute.

Leo got up to relieve Jennifer. The priest was outside blessing the property. Jennifer told him what happened as she was leaving, and then she told Leo. The priest went in to say prayers and threw holy water again inside the fireplace. Then he said to Leo:

"I think the hauntings may finally leave this place when the mist of evil flew out of the fireplace attacking the Mansfield Family guest tour. As long as nobody got hurt, thank God! All the mansion and property have been fully blessed and you should be all right now. If the hauntings continue, keep saying the one-minute prayer like I told you before. If the evil leaves or not, I will see you on Thursday for the exorcism."

Then the priest left.

Leo went outside to check the grounds and saw the branches and leaves moving in some of the big trees. "Man, that's strange," he said to himself. The time was 4:02 p.m. when the evil made the tree branches and leaves move. It all stopped a minute later.

Then Leo went back inside and to the front desk. People were checking in. Waitresses, waiters, and the bartender were getting

16

ready to open the restaurant dining room for dinner just before 5 p.m. Then a table was set up for twenty guests when suddenly the tablecloth flew from under all the dishes and glass on the table, and everything fell on the floor and broke. Then the large table flipped over and slid up against the bar and kitchen, blocking the exits. Dishes and glasses went flying, breaking and throwing up against the wall. It only took one minute for all this damage to happen. The time was 5:02 p.m., as soon as the restaurant opened, when this happened.

All the kitchen help and bartenders were screaming and finding a place to hide because of flying dinner plates and wine glasses. The priest came back to bless the restaurant and dining room.

Two women arrived to check into the mansion. One lady said to the other, "Jean, look at the fireplace — it's huge and very scary looking!" Then they heard a voice:

"Get out!"

Then it got louder:

"Get out!!"

They heard it again, much louder:

"Get out!!!!!!!!!!!!!!!!!!"

It was so evil.

"Colleen, let's get out of here. We're not staying here!" Jean said, and the ladies left. The time was 6:02 p.m. The restaurant was closed for the evening.

Then a storm came with lightning flashing around the mansion and thunder roaring loud. The time was 7:02 p.m. The rain came down hard, flooding outside, then the power went out. The time was 8:02 p.m.

One hour later the power came back on at 9:02 p.m. and the rain stopped and the storm was over. The generators had come on when the mansion lost power. During the power outage black shadows were flying around the lobby ceiling like witches flying. Between 8:02 and 9:03 p.m. the ghost shadows vanished.

Leo was walking through the mansion lobby and saw white and yellow orb lights flying above the fireplace. The time was 10:02 p.m. A bright white mist appeared, and the lights followed, flying in circles around the ceiling and vanishing a minute later.

Leo said, "You must leave this place in the name of Jesus Christ, amen. The priest told you to leave. I am the owner of this mansion and you have to leave!!!!!!!!!"

One hour later Leo was watching a football game on the flatscreen TV in the lobby when suddenly he saw the orb lights again above the fireplace.

"Hey! Didn't I tell you to leave? Get out of here now! In Jesus' name, amen."

The time was 11:02 p.m. The orb lights dropped down and went in the fireplace and disappeared. Leo kept watching the game on TV until Marvels came in for the night shift.

"Good evening, Leo. Who's winning the game?"

"It's tied 31 to 31 in overtime."

"Who's playing?"

"It's UCLA against Washington. Marvels, it was a very bad day today and a lot of evil is happening and it's not leaving. I keep seeing orbs and mist flying around here in the lobby. There was an attack in the restaurant with tables, chairs, dishes, and glasses thrown around the dining room like missiles, trapping the help. I had to close the restaurant tonight again. The band Radio Badlands tour was canceled because of the damage in the club. We had a bad storm and lost power for about an hour. A group tour arrived around 3 p.m. to view the mansion and check in, meeting in the lobby, and while they were waiting something exploded in the fireplace. The damper popped open and soot — a black mist — poured out, attacking the tour guests, covering them in this shit, chasing them out. They boarded the bus and left. Fr. Richard Harris was here all day blessing the property. He witnessed the fireplace exploding. I went out to check the grounds. I knew we were getting a storm this evening and I was checking all the benches and making sure the gates were closed and locked except the main gate. I saw the trees and leaves moving and blowing around, and there was no wind blowing.

"Marvels, I never believed in ghosts, but until I see it for real I will not believe. However, what I have seen, I do believe in evil spirits. But I have not seen a figure with a face, eyes, mouth, or a person from the dead. Yes, I'm frightened, but these visions have not hurt me. The spirits seem to show themselves at two minutes after every hour. It's strange! But it's very annoying when they keep waking you up and you can't sleep! Are these spirits from the dead? I don't know. I still believe it's something to do with the Earth's magnetic field. According to Fr. Harris, he says they're ghosts and this mansion is possessed by the devil. Have a good night and be careful. It's 12:09 a.m. I didn't see if anything else happened," Leo said.

Leo and the night person Marvels watched football games on TV until 2 a.m. Then Leo went to bed. 1:02 a.m., 2:02 a.m., the mansion was quiet.

"Marvels, it's after 2 a.m. and nothing happened. I hope the orb lights and white mist finally left, taking the evil spirits with them. Good night," Leo said.

Leo washed up at the sink and looked at the alarm clock. The time was 3:11 a.m. It was quiet. He left the bathroom door partly open to have a little light in case he saw something in the room. Then he fell asleep. The time was 3:25 a.m.

At 4:02 a.m. Leo woke to a rotten stench of death.

Suddenly, a black mist appeared, crawling along the ceiling. A big black arm with clawed fingers pinned him down on the bed so he couldn't move, clawing his chest and leaving streaks of blood. A second hand came out of the mist, choking him so he could not move, scream, or do anything! Then the mist formed the face of the devil with big horns, bright red eyes, and it opened its mouth, showing vampire-like shark teeth and pointy ears. It started blow-ing a red mist on him that smelled like death!

Four or five more hands came out of the black mist, filling the room with evil. The hands dug into his ribs, pulled him out of bed, and threw him onto the floor against a wall. Finally, he let out a scream!

Marvels went to his room, turning on the lights in the apart-ment where Leo lived in the back of the main counter. He quickly ran to Leo's bedroom, turned on the light, and the mist-creature devilish-looking monster vanished! When Marvels got to him, the room was dark and misty, then brightened like nothing had hap-pened. Marvels found Leo on the floor pinned against the wall, then helped him up.

"Marvels, I was just attacked by a devil ghost! I'm out of here. I have to go to a motel for the rest of the night. I will not be coming in tomorrow. Check everyone out in the morning and don't check anyone in. If you want, you can go to the rooms that checked in and tell them to leave. Make sure everyone is out, then close the mansion and lock all the gates. We're closed until priests come to do the three-day exorcism! It's 5:15 a.m. now. Do not go inside my apartment and watch your back."

"Leo, what did this devil look like?"

"I can't explain it right now. I just want to get out of here before I get killed!" said Leo Davies, and he left the mansion.

About three rooms had checked in, and Marvels went to each room asking them to leave, beginning at 6 a.m.

"Are you the Angel family of five?"

"Yes. Why are you bothering us at six in the morning?" a woman said.

"We have a poltergeist attacking people in the hotel, and I don't want to see anyone get hurt or killed. Come down to the lobby and I'll refund your stay," said Marvels.

Then he called the other customers on the phone while checking out the Angel family.

"Hi, Mr. Danny Valley. This is Marvels Marvin at the front desk. I hate to disturb you at six in the morning, but an evil poltergeist attacked one of our employees, and I would like you and your family to come down and check out before someone else gets hurt or killed. I will refund your stay. Sorry for the inconvenience."

They came down to check out. Then Marvels got everyone out of the mansion, locked up, and left the property, locking the front gate.

Jennifer got a call on her loud cell phone. The time was 7:02 a.m.

"Jennifer, Leo Davies. Don't go into work at the mansion. I was attacked by a devilish poltergeist in my bed about four this morning. Just after 3 a.m., I went to bed only to wake up to the smell of death! I saw this black mist with hands and arms coming down. It choked me, left scratch marks on my chest and stomach, and a bunch of black arms with claws pinched me in the ribs, holding me down in my bed so I couldn't move, scream, or do anything! Then the head of the devil appeared, opened its mouth showing fangs like shark teeth! It had bright red eyes blinding my vision, then it spewed up a red and pink liquid mist in my face that smelled like rotten death! It had pointy ears and a pointy nose. Then it pulled me right out of bed, covers and all, and threw me on the floor, pinning me up against the wall! I was able to let out a loud scream, and Marvels heard me and came in to rescue me! I told him to get everyone out and leave the mansion, then lock the front gate until the priests arrive Thursday morning."

"Jesus, Mary, and Joseph, Leo! I bet you believe in ghosts now! Are you alright?" said Jennifer Strings.

"Yes, I'm okay, I just have three scratch marks but they're not bleeding, thank God. I called the priest and told him what happened, and he told me to close the mansion and get out of there until he comes next weekend. I told Marvels Marvin to get everyone out and lock up," said Leo.

Everyone showed up at the mansion early Thursday morning at daybreak, 6:30 a.m. Leo opened the front gate and the main entrance to the mansion. Leo, Jennifer, Marvels, and the Salve Regina Chaplain Catholic team with Father Richard Harris and a paranormal investigating team were there to help with the exorcism.

That night, a couple was having dinner at the LaForge Restaurant on Bellevue Avenue in Newport. A white mist was flying along the ceiling.

"Jimmy, what's that smoke crawling along the ceiling?"

"I have no idea, Debbie," said Jimmy.

The couple continued talking while waiting for their server.

"Hi there, I'm Michael, your server for this evening. What are you having to drink?"

"I'll have a Grey Goose vodka martini, and she'll have a red wine," said Jimmy.

The waiter brought the drinks. "What are you having for dinner?"

"I want the sirloin steak, and she wants the chicken dinner," said Jimmy.

"What are you having for your sides?"

"I want a baked potato and mixed vegetables, and my wife Debbie wants string beans and sweet potato fries. Thank you," said Jimmy.

"The meals come with a house salad," said Michael.

"Sir, what was that white fog flying around the ceiling earlier?" asked Debbie.

"I don't know. It could be food smoking."

Then Michael went to the kitchen to get the couple's dinners. A pan rolled off the stove by itself and fell on the floor, white chowder spilling everywhere. The gas flame went out.

"Richard and Debra, there's an accident in the kitchen—a pan full of chowder fell on the floor!" said Michael.

Michael brought the salads to the couple, then went back to the kitchen to get the dinners. Kitchen help was cleaning up the mess when they smelled gas and shut the stove off.

Jimmy grabbed the steak knife and began cutting into his steak. Blood poured out of the meat and squirted all over him! His martini tipped over by itself, spilling the drink, and the glass broke on the table. Debbie's chicken dinner lifted off the table and struck her in the face. The meat, sweet fries, and vegetables went all over her as her wine spilled. The glass flew off the table and smashed against a wall!

Debbie screamed, "AHHH!"

Jimmy was stunned, watching the horror unfold! Michael saw what was happening as he came out with a tray of dinners and drinks. The remaining customers saw the haunting and ran out of the restaurant. Michael put the tray down as help arrived to clean up Jimmy and Debbie.

Meanwhile, in the Irish Room next door, a bartender grabbed a bottle of Hennessy to pour for a customer. The bottle slid by itself on the bar. The bartender caught it before it fell, but the glass flew off the bar and smashed against the wall. The customer walked out!

Kitchen help was preparing meals when suddenly pots and pans fell, dishes flew off counters like missiles, and food went everywhere. Dishes and glasses flew off racks and carts, breaking all over! The help ran out screaming:

"Help! Evil is in the kitchen!"

Jimmy said to his waiter: "Michael, I hope you don't expect me to pay for this after what happened!"

"No, sir. You and your wife will get a free meal the next time you come. Go to Spring Cleaners to wash your clothes—on us. I don't know what's going on, because nothing like this has happened here before!" said Michael.

Then a fire started in the kitchen, and the Newport Fire Department was called. The restaurant was closed down.

Newspapers read: *Evil Spirits Attack a Restaurant as Part of the Newport Series of Hauntings.*

Fr. Harris was called with a paranormal team to get rid of the ghost at the LaForge Restaurant.

The Newport Police and Salve Regina Campus Police were investigating a lot of noises at the former De La Salle High School, which now belongs to Salve Regina University. The building was being used as a storage area for maintenance workers and custodians to get supplies and store orders. A poltergeist was hiding inside, appearing whenever people came around. The police and campus police entered the locked building to see what was going on; they searched in every room and found nothing.

A bunch of dead bodies' bones were laid under a heavy compacting unit. The bones had been there for years because the old school was built over an Indian burial ground, and the poltergeist was raising them from the graves.

Then the police and campus police left. One cop said to another, "Did you hear what happened at the La Forge Restaurant last night? Some kind of evil is rising from the dead here in Newport. The Salve Cliff Mansion has a poltergeist haunting the new bed-and-breakfast resort, the Cliff Walk is collapsing, and people are being killed. Now we keep getting calls almost daily about loud noises and the smell of death at this building. In 1979, after De La Salle Academy closed, kids and tourists were breaking in and were never heard from again."

The other cop said, "I wouldn't be surprised if the evil is coming from under the ground, haunting these places. The devil, maybe."

Back at the mansion, after the exorcism was finished, it was open for business. "Leo, Adam Butler from Paranormal Investigators here. The exorcism and our paranormal team have finished our work. You had a poltergeist here from the devil. I don't know how it got here; maybe it's been coming from the center of the Earth for years and picked Newport to unleash its evil. We removed all the evil in this mansion, and this place is much brighter inside, and you should be okay. If the evil comes back, it will be a lot worse than ever! No professional help will assist you, and you will have to leave! Within the next two weeks, you will find out if the evil returns. If it doesn't, you're in good shape. But if it does, get out because it may kill you this time!" said the paranormal investigator.

The clergy left. "Leo, do not talk about what happened here. Just let it go and start a new life in this mansion. Crosses and statues of the Virgin Mary have been placed in every room. Don't tell customers or warn people about the hauntings because if you do, it may come back. If customers bring it up, tell them you don't want to talk about it. Good luck, and if you have any problems, you call me. Remember, keep your mouth shut and tell your help." Said Fr. Richard Harris as he left.

The mansion was quiet for now. At 11:02 p.m., Leo was watching the clock, and nothing happened. He was at the front desk. He looked at the clock again, and the time was 11:05 p.m. He felt safe. When he went to bed after his shift, he slept with the lights on.

Days later, construction workers were knocking down part of the old De La Salle and found hundreds of human bones and underground grave sites. All the spirits traveled in a white mist and settled in the basement of the Salve Cliff Mansion, where they stayed. The mansion had just been cleared with a powerful exorcism.

One worker said to another at the old De La Salle building, "Oh, my fucking God! Look here! Human bones and old grave sites!"

"Holy shit!" said the other workers.

The workers notified the police and the Salve Regina Campus Police.

"Jesus, Mary, and Joseph! Please come down from St. Peter's Gate to rescue all these poor souls buried under the old De La Salle before they travel to the Salve Cliff Mansion next door. In Jesus' name, call Fr. Harris!" said a campus police officer.

Then the same campus police officer started choking, had a heart attack, and dropped dead, collapsing over the grave site on top of a skull from, I guess, a missing person.

"Everyone, get away from the grave site before someone else dies!" said a Newport Police Officer. A rescue arrived to take the dead campus police officer to the hospital.

Fr. Harris and a few Catholic priests arrived with a paranormal team to perform an exorcism. The bones and the grave site were removed, and the old De La Salle building was knocked down. The bones and old grave sites were taken to the Rhode Island State Morgue in Cranston to be identified.

A few days later, a tour was visiting the mansion, and a few people from the tour went on the Cliff Walk to take pictures of the ocean and the buildings just off the Salve Cliff Mansion lawn. Suddenly, the cliff where people were standing gave way and collapsed into the ocean below, killing eight people. The rest of the tour, about twelve people, saw the ground give way and ran for cover back to the mansion.

The Newport Police, fire trucks, and rescues arrived. The mansion was evacuated again. Rescue helicopters and Coast Guard boats arrived to rescue the eight victims, who were pulled from the rocks, mud, and water; they were all dead. Fr. Harris was there with paranormal investigators, and they found no signs of evil activity and they left.

The ghosts of De La Salle were not active yet. They wanted to see the city by the sea and visit other grave sites before settling in the Salve Cliff Mansion basement.

A kite tournament was being held in Brenton Park. Around 9 a.m. on the same day the tour victims died at the Salve Cliff Mansion cliffs, a couple was arriving. The man saw a white mist coming in from the ocean and following their car to the loading site to launch the kites.

"Linda, look at this strange fog coming off the ocean. It looks like a ghost with black eyes, a nose, and a smiley mouth."

"Yeah, Henry, it looks like a thunderstorm might be coming. It's going to be a rainy day. Be careful; you have a big kite, and it's very windy outside right now."

The husband was getting the kite ready off a trailer hooked to the back of his car and wheeled it up to the loading site, pointing toward the ocean. The kite looked like a small airplane and was the size of one. The kite had a battery-operated propeller to give it that extra push when it was released.

"Ready for departure," said Henry. The wind took hold of the giant kite, and Henry was trying to hold it down to reset its position before launch. His wife or girlfriend was laughing. A crowd was cheering. Suddenly, the rope holding the kite wrapped around Henry, and the kite went airborne. Henry was left dangling from the rope, and the kite carried him out to sea for more than a mile. Henry tried to free himself and jump into the cold ocean, but he couldn't. A wind blowing from behind broke the kite apart. Henry disappeared out to sea in fifteen-foot waves, then a shark ate and killed him. His other half, Linda, went from laughing to screaming and crying when the giant kite took him away.

The time was 10:02 a.m. Coast Guard helicopters and rescue boats went looking for him. They found the damaged kite, then divers went in, searching for him where the kite went down until dusk but were unsuccessful.

During that same day, golfers were playing at the Newport National Golf Club after the sun returned after a rainy morning. The trees started moving as if they were coming alive. The leaves were spinning, turning, and falling off some of the trees. One man hit a ball, and it struck a tree; the ball ricocheted and hit the golfer in the head. He had to stop playing.

Later in the day, it clouded up, and rain was expected. Golfers were finishing up their game when suddenly thunder roared. Then a bolt of lightning struck a man dead as he was trying to make a putt. A second bolt struck a crowd watching, and a third bolt struck a cart carrying golfers back to the clubhouse. Another bolt struck a tree. The haunting storm began at 3:02 p.m. and all this action lasted only one minute, then it was over.

Several golfers were hurt. Rescues and helicopters arrived to take the dead golfer and the injured to the hospital. Other golfers continued playing until they finished.

The same day at dusk, ghosts went to visit Fort Adams State Park. Before it got dark, tourists and visitors were visiting by boat, bus, walking, and driving to see the Forts. When suddenly, strange things began to happen. A man ordered a hot dog from a food truck, and a seagull landed on his shoulder and took the hot dog from him and flew away.

"A seagull just took my hot dog!"

The man yelled! One lady saw a white mist flying, following her as she walked toward the forts. A fireball came flying out of one of the guns in the fort, striking a yacht and setting it on fire. People on the yacht had to jump into the water to get away! The mist landed in front of the lady, formed into the White Lady, and vanished! She said to a crowd of people walking, "Did anyone see that ghost?" People walking thought she was nuts. "I just saw the White Lady ghost that's been on the news lately," she said. The crowd ignored her and kept walking.

A boat coming into Fort Adams full of people sank offshore, and everyone ended up in the water. Later, the food truck was attacked by a bunch of aggressive seagulls, pecking and stealing food while the owner of the food truck was cooking. One man heard gunshots and blasts from cannons. The park had to be evacuated because so many hauntings were happening all at once. Police, fire trucks, and rescues came. Coast Guard boats came to rescue people in the water; others swam to shore. Then all the hauntings stopped.

It was beginning to get dark, and police were escorting everyone out of the park, using flashlights and floodlights from police boats so people could see where they were going. A greenish-white fog flew over Newport Harbor, flying over the boats into downtown, and vanished!

Back at Fort Adams, one man said to police, "Someone is firing the cannons, sinking boats and setting them on fire; they're going off everywhere!"

The National Guard arrived from Salve Regina to go through the fort to see who was firing the guns inside the fort, searching for hours and finding nothing. The National Guard troops said to police, "Nothing has been fired from these cannons; they're all plugged up and can't fire! The gun fire is coming from somewhere else! Somebody may have gone in the forts, firing a big gun to do damage like this."

Police said to the troops, "A man witnessed cannon #4 shoot a fireball, striking the Mason's Yacht, setting it on fire and sinking. Another boat out at sea was struck by gunfire or a rocket!"

"That's impossible because you can't fire these cannons. We spent hours taking them apart; they're all fake. A sniper must have been on the roof or managed to break into the fort, firing a big gun or rocket launcher," said the National Guard.

The park was closed off with police tape. A man was found dead in the camping area. A dead shark washed up on Fort Adams Beach. The military was called in, looking for the shooter and policing the fort all night. The time was 10:02 p.m.

THE NEWS: "Good evening; we have breaking news from Newport. A bunch of strange happenings in Newport today leading to several deaths and injuries. We begin at the Cliff Walk on the Salve Regina campus earlier today when the cliff gave way, and eight people from a tour visiting the Salve Cliff Mansion were presumed dead. A man at the Brenton Park Kite Festival was taken out to sea when he was trapped by the kite he was launching, and he was tangled in the rope. His body was never found when the Coast Guard rescue found the downed kite. Two men were killed after being struck by lightning at the Newport National Golf Club. Police in Fort Adams National Park found a dead man in a camping area. Several people were injured when gunfire or rocket launchers struck boats, sinking them and setting them on fire. Visitors in the park witnessed cannons from the fort firing fireballs at the boats. According to the National Guard, snipers on the roof may have caused all the damage. Lisa Storm reporting on WJAR Channel 10 News in Newport."

We continue our story in Newport. Several people are reporting strange things and ghosts haunting hotels and mansions. Witnesses the other night reported strange evil at the La Forge Restaurant and seeing a ghost in the Tennis Hall of Fame next door. Workers at the restaurant reported plates, glasses, pots, pans, and kitchenware flying around, striking the walls. Food flew everywhere, and stoves were turned on until the restaurant caught fire and was forced to close.

These hauntings began after the old De La Salle High School, which now belongs to Salve Regina, was under construction and hundreds of human bones were found and the rest of the building had to be destroyed. The human bones were removed and taken to the Rhode Island State Morgue in Cranston. WJAR News 10 reporting.

Tourists visiting the mansions had their last stop at the Tennis Hall of Fame, and there were several visions of ghosts there, black shadows that looked like the devil! The White Lady and gray and green mist flew above them, followed by a cold, fast-blowing wind. After several complaints there and more strange things happening at the La Forge Restaurant, the Salve Regina clergy priests and a paranormal team had to come in and clean up the evil.

Back at the Salve Cliff Mansion, it reopened in mid-November 2022. After the eight people were lost in early October, the mansion was quiet, and a Christmas tree was set up and decorated on each side of the fireplace. "Open for business, happy holidays, and no more ghosts!" one man said while checking in. The same crew was back working at the mansion, and there were no hauntings.

On December 11, 2022, strange things began to happen at the mansion again. All the students were gone from the Salve Regina Campus for winter vacation, and Newport was quiet. Not many people or tourists were checking into the mansion because of its past history, but it was getting a little better because the holidays were coming.

Tuesday, December 13, 2022, a custodian was washing floors in the basement, and maintenance was fixing a leak in the basement. The custodian was dipping the mop in the mop bucket and walked up to the other end of the mansion's basement, washing the floor and making his way back to the mop bucket, and it was not there. He looked at his watch, and the time was 9:02 a.m. The mop bucket was in another room. The custodian questioned the maintenance worker, "Henry, did you move my mop bucket?"

"No, Scott, I did not!" Then the custodian grabbed the mop bucket, and he went back to finish washing the floor. Then he swept and washed the room where he found the missing mop bucket. When he started washing the room, the mop bucket disappeared again! When the custodian washed his way back to the bucket, it was not there! He went looking for it again, and it was in the middle of a wet floor he had previously washed.

The maintenance worker was fixing a leaking pipe when suddenly he saw a black shadow zip right past him! He looked at his watch, and the time was 10:02 a.m. He continued working after a brief break. The custodian came over to him, and he said, "Henry, something strange is going on down here. I don't believe in ghosts, but I was washing the conference room, and I placed the mop bucket in the library, and when I returned, it disappeared again. I found it in the middle of the hall I just washed!"

"Scott, you're right. I saw something! I saw a black shadow go by me while I was working. I believe in ghosts, and this place is haunted. If you don't believe, you better think again!"

Then the custodian finished what he was doing, and he put the bucket in the custodian room. While he was rinsing out the mop, he heard a voice, "Get out!" He went up to the front desk and he said, "Jennifer, do we have ghosts here? My mop bucket is playing games, disappearing from me downstairs, and I heard voices telling me to get out in the custodian room, and it's only me in there?"

"This mansion was haunted for years, but the Catholic Priest and a paranormal team got rid of them a couple of months ago. I hope it's not coming back. I will take your report and tell Leo when he comes in at 4 p.m.," said Jennifer.

On December 15, 2022, a Friday night, people were checking in for tomorrow night's Christmas party in the lobby lounge.

"Good afternoon, Mrs. Strings. My wife and I would like to check in for the weekend because we will be going to the Christmas party tomorrow night. My name is Earl Bayside, and my wife is Evelyn."

"Yes, you have one free night, and the balance is $600," said Jennifer.

The couple checked into their room, and the bellhop brought them their luggage. Evelyn looked at the alarm clock in the room, and the time was 4:02 p.m. Jennifer left for the day, and Leo Davies checked in for his shift. When Jennifer was leaving, it was raining hard and flooding.

The couple went for dinner. They had swordfish, a few drinks, apple pie, and coffee. Then they went to the lounge to sit in front of the fireplace before going dancing later in the evening at the nightclub. Then they went to bed at about 1:30 a.m.

A big rain and wind storm was brewing outside while Earl and

Evelyn Bayside were sleeping in bed. The strong wind blew over a big oak tree, and it crashed through the window of their room. A big tree branch pinned both of them in the bed. A branch was driven right between Evelyn's breasts, pinning her against the headboard, and her blood was splattered all over the room. The rest of the big tree branch ripped Earl's stomach open, and his heart was pulled out of him, resting in a pool of blood. Both of them were killed.

People staying in the room below woke up to a loud crash, and blood and water were dripping down the walls in their room. They called the front desk, but no one was answering the phone.

Leo heard the crash of glass breaking, and he went out in the pouring rain and strong winds to investigate. He found the downed tree and broken windows in about three rooms. Then he went back to the front desk, and a man was there waiting. He said, "Hi, Mr. Davies. Bruce Armstrong, staying in room 203. I heard a big crash, and blood and water are dripping along the wall. Someone staying above me may be hurt from the storm."

"Stay here; something evil may be going on," Leo said. Leo and the night person, Marvels Marvin, went to investigate the room damage in 203, and blood was still dripping down the walls. Then they went to room 303 and they found two dead bodies with a big tree branch driven through them and a waterfall of blood pouring from the bed they were sleeping in. Leo threw up.

"This is not evil; they were killed by the storm. But we will find out pretty soon if it has something to do with this mansion's past. Sorry for puking on your shoes, Marvels." Then Leo called 911.

Then he and Marvels went back down to the front desk. He said to the man, "Go get your wife and check out. We might have something evil going on here again. Two people above you may be seriously hurt or killed. I will refund your stay. The Christmas party tomorrow night is still on." Bruce Armstrong and his wife left.

The Newport coroners removed the dead bodies in room 303,

and hotel workers came in to clean up the room. The police and rescue workers were there, writing up the report while Leo was checking damages in other rooms. Luckily, no one was staying in three other rooms where windows were blown in.

"These people are dead. Can you identify them?" said the coroners.

"The victims' names are Earl and Evelyn Bayside from Indian River, Florida," said Marvels.

The next morning, Fr. Harris arrived at the scene of the dead bodies. "It does not appear that this was evil. I believe it was a freak accident from last night's storm," said Fr. Harris.

The news reports: Two dead, two injured from last night's storm at the Salve Cliffs Mansion.

Jennifer came in to relieve Marvels Melvin, and he told her what had happened during the night. He gave the priest a print-out. Fr. Harris was still there, saying prayers and throwing holy water with paranormal investigators in the basement. The printout read: "The maintenance man saw black shadows in the basement, and the custodian's cleaning equipment went missing and he heard voices telling him to get out."

"We have something down here. I believe this mansion is built over an Indian burial ground. I think there are several grave sites buried under all of Newport. Hundreds of human bones were dug up at the old De La Salle High School, which now belongs to Salve Regina. Several hauntings here in Newport have been happening since the De La Salle bones were dug up and people were dying. It could be possible graves could be buried under this mansion. I don't believe the shadow sightings and the voices will hurt you. I think they will go away soon because I feel it's only down here in this conference room and basement hallways. If the evil does start up again, you may have to dig up the basement floor to see if there's a grave site, or you have to get out! I would stay out of down here for a while because you still have a little activity. The deaths and injuries have nothing to do with the hauntings here. Accidents happen. We had a bad storm last night, causing lots of damage. I will see you tonight at the Christmas Party with Cardinal Richard Hurts," said Fr. Harris.

Jennifer Strings was in the lobby lounge, preparing for the Christmas party, lighting the Christmas trees and filling the fireplace with wood and lighting the fireplace. A catering company brought food, and the lobby was set up and ready for guests to arrive. Leo Davies arrived for people checking in and hanging coats. "Christmas Party," the guests began. They had a few drinks, and a buffet was being served, and a nice fire was burning in the fireplace. Fr. Harris said a prayer before the meal was served. After the meal, kids were toasting marshmallows in the fireplace while Christmas carols were being sung. Groups of people were sitting at tables, eating Christmas cookies.

Suddenly, there was a loud scream, getting everyone's attention and looking around. The scream was heard above the fireplace, between the Christmas trees. Suddenly, a fireball flew out of the fireplace, striking a group of people sitting at a table, setting them on fire. They ran out of the mansion on fire, jumping into the snow outside. Fr. Harris and Cardinal Hurts watched in shock. Then the damper blew open, dumping black soot on the fire, putting the fire out. Everyone ran out of the mansion without their winter coats.

Fr. Harris went over to the fireplace to say prayers and throw holy water into the fireplace. A roar of the devil sounded in the fireplace. The lights were blinking on and off. Suddenly, Fr. Harris was sucked into the fireplace, and the damper was swinging open and closing, and he disappeared, being sucked up the chimney. Then the ash trap opened, throwing wood ash and black soot under the wood rack, and human bones were flying out, covering the lobby floor.

Cardinal Richard Hurts cried, "Fr. Harris! Fr. Harris! Fr. Harris! Please come back! Oh! MY God!" Then a strong gust of wind blew out of the fireplace, blowing black soot at Cardinal Hurts. While he was saying prayers and calling for Fr. Harris to return, burning wood rolled under the Christmas trees, setting them on fire. He left, covered in black soot.

Several rescues arrived to take the burned victims to the hospital. Fire trucks arrived to put out the fires, and the mansion was closed off by police. Roads were closed, and it was snowing heavily. Cardinal Richard Hurts was okay; he would need a long shower when he got back to the rectory. Leo Davies evacuated the mansion, escorting guests out a back entrance because the lobby was on fire. The guests had to walk in eight inches of snow to get to their cars. Police directed the guests out of the mansion parking lots. The Newport Fire Department was putting out the fires in the lobby.

Fr. Harris is dead; his bones are somewhere in the fireplace. When daybreak came, reality set in. Police, fire trucks, rescues, and snowplows were there all night. The plows were clearing snow in the parking lots so people could get out and clearing walkways and the main gate entrance so the firemen could do their work. The fire department swept out the fireplace and boarded it up. Then a coroner's team arrived to move the human bones scattered all over the lobby. Fr. Harris could be among them. The bones were taken to the Rhode Island State Morgue in Cranston to be identified. The Salve Cliff Mansion lived up to its name: closed and chained up again for good. Newspapers read: "5 dead and 13 hurt at the Salve Cliff Mansion Christmas Party. Olympic Builders will have to find another buyer."

TWO

HAUNTING AT THE MISERICORDIA

ood morning, ladies and gentlemen. Welcome aboard UMASS
Tours. My name is Danny Duke, U-Haul Science Coordina-
tor. We are going to the Misericordia House bed-and-breakfast in
Great Barrington, Massachusetts, to find ghosts there. We will be
staying there for a week before we break for Christmas vacation.
We will identify what's haunting this facility. Sit back and enjoy
our trip."

The UMASS bus arrived at the Misericordia. "Good afternoon.
Danny Duke, tour guide from UMASS Tours."

"Pleased to meet you. My name is Marie Martha Madonna,
the Mother Superior. Just call me the Triple M! Welcome to the
Misericordia House. How many people do you have?"

"I have 15 students from the University of Massachusetts."

"Come inside and I will give you a tour of this facility. The
main gate leads to these big French doors. Come in and make
yourselves comfortable. The lobby has velvet and leather furniture,
and we have an 8-foot-wide fireplace and it's 6 feet high. The lamps
and chandeliers have gold and silver surroundings. The Christmas
tree stands 20 feet high with 10,000 colored lights and was put up

on November 1st, and it takes 5 weeks to decorate it. The lobby stands 23 feet from floor to ceiling. A nice fire is burning in the fireplace on this very cold day. We have four floors in this facility. We have 6 rooms on each floor. The fourth floor has a conference room and special guest rooms. Each room has two queen beds and a pull-out sofa that sleeps two. Six people can sleep in each room. The maximum capacity is 128 people. The rooms all have a bathroom with a Jacuzzi, gold faucet fixtures, a sink, and a toilet. A linen closet and a shower house coat are inside. All the furniture is mahogany, and there are stained-glass windows in each room. And oriental rugs.

You're visiting room 305. We have a ghost that visits this room almost every night that looks like a heavy-set woman with very large breasts known as the Mother Superior Misericordia Ghost from the 1600s. If you see her, she may not let you sleep. She may spit at you, show you her private parts; her nipples light up like Rudolph the Red-Nosed Reindeer. Red, red, red! She may appear as bright as Black & Decker lights, and she appears in the French mirror above the bureau.

Sometimes you may see yellow, green, and blue orbs flying around the room. We have gone through several renovations and construction here at the Misericordia in the last 8 years and are frequently visited by bears. We have a lot of black bears roaming around our property. We have been broken into a few times by bears looking for food.

All these rooms are beautiful! There's no guarantee that you will see a ghost because visions have not been seen very often lately. Your only chance you may see one is if you stay in room 305. The room is open for you to check in. We have had some injuries from ghosts here and bear attacks in the past. We have had exorcisms and paranormal teams remove ghosts here. They come and go every once in a while. Now it's winter time when ghosts are seen often here.

Let's go up to the 4th floor before we check in. Up here are conference rooms and guest rooms we rarely use. Let's go to the basement. Down here is the laundry room, storage areas, and emergency shelters because we get tornadoes during the summer months. I will not go over with the outside right now because everything is covered in snow, and it's only 8 degrees outside. Let's go upstairs and check in, and you can warm up in front of the fireplace before dinner. A ham dinner will be served in the dining room at 6 p.m."

"Tomorrow morning you get a free continental full breakfast in the dining room from 6 a.m. until 11. Lunch is served from 12 noon until 2 p.m., and the tea party is served from 2 to 4 p.m., and dinner is served from 6 to 9 p.m., and music is being played until 1 a.m. with a band or DJ. In the dining room with a full bar and dance floor. Tonight we have a band. 'The K-9 Rockers' is the name of the band playing rock & roll music. Let's check in then you're on your own!" said the house madam, Marie Martha Madonna.

"One more thing before you go to the lounge or rooms, check out the gallery near the dining room," said the house madam.

The UMASS tour was in the lounge warming up in front of the fireplace before dinner. The tour later went to dinner. A ham dinner was served with mashed potatoes, corn, and brown bread. Apple pie was the dessert. A black bear was looking in the window while everyone was eating, but it was too dark outside to see it. The bear was licking its chops, moaning, and crying in the freezing cold, watching everyone eat from behind an electric fence protecting the property around the Misericordia House.

The bartender was getting the bar ready, and the band was setting up for tonight. The bottles and glasses were moving on the bar, ready to fall, and the bartender was grabbing them. He said, "Mother Superior! Stop busting my balls and stop what you're doing!" He was talking to the ghost. The bartender was alone in the bar area of the nightclub. The activity stopped. The time was 8:02 p.m. An hour later, when the nightclub was opening, the bartender looked at his phone, and the time was 9:02 p.m. Nothing happened when he looked at his phone again two minutes later. He knew the Misericordia was still here and her hauntings happen at two minutes after every hour when her activity is active.

"Ladies and gentlemen. After dinner, I will show you the gallery," said Danny Duke, UMASS tour guide. After dinner, the tour got together to go to the gallery. "Ladies and gentlemen. This is what the grounds look like during the summer. There's a swimming pool here, tennis courts, basketball courts, and a miniature golf. The fence around the property keeps the bears out because of recent attacks. The fence is electrified like a jail setup. In the spring, you have a Chinese Garden with thousands of all kinds of flowers, and during the fall, you have a sunflower field. For the rest of the night, you can go to the club to see the band play and dancing, or go and relax in the lobby and get in front of a warm fireplace, and we will meet tomorrow morning for breakfast about 8 a.m. in the dining room. Meanwhile, make yourselves comfortable or go looking for ghosts. If you see something, take pictures and write up reports; that's why we're here for a week," said the tour guide.

Late in the evening, around 2 a.m., some of the tour was still in the lounge, sitting in front of the fireplace playing cards. The fire was acting strange, making shapes, and the wood was turning, rolling, and burning, and it looked like a roast in the fireplace. One girl said to another from the UMASS Tour, "Debby, look at the fire, it's forming a face that looks like the devil."

"Oh, my God! Robin, take pictures. The fire has a face with black eyes, a red nose, purple pointy ears, a blue-colored mouth, and blue horns above the fire and burning green below, and the wood is turning and moving. It looks like we have the devil here!" said Debby. Everyone was taking pictures with their smartphones. Suddenly, a loud roar was heard, and the fire blew out in the fireplace, and the room filled up with smoke. "Everyone, we have to get out of here before someone gets hurt!" one man from the tour said.

The tour guests went to the front desk to show the pictures. "Holy shit! I believe we have the ghost of the Misericordia here, but I never saw anything like this! It looks like the devil coming up from Hell; this is evil! I will call the Mother Superior," said the night clerk at the front desk.

The UMASS students wrote up a report and showed the pictures to the tour guide, waking him up at 3:30 in the morning. The clerk at the front desk called the mother superior.

"Marie Martha, David Shaw calling from the front desk. I am so sorry to call you at 3:30 in the morning, but we have something evil here in the lobby foyer. A group of the UMASS tour took pictures of a devil-like face forming in the fireplace, and the fire quickly went out and the room filled up with smoke. The students heard a loud roar chasing everyone out. I heard the roar myself, and it sounded like a wild animal in the fireplace chimney. I'm sending you some pictures to your phone!"

"David, check the fireplace and see if it's still burning and throw buckets of water on it to put it out! Thank you. When I come in in the morning I will get a priest to remove the evil," said the Mother Superior, Marie Martha Madonna.

The clerk went to the fireplace and it was still burning with wood but no flame; the fire was almost out. The clerk threw water on it to put the fire out for the night. Six ladies from the UMASS tour were staying in room 305 and never saw a ghost. The ladies kept calling for the Mother Superior Misericordia, looking at the big French mirror, but nothing was happening. They were looking at the alarm clock and their phones, and the time was 4:02 a.m. One minute later nothing was happening.

The next morning everyone in the tour met for breakfast, then met in the lounge after. "Ladies and gentlemen, five members of the UMASS Science Team Tour saw a positive identity of a ghost here during the night, and they took pictures. The Mother Superior will show you the uploaded pictures on the video screen. My name is Pastor Joseph General, an all-denominational church priest and paranormal investigator. Two years ago, my team and I removed the Mother Superior Misericordia ghost, and since then, she has not been seen here! The madam, Marie Madonna, was thinking about changing the name of this bed-and-breakfast facility but she decided to keep the name because she liked to show her private parts, appearing in bright lights with her colorful orb balls flying around the room. But she was a nuisance, keeping people awake at night until things started getting violent, so we had to get rid of her through exorcisms. But she's not the cause of all the violence. We found evil. Look at this video. It looks like the devil is rising up from hell right here in this fireplace. I will be rescheduling another exorcism to get rid of this evil ghost in this room. I am here with some private paranormal investigators. Here is Eric Mancini, Chet Armstrong, Louie De Dinardo, and Pamela Fisher. We will be performing an exorcism right now and a national three-day exorcism right after the New Year! The building will need to be evacuated for three days when we come back after the holidays. Before we start, everyone has to leave this room, and I need the Mother Superior of the house to lead me to other parts of the building where fireplaces are located. We do have some kind of devil haunting this room, and if we can't get rid of it, people may get hurt! The Misericordia House has had issues of ghost sightings coming from this fireplace before many times, and we have been here several times before, moving ghosts in this mansion. But by the looks of these pictures and showing on the video screen, I have never saw evil like this in my 29 years of priesthood: it looks like the devil rising from hell! Mrs. Marie Madonna, please light the fireplace? Everyone please leave this room. When the fire gets going, the exorcism will begin," said Pastor Joseph General.

"Pastor, did you hear what happened in Newport, Rhode Island?" said one of the paranormal investigators.

"Yes, I did! There was some kind of devil in a Salve Regina University mansion that killed people there! We have the same thing happening here, and we have to move it before more people get killed!" said the pastor.

The fire in the fireplace was roaring and oak wood logs were popping and had a nice fireplace smell to it. The fire burned normally, and the pastor and paranormal investigators found no evil. They performed an exorcism and everything was okay. A meeting took place with the guests and the staff after prayers were said and holy water was thrown in every room in the Misericordia mansion. After the pastor said, "I want all guests and staff to meet in the dining room for a brief meeting," said Pastor Joseph General. After lunch and tea time were over, and before dinner, the meeting was held.

"Good afternoon, did everyone enjoy the spinach pie lunch and Tea Party?"

"Yeah! And yes!" said the guests and staff.

Then the meeting was held and the pastor continued. "Good late afternoon, early evening. The exorcism was successful in the lounge. Last night's haunting happened at 3:02 a.m. as you've seen on your phones. Tonight, put the fire out before that time and don't leave a fire burning late at night. After the exorcism, I did find activity throughout this mansion, nothing threatening, but something else is here. The paranormal investigators and I said prayers in every room and the basement. You should be okay. Beware of bears in the area; you have black bears and big brown grizzlies. I found activity with weather in this area since 1995. On May 29th, this area of Great Barrington surrounding the Misericordia has been hit six times by tornadoes on this same date: May 29th, 1995, again in 1997, 1999, 2005, 2011, and 2018. The air here is thin, and the Misericordia House sits in a valley where wind storms spin in all directions. The thunderstorms and snowstorms are stronger than usual, which could be caused by evil spirits! We cannot prove it, but there is activity surrounding this property and that may be attracting so many bears during the summer months. Be aware of your surroundings if you leave this resort. We have a lot of wildlife here, including mountain lions! Something is attracting these animals to this area, and we do not know why, because Great Barrington and the gateway to the Green Mountains of Vermont and the vacation way to Upstate New York is one of the most populated places to visit. Once again, my name is Pastor Joseph General. Call me if you have any more ghost issues here, and enjoy your stay here at the Misericordia."

At 6:02 p.m., the madam lit the fireplace in the lounge, while everyone was eating dinner. Nobody was in the lounge, but people would be going in there after dinner. The devil's ghost face appeared again briefly in the flame like before, but no one saw it. The fire burned normally for the rest of the night. A Fish & Chips dinner was served on a Friday night.

Five days later, the UMASS tour had not witnessed anymore ghosts until the night before they were leaving. Five women staying in room 305: Debby, Ellen, Betty, Beth, and Yates. Five women whose first names spell out DEBBY. Debby was going into the shower and she turned the water on and it was pouring out black mud! She turned the shower off, and she said, "Ladies, don't take a shower, the water is coming out black!"

Then Debby called the front desk. A maintenance worker came up to check the shower and it was running clear. "Ladies, you may have got rust build-up in the shower head. Let it run for a while; the water is coming out normal now," said the maintenance worker.

Debby went in the shower and the water was okay this time and she took a shower. While Debby was in the shower shampooing her hair, Ellen was combing her hair and the comb slipped out of her hand and fell behind a couch. She moved the couch and an owl leaped off the floor behind the couch and went right for her throat! Ellen let out a loud scream then the owl attacked her! Beth, Betty, and Yates saw the attack and they screamed hysterically! "AHHH!"

Ellen collapsed on the floor in a pool of blood with the owl still attacking her, flapping its wings! Debby came out of the shower wrapped in a towel and she grabbed the owl off of Ellen, wrapping it in the towel, and she choked the owl until it was dead and she threw it out a window, then she called for help!

The other three ladies were trying to get out of the room, but the door locked from the inside. Ellen was dead. While the rest of the four women tried to get out of the room, it filled with black flies and bats that attacked them as they screamed for help. The man covering the front desk had the room key and tried to use a key card to enter the room, but it was not working. The maintenance worker had to break the door down to get into the room. The women were covered with blood from the bats biting them. When maintenance busted the door down, the flies and bats retreated and disappeared. The women were covered in blood.

Debby cried, "An owl killed my best friend, Ellen! I threw it out the window!"

Rescues, fire trucks, and police cars arrived by the hundreds to take the injured and the dead lady to the hospital. Meanwhile, the tour guide had to get his crew together and evacuate the Misericordia House at three o'clock in the morning. Before help arrived, the bus driver went to get the bus from a parking lot across from the Misericordia House in a snowstorm, and he saw two black bear cubs rolling and playing in the snow. Suddenly, the mother black bear came out of nowhere, attacking the bus driver, pinning him against the bus and biting his head off, and killing him. Mama bear and her two cubs ate part of his body for a quick meal before disappearing into the woods. When help arrived, the Misericordia was being evacuated. The bear cubs even ate his keys.

Phones rang in everyone's room, telling them to check out and leave. "How can we get out of here with a foot of snow on the ground?" said one couple.

"A lady was killed by something evil in room 305. For your own safety, I'm asking everyone to check out and go to the Hampton Inn up the street. The Misericordia is being evacuated!" said the receptionist at the front desk.

The rescue workers said to each other, "What hospital are these victims going to? Mass General in Pine View?"

"No, they will be treated at Hannibal Hospital in Vermont. The dead victim went there, too," said another rescue worker. "Change of plans: Take the injured to Mass General, and the dead victim is going to Hannibal in Vermont."

The rest of the UMASS tour waited in the lounge, warming up by the fireplace and taking naps until the bus pulled up to get them. Two hours later, the bus never showed up. The madam, Marie Martha Madonna, got a call at 3:30 in the morning about what happened to the ladies staying in room 305. "Danny Duke, please come to the front desk!" The madam called his phone, but there was no answer. One person from the UMASS tour went to his room, and no one answered the door.

"Mrs. Madonna, Shirley Martin from UMASS Tour. Danny Duke's not answering his phone or in his room."

"He might be warming up the bus. Go to the lounge and wait; the bus will be coming soon," said the madam.

The police and rescue never knew what was happening across the street. Three hours later, still no bus. Shirley Martin went out in the bitter cold and blowing snow to investigate. When she got to the bus, she saw the bus driver's dead body torn apart, lying in a pool of blood in the snow. His head was bitten off; Mama Bear ate that! A leg was bitten off; one of the cubs ate that! And his right arm was torn off; the second cub got that! And his keys! Shirley screamed hysterically! "AHHH!" Then she ran back across the street to the Misericordia House, screaming and crying. "The bus driver's dead! He was killed by a wild animal! Please help!"

The madam called the Mass Transit Authority to hire shuttle buses so people could evacuate and go home. Police and rescues arrived again to move the dead body. "Mrs. Madonna, no buses will be going out for a couple of days because of the storm," said Mass Transit Authority.

Shirley Martin met with police and rescue at the dead body, crying. "The victim was killed by a very big, hungry bear!" said a rescue worker.

Then they went looking for his keys and wallet, but they were in one of the cubs' stomachs. A good part of the bus driver's leg and thigh was gone. The police said to Shirley, "Go back inside and go to his room to see if he might have left his keys and belongings."

A second cop said, "If you can't find them, maybe the bear ate them!"

Shirley went back inside, and maintenance went to his room and found nothing; the room was empty. The rescue removed the dead body, and the bus was left behind. Maintenance locked the gate so no bears could get on the property. Before the gate was locked, police broke a window to crawl into the bus, looking for the bus driver's keys and found nothing but road maps.

While the horror show was going on outside, the madam was spreading the bad news inside. "Good morning, and I am so sorry about what happened here during the night. One girl was killed by an evil owl in room 305, and four others staying in that room were hurt. The UMASS tour bus driver was killed by a vicious wild animal going out to the bus. I assume he may have been killed by a large bear! My name is Madam Mother Superior, Marie Martha Madonna, the owner of the Misericordia House bed-and-breakfast. I have officially evacuated this building due to the fatal hauntings. However, we are currently in a winter storm warning for the next two days here in Great Barrington, expecting more than three feet of snow, and travel is shut down until plows can clear the roads. Only emergency vehicles can get through, followed by a plow in front of them! Sorry for the inconvenience! The dining room is open for breakfast and do what you have to do, and I will give you your keys back to go back to your rooms until Mass Transit Shuttles can get you out of here! If you have any issues with ghost hauntings, I will give you another room. All meals will be free until you leave. Thank you for your cooperation," said the madam.

Ellen and the dead bus driver's body parts were taken to the refrigerated morgue unit at Hannibal Hospital in Vermont. The other four women were taken back to the Misericordia House by helicopter from Mass General in Pine View. The chopper landed near the front entrance of the Misericordia House.

"Debby Wagner, Beth Brown, Betty Bryant, and Yates Cornell, welcome back. I am glad to see you ladies are okay. The evacuations here at the Misericordia have been delayed because of the snow-storm. You heard about what happened to the bus driver, being killed by a possible bear attack! I am so sorry! And sorry about Ellen Shilling! You ladies will be staying in room 101. Room 305 is shut down and boarded up! If you have any issues with hauntings, I will give you another room. Meet the rest of your tour eating dinner in the dining room. All meals are free until you leave," said the Madam, Marie Martha Madonna. Shirley Martin gave the four ladies hugs and told their stories in the lounge after dinner.

Mama bear and her two cubs managed to get on the property during the night, hiding behind a shed out of view from the public.

"Shirley, Ellen was killed by a bat owl with vampire teeth when she moved a sofa when her comb fell behind it while she was combing her hair. I grabbed the owl, choking it with a towel and threw it out a window. I was bitten on the ear by a vampire bat when the room filled up with bats and black flies," said Debby.

"I was attacked by a swarm of black flies the size of bees between my legs under my house coat," said Beth.

"I was attacked, bitten by bats, and stung by the black flies!" said Betty.

"I was covered with black flies, biting and stinging me, until I passed out! I tried to get out of the room, and the door locked so we couldn't get out; maintenance workers had to break the door down to get us out! We all went to the hospital," said Yates.

"I went out to see what was taking so long before the bus came to get us, and I found the bus driver's body. It looked like he was attacked by a grizzly bear or a big wild animal," said Shirley Martin.

Night time. All evening activities were canceled. Snacks were served, and the bar was open for drinks. A priest was there in the lounge, saying prayers. The fire was burning normally in the fireplace with a priest there; no devil in there tonight. At bedtime, the four women victims from last night's attack were staying in room 101 near the front desk.

Debby said, "Ladies, if anything happens tonight, I am going to hijack the bus and we're getting the fuck out of here!" The women slept with the lights on. Before going to bed, the ladies moved things around to see if something else would come out after them. The room was quiet.

At 3:02 a.m., people woke up to a lot of loud noises coming from room 305. The maintenance worker removed the boarded-up room, and the room was quiet. The French mirror was taken out of the room, and maintenance moved furniture and beds around and found nothing. They boarded up the room again and brought the French mirror down to the main office near the front desk. The noises in that room lasted only a minute but were loud enough to wake people up.

Two days later, plows plowed all the roads so people could go home. Mass Transit shuttle buses arrived to take everyone out of the Misericordia House. The UMASS tour bus was towed back to the University of Massachusetts. A week later, there were no more hauntings, allowing the Misericordia House to reopen during Christmas week.

On a quiet Tuesday night, a large tour was having a Christmas party dinner in the dining room when suddenly, a black bear crashed through a window into the dining room, helping itself to the Christmas dinner buffet. Then a second bear arrived to help itself. Everyone ran out screaming, "Help! Help! Help! Help! There are bears in the restaurant!" The tour ran back outside to get into the bus to safety. The two bears ate the entire buffet and knocked tables and chairs over. Kitchen staff started throwing things at the bears, hitting them in the head, but the bears just kept eating. A bartender threw bottles, breaking them over the bears' heads, but it didn't matter; the bears continued to clean up the buffet. No one was hurt, and the dining room was destroyed. Tables and chairs were busted into pieces while the two bears kept chasing after food droppings, knocking tables over to eat all the food until nothing was left, not even a glass of orange juice.

Police arrived with shotguns to kill the bears! When help arrived, the bears retreated back out the window they crashed into and disappeared! The police, K-9 units, and animal control arrived, searching the property to find the bears, and they were long gone! The tour checked out and left. Once again, the Misericordia House had to close down. Police and the animal control unit were there all night, keeping people safe and looking for the intruding bears.

Pastor Joseph General arrived, and the mansion management and police got together. The pastor said, "Good evening, officers and K-9 units and management. The Misericordia House is haunted by a series of ghosts, but lately, guests have been getting hurt and killed. A girl was killed by a vampire owl bat in room 305 about 10 days ago, and four other girls were hurt by vampire bats, black flies biting them and stinging them! The UMASS Science Ghost Tour girls were the victims of these attacks. Their bus driver was killed by possible bears in a snowstorm. The UMASS tour witnessed a view of the devil in this fireplace, so a professional paranormal investigating team, me, and several Catholic priests had to perform a three-day exorcism to move and get rid of the evil here! It's been quiet the last two weeks, and now the Misericordia is getting bear attacks and break-ins. This property and the Pine Cemetery next door are built on top of an Indian burial ground, and this area has a lot of bears because they can smell the dead. Bears have been knocking gravestones down, raising the dead. This may explain all the evil here lately. If the evil keeps returning here, you will have to close the Misericordia for good because we can no longer help!" said Pastor Joseph General.

THREE

Hospice Haunting in Connecticut

Moodus, Connecticut. March 2023. A hospice unit moved into a former mental institution in Connecticut. Nurses, counselors, doctors, social workers, etc., arrived looking for work at the newly renovated hospital. A group was waiting in a lounge with a fire burning in the fireplace. The flame was forming into a devil-like figure, but no one noticed and was not paying attention to the fireplace. A man came into the lounge with 50 people to begin interviewing them for jobs at about 9 a.m.

"Good morning, ladies and gentlemen. My name is Doctor Marshall Law, and I am here with the head nurse, and her name is Mrs. Mary Burnstein. Welcome to the 'University of Connecticut Hospice Center,' formerly known as the Boardmen Institute of Mental Health. This building and campus around this hospital have been vacant for about 40 years until UCONN Health took it over and built this place into a hospice center. I am looking for nurses, social workers and doctors, maintenance workers, custodians, meeting counselors, and kitchen help. Mrs. Burnstein and I will begin passing out applications for you to fill out. Then I will go over the past history of the former Boardmen Institute and then will go on a tour. Patients will begin coming in on April 1st," said Dr. Marshall Law.

Everyone was filling out the paperwork, then the head nurse spoke. "Good morning. My name is Mary Burnstein, and I used to work at the Boardmen Institute back in the late 1980s before retiring and now I became a hospice nurse to help people who are dying. The past history of this campus has not been good. The Boardmen Institute of Mental Health was a psychiatric nuthouse! Sister Claire Thomas will take your paperwork, and I will finish talking about the past history of this place and we will go on a tour," said Nurse Mary Burnstein.

Sister Claire gathered up all the paperwork, then Nurse Burnstein continued her speech. "Ladies and gentlemen. Back in the late 1970s or early '80s, an asteroid from outer space crashed into Moodus, Connecticut, and a rock-like creature came out of it that looked like the devil, and it killed many people and animals. The creature was a female, and she had several demon-like creatures and siblings that delivered a powerful venom that made a lot of people sick and killed a lot of animals, turning them into creatures, werewolves. Many people and animals have died from this venom. All these space-shot creatures had a scorpion stinger tail and were killing machines. The creatures were called the devil coming from hell, from the heavens! The government did not talk much about the global threat, because did this really happen or was it all fake? According to Air Force blue laws, this never happened! If it happened or not, the Boardmen Institute housed a lot of very sick patients infected by a substance Moodus Police described as the "Pink Blob slime Jelly Orange Sand!" A deadly bacteria worse than "Orange Agent," used in the Vietnam War! We had patients who were possessed by the devil. Exorcisms and paranormal practices happened here. Patients infected by the pink blob jelly deformed into indescribable creatures of the unknown! Some patients turned into werewolves or a devil-like creature or from a human to an animal while they were possessed with this pink blob jelly virus. Many people have died in the Boardmen Institute, and their ghosts were present. The issues here were so bad it was like treating the devil! We had isolation rooms and a jail to lock patients up from attacking and killing other patients! Some patients had to wear straitjackets or were chained down. The Boardmen Institute was the mental health nuthouse capital of the world! The worst of the worst, we had it here!

Now let's go on a tour. Here is the lounge, front desk area, next is the dining room and kitchen. Then a game room with pool tables and a one-lane bowling alley. Ping pong tables, corn hole, pickleball, and hopscotch and small games for kids to play. Outside, we have tennis courts, basketball courts, and miniature golf and a softball field. Outdoor pool and restrooms. Now I will show you the rooms where the mentally retarded and the special needs stayed. These bedrooms will be the hospice center where patients will stay until they pass away. This is the hospital unit and our name is: 'The University of Connecticut Hospice Center.' The next set of rooms were isolation rooms and chained-down bedrooms where crazy patients stayed and were locked up, but now they're regular rooms to host hospice patients. The next area: This used to be a jail, now it's a storage area. Then we have a library that used to be a museum of demons from the so-called 'Moodus Connecticut Devil.' The basement area we had deformed animals staying here, but now it's the hospice morgue and coroners' stations and freezers to hold the dead before they're buried. We have a hospital storage area down here, too. But we have no deformed animals or demons locked up down here! Come outside, and we will go to the next building. Here we have an auditorium/movie theater and conference rooms, classrooms, offices, etc. You will be here later today to watch videos and learn how hospice works, and know how to handle patients before they die. This area is the 911 unit with more rooms for patients to be admitted to a hospital or here in hospice. We have a hospital here for patients in palliative care. The next building is the facilities' security and the Moodus Police sub-station. This is the area you check in before coming to work. We had a 15-foot electrified fence surrounding the property when it was the Boardmen Institute to keep crazy people and animals from breaking out! Part of the fence still stands along the woods to stop bears and deer from coming on the property. Building #4, is the water and power unit and generators and backup boilers to heat and light all buildings in case the power goes out. The fence is no longer electrified, and we have no more crazy people or animals here! We will go back to the main building to have lunch in the dining room, then we will meet in the conference room in building two to watch a video before you get hired. Thank you for your cooperation. Is there any questions?" said Nurse Mary Burnstein.

"Yes, are there still any ghosts here?" said one lady.

"The Connecticut Catholic Clergy and national paranormal investigating teams performed exorcisms to get rid of all the evil before this hospice center was allowed to open. We have been here for two hours, and we haven't seen any ghosts at this interview!" said Nurse Burnstein. On the way to lunch, a thick fog formed.

One lady said, "Mrs. Burnstein, what's this thick fog following everyone?"

"We're near the Moodus River, and it gets pretty foggy on cold March days," she said.

About three weeks later, the new hospice center was open for business, and the old Boardmen Institute ghosts can't wait to make a visit! One nurse was in the laundry room washing and drying bed sheets and blankets at 10 o'clock on a Saturday morning. Suddenly she saw a big black shadow of a man from floor to ceiling walk into a wall. She screamed and went over where she saw the shadow, and nothing was there. She felt the walls, and part of the wall was cold, and part was warm. She shook her head, and she said to herself, "I know I didn't sleep well last night, but I saw what I saw!" Then she told the nun, Sister Claire Thomas, who was working Hospice on weekends. The nun went to the laundry room to say prayers, and she saw nothing. Then she left.

Another nurse was doing laundry when she heard scratching noises. The nurse was putting clothes in a washing machine when she heard the scratching sounds, and it looked like someone was clawing, trying to break through the wall, then a growling sound like a mean junkyard dog! Then it stopped. The nurse was not paying attention until she heard the growling; she saw nothing, and she left the laundry room as fast as she could! She said, "Sister Thomas, there's a wild mean dog or a wild animal in the laundry room!"

"Let's take a walk, Vicki; I was just there! Mary Allen said she saw a black shadow of a man walking through a wall! I went to the laundry room and I didn't see anything there. Mary and Vicki, you need to get your sleep, you're hearing and seeing things!" said the nun and she left.

Sister Thomas was walking the hallway on her way to a meeting just after lunch, and she saw a black shadow that she could not describe follow her and leap over her, and now it was in front of her. The hallway went dark, then it disappeared as she screamed! Then the apparition was gone, and the hallway brightened. She ran to the conference room in a hurry and she shut the door and held her meeting, and before she played a video, she said, "Vicki Hicks and Mary Allen, you're right; there is something evil here! On my way here, a dark black shadow that looked like a jet-black spinning and rolling fog followed me in the hallway, and it went above my head, and it landed in front of me, and I went through it, and the hallway went dark like night! Until I screamed, the black fog/mist, or whatever you call it, went away! Let's forget about it right now and finish our lecture. Later, I will call a priest to come after Nurse Burnstein finishes our meeting," said Sister Thomas.

"Sister Thomas, this is the hallway where a man was attacked by the shadow you're describing, and it got in him and he was torn open and black flies, spiders, and snakes ate him alive and killed him when this hospital was the Boardmen Institute!" said Nurse Bernstein.

Sister Thomas fainted! Nurse Bernstein held the meeting. When Sister Thomas recovered, she called a priest. "Father Henry Lord from St. Michael's Church in East Haddam, Connecticut, speaking."

"Hi, this is Sister Claire Thomas calling from the University of Connecticut Hospice Center, formally known as the Boardmen Institute. Gray Stone Building main hallway. We have a black, evil, devilish-looking ghost roaming in the hallway that nearly attacked me, but I was able to pull away from it. This thing was chasing me and flew over my head, and it fell in front of me, and I walked into it, then everything went black as night until I screamed; finally, it released me. A couple of nurses saw a black shadow of a big man in the laundry room; a second nurse reported a mad dog growling and scratching in the walls in the same laundry room," said Sister Claire Thomas.

"Give me a couple of hours, and I will stop by," said the priest.

Two people were visiting a patient in room 222 who was ready to die when suddenly saw a purple shadow appearing on the back wall of a man. A man and a woman saw the shadow and the dying woman, who was about 90 years old. She screamed, "Get out of here! Get out of here!! Get out of here!!!!" in a high-tone voice.

"Excuse me, sir, but you do not belong in here! Leave!" said the woman visiting.

The apparition roared like a bear and showed vampire fangs, while the patient kept screaming, "Get out of here!"

"Frank, call the nurse!" said the woman visiting.

The nurse came into the room, and the purple ghost disappeared. The dying lady was still screaming then she stopped when the nurse came in the room. The lady in the bed died.

"Nurse, me and my friend saw a purple ghost appearing on that wall, and it growled and roared like a mean bear, showing mean teeth, and it charged at me and my grandmother, Elsie, in the bed, and suddenly vanished when you came into the room. My name is Emma, and my friend's name is Frank."

"Pleased to meet you, my name is Mindy Martin, the head nurse here in ward 5. I heard Elsie screaming while I was far down the hall. I am sorry, but I think she passed!" said the nurse.

Then a loud roar again! "I think we better leave before someone gets hurt," said Frank.

"Frank, I think the devil took my grandmother. She was not a good mother, and she had her four kids taken away from her, and she was working for the mafia, and she was always abandoning her children, and she spent 20 years in jail because she had her son, Richard, killed! I strongly believe that ghost in her room took her; it was the devil!" said Emma.

A nurse was in the basement getting medication out of a storeroom when suddenly she saw a black fog forming along the floor, and it formed into a human figure with big horns and it looked like the devil. She left the medication where she found it, and she ran out of the room and closed the door, and she got out of the basement in a hurry! She said to the nurse working in her area, "Mindy! Sheila Swallow. We have a devil downstairs! I was getting some medication to give to the patients in the basement storage, and suddenly a black fog formed into a devil-like creature! I left the medication there and left the room," she cried.

"You're the second person who saw something tonight. I will call Fr. Henry Lord from St. Michael's Church. Elsie Berlin in room 222 and her granddaughter and boyfriend saw a purple devil-looking monster in her room, then she passed away!" said the nurse Mindy Martin.

The priest came to bless the rooms, and he found nothing. He said, "Mindy, when people are dying, spirits come to get them. Some of them are good, and some of them are bad. Then they pass. Just say a prayer to St. Michael the archangel that gets rid of evil spirits."

"Father, what about the black devil I saw in a storage room; there's no one staying in that room!" said Sheila.

"If you're taking care of a dying patient and a spirit, good or bad, is trying to get her soul, it may follow you until that patient dies. Just say the prayer I told you: 'Go away in the name of St. Michael, the angel of Jesus Christ!' Stand your ground and stay in front of the ghost saying that prayer. Do not chase it or challenge it. Don't show fear, and when it follows you, you face it and act like you're the boss, because if you show fear and not say that prayer, the ghost can get into your body. If the ghost catches you or tries to hurt you or make things difficult, just keep saying that prayer until it goes away. Let's go to those rooms one more time together. When I was there myself, I found nothing threatening. If I see something, I will get rid of it! You heard about the history about this hospital being haunted when it was the Boardmen Institute; a lot of bad things happened here! Some of the spirits may still be here, and they were forced to leave when exorcisms were performed. Now a new hospital opens may have activated the lost spirits trying to make a comeback because you have people dying here! This hospital was a former mental institution nuthouse, and now it's opening up to a hospice center! People are dying here, and the ghosts want their souls. I have gone through all 4 buildings today, and I have not found anything evil. Here's room 222; the Connecticut coroners are removing the dead body right now. I said prayers over her dead body earlier. There's nothing evil in this room now," said Fr. Henry Lord.

"Father, is it possible the purple devilish ghost killed her!" said Nurse Mindy Martin.

"I can't really answer that, because all evil and good spirits go after the dead when people die. If the evil spirit showed its presence, it's usually weak. If you see a white mist or brightness in the room, it's a good spirit. If she was a nice lady, the good spirit will guide her soul to heaven. If the bad one got her, she'll go to hell! Nobody knows! Let's go back to the storage room where the black mist/fog was spotted? There's nothing here, Sheila. Just because a bad spirit passed through here does not mean it's coming back. It was probably checking the room out to see what's here, then it leaves. Get what you need while you're in here. I will stay here until you leave," said the priest.

Sheila got the medications she needed, then she and the priest and Nurse Mindy Martin left the storeroom. Minutes later, the black mist formed again, but no one saw it. The time on the clock in the storeroom was 11:02 p.m. The black mist vanished a minute later!

12:02 a.m., a nurse heard a patient throwing up. When she went to her room across from the nurse's station, she was still puking up green vomit, then the woman turned purple and then blue, and then she died as the nurse watched in horror!

1:02 a.m., after cleaning up her mess, the nurse heard a voice, "Get out!"

2:02 a.m., a man choked in his bed and died!

At 3:02 a.m., a woman was in her bed dying, and a devilish black mass was over her body, sucking out all her energy out of her mouth until she died!

At 4:02 a.m., Nurse Mindy Martin, working the night shift, felt something go inside of her. She called the priest. "Father, sorry to bother you in the middle of the night, but I just felt something go through me! I did not see anything, but it was strong enough to knock me down!"

"Just keep saying the prayers until it stops," said the priest, and he hung up the phone.

5:02 a.m., another woman choked in her bed and died!

At 6:02 a.m., a man was in his bed, and he took his last breath, and blood poured out of his mouth, and he died!

At 7:02 a.m., coroners arrived at the hospice center to remove the dead bodies!

8:02 a.m., Father Henry Lord arrived to bless the rooms from the dead!

9:02 a.m., a meeting was held with the hospice staff with a doctor. "Good morning, my name is Doctor Marshall Law. About 6 people have died during the night, and there have been several ghost sightings, and Father Henry Lord is here right now blessing rooms where patients have died overnight. He has been here several times since opening day, trying to remove the evil from the previous owner: 'The Boardmen Institute.' The problem we're having here since hospice opened, the ghosts from the past are returning because we are a hospital for the dead, and the old evil is trying to get in their bodies. Now we have help leaving because of the issues here. I think we have to live with them and follow the priest's instructions until a paranormal team and the Catholic Priests perform an exorcism! If it does not work, we're stuck with them! People are dying here attracting ghosts!" said Dr. Marshall Law.

While he was holding this meeting, a paranormal investigating team arrived with the Connecticut Catholic Clergy, and they arrived at 10:02 a.m. One hour later, an exorcism was being held. Fr. Henry Lord looked at his watch, and the time was 11:02 a.m. A gray mist was floating around the hospice campus since Fr. Lord arrived at 9:02 a.m. It turned white at 10:02 a.m., and it turned green at 11:02 a.m. during the exorcism. At 12:02 p.m., the mist was black with arms, teeth, and grabbing hands were reaching out, trying to grab someone, but the mist was not strong enough to hurt people because the exorcism was too strong because priests and paranormal investigators were trying to remove it! Then the mist vanished a minute later.

1:02 p.m., the exorcism was over!

At 2:02 p.m., the priests and paranormal investigators were there all day, saying prayers in all the rooms throughout the hospital before leaving. At 3:02 p.m., a meeting was held with the priests and paranormal investigators. "Good afternoon, ladies and gentlemen. My name is Gordon Bryant, the head leader of the Paranormal Investigating team. We have found a dangerous Poltergeist here strong enough to hurt you or kill you! A violent mist that changes colors; known as a poltergeist. The mist looks like fog, then it gets thicker, and when it darkens, it can be as black as the ace of spades, and that's when it can be dangerous! We saw visions of dead people in this black mass mist. We saw arms, grabbing hands, and vampire-like teeth rolling around like in a ball bouncing off the walls! We had to say strong prayers to get rid of it! Had we not got here this morning, a lot more people may have died. We did what we had to do to remove this nasty poltergeist. After today, you have two choices: #1, if the evil spirits continue to happen, you will need a national exorcism with Friars from Providence College and Cardinals of Georgetown University. #2, you live with them! If we can't get rid of them, we no longer can help you. The problem should be solved here! If not, you have to go to plan B! Do not talk about them or challenge them because you may open up a new portal." Thank you," said Gordon Bryant, paranormal investigator.

4:02 p.m., the priests and paranormal team left the hospice center. 5:02 p.m., the poltergeist is still here, floating around, but no one saw it! The ghost was in the basement, and no one was down there at the time.

6:02 p.m., pans, pots, cups, and dinner plates started falling when a shelf in the kitchen gave way. The cooks and kitchen staff witnessed the accident. "Hey, fellas, the shelf can't handle all that weight; stop packing too much on the shelves!" said the cook.

A knife flew across the kitchen and stuck in a wall, then landed in a sink full of water while kitchen staff was preparing meals. The time was 7:02 p.m. No one saw it. A security guard at the front gate looked at his watch, and the time was 8:02 p.m. The gate was open, waiting for a rescue when suddenly the gate closed by itself and locked! The security guard went out to unlock the gate, but it wouldn't open, and a rescue vehicle with its lights on was waiting at the gate, so he called for help. "Dr. Law, Officer Billy Banging Beaver, at the control gate. The gate closed all by itself and locked. I went out to unlock the gate, and it would not open. I have emergency vehicles waiting to get in!"

"Okay, Billy, I'll be right there!" said the doctor.

Then the gate opened by itself, and the rescues were able to get through! The security guard was shocked. Dr. Marshall Law arrived at the security gate. "Hi Doctor, something's malfunctioning here! The gate closed on its own and locked for a few minutes while a rescue was waiting. The gate locked, so I went to get the keys to unlock the gate, and it would not open! Minutes later, the gate opened on its own. Something strange is going on here!"

"Billy, maybe the poltergeist that's been haunting this hospital was trying to leave!" said the doctor.

"A poltergeist! Are you on drugs!!!" said Billy.

"We have ghosts here, hurting and killing people! Priests and paranormal investigators have been here for a week, trying to get rid of them! You were not warned about UCONN Hospice being haunted when you were hired?" said the doctor.

"Yes, I was told we have ghosts here, and I attended all the meetings about it, but it's all a bunch of garbage, because I don't believe in those things! Until I see something, I will not believe! I thought it was strange to see the gate close and lock and reopen again on its own, but I did not see anyone playing with the gate! I have been here for two and a half weeks, and I never saw anything or heard anything around here until the front gate started playing games with me! I think it's all bullshit! I heard about the Boardmen Institute was haunted, but until I see something, I do not believe!"

"Well, Billy, you will find out, because something, not from this world, is haunting this hospital!" said the doctor.

Bill closed and locked the gate. Then he went back to his office, and he heard a voice loud and clear saying, "Get out!" he heard the voice three times, and it stopped! He looked at his watch, and the time was 9:02 p.m. The officer's intercom was raised high while he was hearing the voices, and he turned it down. Then he saw a strange shape like a black roaming fog, then it formed like a bear and disappeared into the woods. Billy grabbed his gun to police the area, flashing a bright flashlight, and he found nothing for about 45 minutes. He went back to his locked office, and he saw a man dressed in all black inside!

The man had small horns, and he looked like Batman from behind. The police officer opened his office and faced a crying man and he said, "Sir, you're not supposed to be in here! What's wrong!" The man growled like a roaring bear, showing his vampire fang teeth, and he looked like the devil! Then he disappeared! The ghost went through Billy's body, knocking him down on the floor. Then Billy got up and the main gate blew open, and he saw this ugly black mass going out the opened gate, then it closed and re-locked! The time was 10:02 p.m., and it was all over in a minute! Billy frantically called Dr. Law.

"Dr. Law. Billy Banging Beaver, calling from the front gate: You're right! Something f--ked up is going on here! I believe you, doctor! I was attacked by a devil-like batman in my office! Around 9 p.m. I heard voices in my office telling me to get out! I saw the volume raised up high on the intercom, and I didn't think much of it; I thought I may have touched the wrong button on the PA system. Then I saw a black fog outside, and I watched it form into a bear-like animal running into the woods, then it was gone! I grabbed my gun and made sure the gate was locked and I locked my office and policed the grounds, making my nightly rounds outside. When I got back to my office, I saw a man that looked like Batman inside my locked office. When I arrived, unlocking the door, the man was inside, crying. He looked normal. I said to him, 'You're not supposed to be here, what's wrong!' The man growled and roared like a mean bear, and he started showing what looked like vampire teeth and blood dripping from his mouth at me. I backed up to get away from it, and it vanished, going into me, knocking me down. I felt like I was hit by lightning! Then I saw a black rolling fog going out the main gate, blowing the gate open, then it vanished! It was the scariest experience I ever had! The man looked like the devil! I was afraid to go out and locked the gate, then it closes on its own. I am still in my office, scared out of my pants!" said Billy Banging Beaver, the security guard.

"Billy, just pray, and I will be right there in a few minutes!" said the doctor.

Then Dr. Law arrived, and the security guard went out to lock the gate for the evening. Then they went to the office, moving things around, and they found nothing. "Billy, something seems to happen at two minutes after every hour. Right now, it's 10:32 p.m. In the next half hour, look at your watch, and at 11 p.m., get out of your office and get under a lighted area and pray. Lock the office and stand over near the gate under a light until 5 after 11 to be safe. Call the priest about 11 p.m. There is nothing here that will hurt you; you saw a ghost! I have to get back to my patients," said Dr. Marshall Law.

11 p.m., the security officer left his office, and he waited by the main gate under a light. He called Fr. Henry Lord at the church at 11:02 p.m., and there was no answer. Suddenly, an owl flew out of a tree and latched onto Billy Banging Beaver's throat, choking him and killing him! The security guard was fighting with the owl for ten minutes, trying to get the owl off of him but could not, and the owl tore his Adam's Apple out, and he dropped dead in a pool of blood in front of the main gate, and the owl was still attacking the security guard, then it flew off!

Dr. Marshall Law was checking the security cameras in the main hospital at 11:05 p.m., and he saw Officer Billy being attacked by the owl, and he grabbed a big knife, and he went to the main gate to call for help. He grabbed Billy's gun and keys to open his office and the main gate, and a rescue vehicle picked Billy's body up and brought him into the main hospital; now he's in hospice now! Later, Billy was declared dead by the Connecticut Coroners Team, and he was cremated at the hospice crematorium because he's an only child; there are no Banging Beavers in Connecticut!

The next day, Nurse Mary Burnstein held a meeting with the staff. "Good morning. Security guard, Billy Banging Beaver, was killed by an owl two nights ago, and he reported seeing a devilish Batman ghost attacking him in his locked office before he was killed! Dr. Marshall Law saw the footage on the hospital security cameras. Father Henry Lord, the Connecticut Catholic Clergy, and a paranormal investigating team performed a professional exorcism for a week in this hospital to get rid of the evil here; unfortunately, it's still here! A security guard is dead, and ghost sightings are still being seen on the property. The paranormal team and Catholic priests did what they can do to remove the evil from the past, and they said, if it comes back, 'there's nothing more they can do.' And if they do come back, the evil will be stronger and angrier, because the exorcisms are not working. Therefore, the hospital is given two choices: live with the evil or hire a national paranormal team and Cardinals from Georgetown University in Washington, D.C., and the powerful Friars Priest from Providence College to perform a national three-day exorcism and evacuate the hospital for a week. This will cost a lot of money, but it's better than being killed from the past Connecticut Devil!" said Nurse Burnstein.

"Before we close this meeting, if any more things happen, we will need to have a National Exorcism, before someone gets killed or seriously injured," said a nun, Sister Claire Thomas.

One man said, "I quit working here! I'm out of here before the s--t hits the fan!" The man, a nurse's assistant, walked out.

Nurse Burnstein went to a dying man's room. He was 100 years old, and he started decaying right in his bed! The man's skin was disappearing, and he was turning into a skeleton, and the smell of death was too much for Nurse Burnstein to handle. She closed his room and walked out; the man died.

Another nurse was taking care of a dying man, feeding him his medicine when suddenly smoke was coming out of the man's ears, nose, and throat, then the nurse smelled something burning. The man was farting and peeing in his bed, and a lightning bolt shot out of his a--hole, and he caught on fire and burned to death! The body burned, and the bed and everything else in the room were okay. The nurse screamed, crying, "Help! Help!! Help!!!! A man is burning in his bed in room 113!" Help arrived, and the man burned to ashes, and he died of cause! Nurses and hospice help came in with fire extinguishers to spray over the dead body! Then a black fog formed a devil-like face with big horns and mean teeth, and it roared like a mean bear and sprayed a flame of fire out of the devil ghost before it disappeared! The nurses and the hospice workers witnessed the ugly fire-spraying ghost! And they said, "We're not afraid of you! Go back to hell in the name of St. Michael, through Jesus Christ! Amen!" Then they sprayed the ghost with the CO2 fire extinguishers to choke the ghost, then it was over! "The man died from spontaneous human combustion. This act is from the devil; the devil may have taken him! The man was Asian, and he was 88 years old, and his name is Dik Suk," said the hospice team!

A woman was found rotting away in her bed until she turned into a skeleton and died. Her flesh covered the bed and was dripping on the floor, and three big rats were eating the remains of her flesh and guts! Nurses and hospice helpers watched in shock, screaming and praying! Later, a screaming lady was lying in her bed, and two black human-like figures were hanging on top of her, and hands coming out of the ghosts were grabbing her. A nurse came into the room, saw the horror unfold, and she yelled at the ghosts, "Get out of here right now!" The ghosts vanished, and the woman died!

A meeting was held with nurse Burnstein with the hospice nurses. "Good afternoon, before lunch is served. The Hauntings here, are getting worse; Patients are dying one by one, and we need to shut down for at least two weeks and call for a national exorcism. All patients will be moved to nursing homes and hospice centers here in Connecticut and Rhode Island, before things get worse. I believe the history of this facility is still possessed by the demons from the Boardmen Institute!

I fear more people may die if we don't have a national exorcism, from PC and University of Georgetown. If the national exorcism does not work, we have to live with them or close the facility! A national exorcism was performed at the Boardmen Institute, and it did not work! The devil is taking our patients when they die and we have to find a way to stop it! Fr. Henry Lord will be by later today to say prayers once again until the national exorcism and paranormal investigators arrive. It may take weeks to get all the evil out of here! Then the facility will be cleaned and painted. New floors will be replaced. This hospital will be completely sanitized before the cleaning and renovations are done! Thank you." Said nurse Mary Burnstein.

Employees began to quit and there's always help wanted ads at the 'University of Connecticut Hospice Center.' Then a national exorcism was held and the hospital and patients were evacuated! Catholic Priests, powerful Friars from Providence College', Cardinals of Georgetown University and professional paranormal investigators arrive to clean house of all the evil spirits!

The exorcism was done by May 27th, 2023. Two/three weeks later the hospice center re-opened. The national exorcism, did not work! The evil is still here while renovations and cleaning is being done! The dying patients came back and the hauntings are coming back slowly!

The day before the 4th of July, 2023, a group of visitors were visiting a patient in room 420. A little girl was looking at the wall above the patients bed. "Mommy. Look at the wall! Something's moving behind it!

"Oh, my God! It looks like a person scratching behind the wall trying to break thru! I'll get the nurse."

The mother of the little girl went to the nurses station. "Excuse me nurse. Someone is trying to break through a wall above my grandmothers bed in room 420."

"Oh, no!" Said the nurse, and she went to investigate and nothing was there.

"Hi, nurse Hypervaine, something evil is going on here in this room." Said a man, one of the visitors.

Sister Claire Thomas arrived and she felt the wall and it was warm but she did not see anything. She went to the next room and a fog formed around a lit lamp, and it vanished right in front of her eyes as soon as she entered the room next door. She said to nurse Burnstein. "Something evil is still going on here! I went into room 418 to see what is trying to break through a wall in room 420. I saw a mist clouding around a lit lamp. When I went in the room, what I saw, vanished! No one was staying in that room."

"Sister Thomas. I want you to go to each room patients are in, and say prayers. Whatever the spirits want, they will go after the dead but if people start getting hurt or killed, we will have to leave and vacate this hospital again." Said nurse, Mary Burnstein.

Sister Thomas went to the room of a dying patient and the machine the women was hooked up to, stopped and she passed away! Sister Thomas covered the dead women. Suddenly she was picked up and thrown up against a wall and thrown back down on the floor and slid across the room! She got up and she left that room in a hurry! She told nurse Burnstein what happened. "Mary, I am fucking out of here!" She said and she left.

The ghosts did not bother nurse Burnstein because she's not afraid of them and she knows how to handle them! Nurse Hypervain went to a room to give another dying women, morphine to calm her down. She was cleaning up the room. Suddenly the women's bed lifted about four feet off the floor, turned upside down and the screaming lady was thrown out of bed on to the floor and the bed landed on top of her and crushed her, as nurse Hypervain watched in shock, as she screamed hysterically! "AHHH!" Then she ran out of the room and out of the building! Another man was attacked by a ghost that looked like the devil and he died!

The problem at the hospice center got so bad, a priest and nuns' convent area was installed in the nurses' area to chase the ghosts away, but the problem is not working. The devil is doing everything possible to take away the dead! The more priests and nuns continue to check on dying patients, saying prayers, the spirits keep getting more aggressive!

A priest and a nun came into a room, saying prayers to a woman dying in her bed, and she was decaying at a rapid speed until you could see her bones! The flesh rotted, then a machine she was hooked up to malfunctioned and caught fire. The body caught fire, and her flesh melted to the steel bars of her hospital bed. She roared like a mean bear trying to get out of bed while burning to death! Then she dropped dead!

Nurses came into the room with fire extinguishers to put the fire out. The room stunk so badly, coroners had to remove the bed with the burnt body covered in sheets. The woman's flesh was still melted on the bed bars, and she was a skeleton when coroners took her out of the room.

The priests and nuns screamed, trying to say prayers, but they were choking on the smoke and the smell from rotting flesh until they had to leave the room!

Nurse Mary Burnstein was in the storage area in the basement of the hospital, moving some freight a truck had just let off on pallets. Suddenly, an owl flew out from behind one of the freight cases and into Nurse Burnstein's face, gouging out her eyes. She fought with the owl, grabbing the bird by the throat, but the owl kept scratching her face! Nurse Burnstein lost one eye, and she kept fighting with the owl until she was able to grab a box cutter and stab the owl to death! Then she called 911, and she went to the hospital. Finally, she quit the hospice center.

Later that night, Nurse Burnstein called the hospice center, telling a nurse what had happened to her. She told the nurse she quit. Later, the same nurse saw a light blinking at her desk from room 222. She went to that room, and no one was in there! There were no machine hook-ups; the room was empty.

She went back to her nurse station and said to another hospice nurse, "Marie, a light was blinking in room 222, and there's no one there. The room is empty. How can that be? I turned the light out, and now it's blinking again."

"Maybe a poltergeist is in there! Stay here, Martha, and I will go check it out!" said Marie.

Martha turned off the light from room 222. The blinking stopped, and Marie, the hospice nurse, went to investigate. When she got to room 222, the room light was blinking again. Marie went into the room, and nothing was there. Suddenly, she heard scratching sounds. She looked around the empty room. Suddenly, a crow flew out of a heating duct and attacked Marie, landing in her hair as she screamed hysterically! The crow scratched her face, plucking out her eyes, biting her nose, and taking a piece out of her ears, biting her until she collapsed!

A second and two more crows flew out of the same heating duct in room 222, attacking Marie, going for her throat, pecking and biting her until she was dead! Then all four crows flew back into the heating duct they had come out of and disappeared after getting enough to eat and blood to drink! Marie lay dead in a pool of blood.

The door was open in room 222, and Marie's blood washed out into the hallway, where a mouse was getting a drink! Martha turned the light out for the third time, and she went to the room to meet her. She saw blood in the hallway outside room 222. The mouse ran away! Martha went into the room and saw Marie's dead body, and she screamed, "AHHH!" She saw the heating vent lying on the floor, and a crow flew into the room again. Martha ran out of the room, shutting the door quickly before the crow attacked her.

The next day, the hospice center closed its doors!

FOUR

HAUNTINGS IN MATTAPOISETT

Wednesday, August 18th, 2022

The Mattapoisett Police got a call about a bunch of cars parked at the boat marina. Alarms were going off, and boats were untied and floating out in the harbor. No arrests were made, and the owners had to come and bring the untied boats back in and turn the alarms off in their cars.

The next night, police spotted a giant green glowing monster moving across the Mattapoisett Harbor, and some boats were colliding and smashing into one another! Minutes later, the green ghost vanished, leaving boats damaged. Nearly the whole police force was there, looking for possible intruders.

"Officer Glenn, did you see that? The Green Man ghost!" said another officer.

"Yes, I did. It's called the Green Man, a toxic ghost that owns this town with power, and he will never leave!"

Friday, August 20th, 2022

A massive explosion at the Mattapoisett boat marina burned all the boats and cars parked there! The blast was big enough to burn the town to the ground—maybe all because of this goddamn Green Man ghost! The cause of the blast was unknown. It looked like a nuclear bomb had dropped.

A packed restaurant at the Mattapoisett Inn was having a peaceful tea party at 2:15 p.m. that day. Five minutes later—BOOM! The ground shook like a violent earthquake! The blast blew out windows in nearby neighborhoods, the sky went black as the ace of spades, and a huge fire was visible for miles. Windows cracked, dishes and glasses fell off tables at the Mattapoisett Inn, and people screamed, running out of the restaurant to their cars in a panic.

Mattapoisett residents started running like a marathon up Route 6 toward Fairhaven, with dogs, cats, and farm animals following! The entire town was covered in black smoke in minutes. People began to think it was the end of the world, running for cover in fear. Cars and trucks followed the crowd, trying to escape up and down Route 6. Fairhaven and Marion were the escape routes.

The Mattapoisett Fire Department raced to the scene, followed by Fairhaven, New Bedford, Marion, Dartmouth, Tiverton, nearby Rochester, Cape Cod, and even Providence fire departments. Helicopters flew overhead spraying water. Fire boats parked in Buzzards Bay near the marina, spraying burning boats.

A Tiverton fire truck caught fire and burned like the rest of the vehicles. When the fire was finally put out, the marina, hundreds of vehicles, and countless boats were reduced to ash. Dead bodies floated in the water, washing ashore. The Mattapoisett boat marina looked like the gates of Hell.

Before the fire was out, the smoke created its own weather— thunder, lightning, dust devils at Ned's Point, and waterspouts. Fire trucks, police, and rescues crowded the town, driving through firenadoes. Several buildings were destroyed. For three days, fire crews and boats worked 24/7 putting out smoldering ash. Burned and damaged boats were pushed to shore for disposal. Tow trucks hauled away burned cars so the area could be cleaned and rebuilt.

The site was closed off with *No Trespassing* signs, and streets were blocked. Evacuated residents had to return home on foot, guided by police. No vehicles were allowed in until Monday, three days after the fire.

The day after, around midnight, the Green Man ghost appeared over Mattapoisett Harbor, and fire boats sprayed water at it. The Green Man disappeared.

July 15th, 2023

A couple was in town looking to buy a house. They visited a brown Cape Codder, waiting for the realtor. A 2020 Mercedes pulled up, and a lady stepped out.

"Good morning. My name is Sally Winters from Fall River Realtors."

"Hi, Sally. Andy Gillette and my wife, Alex."

"Pleased to meet you both. Come inside, and I'll show you the house.

This is a brown Cape Cod with a two-car garage, at 9 Milk Coffee Way. Only three homes are located on this dead-end street—3, 6, and 9. They're spread out, so you'll have privacy and plenty of room. Look in the woods—you've got company. A couple of deer!

Come inside. The front door leads to the living room, then the dining room, then the kitchen. Here's the porch, which exits to the backyard and connects to the garage. The garage has a long workbench, a paved cement floor, and storage.

This door leads to the basement. Wood stairs go down to a cement floor and a bulkhead out to the yard. Washer and dryer hookups. Gas heat and hot water.

Back upstairs, you've got the master bedroom with walk-in closets, a gas fireplace, and two windows. The bathroom has a jacuzzi, toilet, sink, linen closet, and window.

Upstairs, there's a small bath and two bedrooms, each with walk-in closets and two windows. Back downstairs, the living room has three windows and a gas fireplace.

The backyard has an acre of land with apple trees and pines, plus a storage shed behind the garage. The house has a new roof and has been completely renovated. It's ready now—$450,000. A 15-year mortgage is about $4,125 a month.

Mattapoisett has beaches, parks, restaurants, and the famous Mattapoisett Inn and harbor. Good luck!"

The Gillette's bought the house. Their daughters, Ruth and Debra, helped them move in with friends. Eight days later, trucks delivered furniture and appliances. While movers set up the washer and dryer in the basement, a mist appeared there—but no one noticed.

July 23rd

That night, a violent thunderstorm struck. Alex dreamed of a tornado ripping the house into the sky, sucking her out the window like in *The Wizard of Oz*. She woke up breathing heavily. It was 3:02 a.m. Outside, wind bent the trees, lightning flashed, and thunder shook the room. Minutes later, the storm passed.

At 5:30 a.m., Alex and Andy got up for work. She was a nurse at Saint Anne's Hospital in Fall River. He was a teacher at Durfee High School.

"Andy, do we get tornadoes here?" Alex asked.

"Not in Mattapoisett. Why?"

"I dreamed one hit the house last night."

"That storm was bad. I heard it too."

They ate a quick breakfast and left for work.

"I had a scary dream during last night's storm. Our house was hit by a tornado and we were flying in the air like in the movie *The Wizard of Oz*, and I was sucked out a window into the mean funnel!"

"That storm was bad last night. I heard it too!"

Then the couple had a quick breakfast and they were off to work. Andy had short days until school started in September, and he was getting his classroom ready, ordering books and cleaning up his classrooms.

Sally was in the break room having lunch with a bunch of nurses at the hospital, and she was talking with her co-workers about her new house. One nurse said to her, "You moved to Mattapoisett! Have you seen any ghosts there?"

"I don't believe in such a thing. We had a bad storm last night!"

"Sally, Mattapoisett is the ghost capital of the world! There's a lot of ghosts there!" said the nurse.

Sally laughed. Then lunch break was over and she went back to work.

About lunchtime Andy came home and fixed himself a chicken sandwich, then he went out to cut the lawn. He saw a black figure out in the woods and he said, "Excuse me! But you're on private property!" Then the figure disappeared behind a tree.

He went in the storage shed and grabbed his shotgun and went to where he saw the black figure. He cocked his gun twice and fired one shot into the woods, but he saw nothing!

Then Andy went back to the shed and was pouring gasoline into the sit-down lawnmower when suddenly he heard someone knocking against a wall in the storage shed. He grabbed his gun and went outside and saw a tree branch banging up against the shed, blowing in the wind.

He walked around and behind the shed and garage, but he saw nothing. He went for a brief walk into the woods on his property and he hollered out, "Whoever is roaming on my property, I have a big gun!"

Then he cut the lawn before Alex came home.

About 2:30 p.m. he pulled a grill out of the shed and wheeled it to the outdoor patio because he was going to cook some steaks tonight for dinner. An hour later he saw a big deer in the woods. Andy went to the shed to grab his shotgun and he shot the prancing deer in the ass! The deer ran away like a bat outta hell! He went looking for the deer, carrying his gun, but the deer was long gone. He went back to the shed to put his gun away.

Then Andy heard wings flapping outside while he was in the shed. He went looking outside where he heard the wings. He looked in the trees and around his house, but he saw nothing.

About 4 p.m. he went into the garage to put tools away and he heard a soft voice: "Get out!" He could barely hear the voice. Then he went back to the shed to get a table and chairs to set up on the patio near the grill. He heard the same voice again, very softly: "Get out!"

"Who's out there?" he hollered.

"Excuse me, sir. Are you the new owner of this house?"

"Yes, sir. My name is Andy Gillette, and my wife Alex will be home from work shortly."

"Pleased to meet you. I'm Stanley Smith. My wife is Sarah, and we live at 6 Milk Coffee Way."

"Nice to meet you, Stanley. I would like to invite you and your wife for dinner. I am cooking a few steaks."

"Okay, Andy, thank you. I will bring over a 12-pack and a bottle of wine. Do you like Bud Light and white and red wine?"

"Yes, we do!" said Andy.

Then he started cooking, and he noticed a big bird—a hawk— sitting on top of his house. Then the hawk flew off. Andy went in the house to bring out some hot dogs and hamburgers to put on the grill. Then he put potatoes and peppers to cook on the grill, then went back in the house to bring out hamburger and hot dog rolls and cheese.

Suddenly a hawk landed on the grill, eating the steaks, and its wings were catching fire. It flew off with two steaks! One in its mouth, holding the other with its front claws, flapping its smoky wings—and vanished! Andy could not believe what he had just seen.

He went to the shed to get his gun. Suddenly a second hawk grabbed another steak and flew away! Andy shot at the second hawk and missed.

Then the couple next door came over and Stanley introduced his wife Sarah.

"Pleased to meet you. I am Sarah Smith."

Then Alex arrived home from work to meet the couple next door.

"You're not going to believe what just happened!"

"You're not going to believe what just happened! I cooked four steaks to have tonight, and now only one remains! Two hawks came out of nowhere and grabbed the steaks off the burning grill! One hawk caught fire attacking my grill. I watched in shock while bringing out the buns and cheese, and it flew off with two steaks— one in its mouth and one in its claws!"

"Sarah, you can have the steak. The rest of us will be eating hamburgers and hot dogs. I have my gun at my side in case the hawks come back. I almost shot one, but I missed! Alex, strange things have been happening to me today when I got home from Durfee High School. First I saw a man dressed in black with no face. I don't believe in ghosts, neither does my wife. But it was a strange being. I told it to leave because it was on private property. Then it suddenly vanished! I fired several shots out into the woods to scare it away. Then I heard someone knocking on the shed wall, only to find tree branches banging against it. Then I saw a big hawk on the roof of the house and heard voices that I can't explain. And then two hawks landed on my burning grill to steal the steaks. One even caught fire!"

"Andy, people at work told me that Mattapoisett is haunted and there are a lot of ghosts here! I don't believe them," said Alex.

"Andy and Alex, if you don't believe in ghosts, you better think again! Mattapoisett is loaded with them. Watch out for the Green Man, a huge green figure about 20 or 30 feet tall. You can't miss him because you'll see him at night. Later tonight let's take a ride to the Ned's Point Lighthouse around 1 a.m. and you may see it. Don't challenge it—just enjoy the viewing—because the Green Man has been known to burn things if you bother it. Last August we had a mega boat marina fire that burned hundreds of boats, cars, and buildings, and 13 people were killed! Law enforcement believes the Green Man Ghost was responsible for the disaster. He almost burned the whole town of Mattapoisett down. Residents here know not to mess with him. We have more dangerous ghosts in Mattapoisett, but the Green Man is deadly!" said Sarah, the next-door neighbor.

"Have you heard any stories from the last people who lived in this house?" asked Andy.

"No, they just saw animals, mostly deer, but they never told us anything strange happening to them," said Sarah.

The two couples ate and had a few drinks, talking about ghost stories. Then they went for a ride to Ned's Point Park late that night to see the Green Man Ghost, and they spent hours waiting— and saw nothing.

"You people are a bunch of bullshitters!" Andy joked.

The next day Alex was off from work and Sarah brought her mail over to her.

"Here's your mail. We were holding it until you moved in. I had a dream last night that your house was hit by a tornado!"

"Oh my God, Sarah, I had the same dream two nights ago! Do we get tornadoes here?" asked Alex.

"We've been living here for about 25 years and we never had one in Mattapoisett, but lately the Cape, Rhode Island, and parts of Massachusetts have been getting them all summer long. We had a lot of rain and storms this summer," said Sarah.

"That's when I had my dream. The tornado took our house away with me and Andy in it. It was just like the one in *The Wizard of Oz!*"

Alex and Sarah talked about their stories all day.

The next week, August began, and Andy and Alex were on vacation from work. Now they could explore Mattapoisett.

They began going to the town beach. After swimming and laying in the sun and having lunch on the beach, later the ice cream truck arrived.

"Alex, do me a favor. Do you want to get some ice cream?" Andy gave Alex some money.

Meanwhile, a lady dressed in 1700s clothing came over to chat with him.

"Good afternoon. My name is Maria Cooper, the town drifter."

"Pleased to meet you. My name is Andy and my wife Alex is getting ice cream. We just moved here."

"Andy, welcome to Mattapoisett Town Beach. You're in danger when next week's storm comes!"

"Excuse me, miss, but I don't know what you're talking about! Do you want a bottle of water? It's a hot day."

"Please, I would like one!"

Andy went in his cooler to get the bottle of water for her—and she was gone!

Alex came back with the ice cream.

"Did you see that lady in the black and white colonial clothes I was talking to?"

"No, Andy. Here's your ice cream."

"I was just talking with her a minute ago. She introduced herself, told me she was the town drifter, and said I'd be in danger when next week's storm comes. I couldn't make out what she was saying very well, and when I offered her a bottle of water, she vanished. It seems like I was talking to a ghost!"

"That's strange, Andy."

After eating the ice cream, Alex heard a voice in her right ear, very softly: "A tornado is going to hit your house very soon!" Alex looked back but saw no one.

"Andy, I heard someone whispering in my ear about the dream I had, about a tornado hitting our house. When I looked around, no one was there!"

"Don't worry, Alex, a tornado is not going to hit our house. It was only a dream," said Andy.

Later Alex went to the restroom at the beach and she saw the lady in black and white combing her hair in front of a mirror. After going to the toilet she went to wash her hands—and the lady was gone!

She told Andy, "I saw the lady you were talking to in the ladies' room."

Later the couple went for a ride through town and went to the Mattapoisett Inn for dinner. Then they went home.

Stanley and Sarah from 6 Milk Coffee Way came over.

"Welcome. Mattapoisett is a nice town with a pretty beach and harbor. We went to the Mattapoisett Inn for dinner and visited Gazebo Park, Ned's Point, and drove around to see the nice homes and the new boatyard. Please join us for wine, cheese, and crackers," said Alex.

"Stanley, when me and Alex were at the beach, I sent her to go get ice cream, and this strange-looking lady dressed in black and white colonial clothes from the late 1600s came over to introduce herself. Maria Cooper, or something like that. She said strange things to me about us being in danger when next week's storm comes. I couldn't make out what she was saying. I told her I didn't know what she meant and offered her a bottle of water, and when

I went into the cooler to get it, she was gone! My wife saw her combing her hair in the ladies' room."

"Andy, you were talking to a ghost! Maria Cooper, the town drifter, who visits the beach and the Mattapoisett Harbor from time to time. She was killed during a shipwreck in 1717, and her body floated into the town beach. She visits new residents and somehow predicts the future for people. She haunts the beach every once in a while!"

"Stanley, when I had that dream about a tornado hitting our house, this strange lady told my husband he was in danger when next week's storm comes. That's freaky!" said Alex.

"We've had some strange things happening at this house, and we haven't lived here more than two weeks. You saw the hawks stealing my steaks off the grill last night, and I saw a strange man dressed in black standing in my backyard. I never believed in ghosts, but this is something I can't explain," said Andy.

"Andy, you and Alex need to do two things: #1, call a Catholic priest to come and bless your home. #2, go to the library after the priest is done and find out the history of this house. Mattapoisett is a nice quiet bedroom community, with nice beaches, restaurants, and parks, but it also has its dark side. This town is a dumping ground for ghosts—we live over an Indian burial ground."

"When you go to the library, you will learn all the ghost stories in this town; even the library is haunted! Good luck," said Sarah, the neighbor from 6 Milk Coffee Way.

After talking about ghost stories all night, the next morning Andy had a doctor's appointment. Then he and Alex went to Oxford Creamery for lunch and afterward they went to the library.

"Good afternoon. My name is Andy Gillette, and this is my wife, Alex."

"Pleased to meet you. I'm Carol Armstrong, the head librarian. How can I help you?"

"We just moved to Mattapoisett three weeks ago. We live at

9 Milk Coffee Way, and my wife and I have been experiencing some strange happenings there. I want to find out the history of this house," Andy said.

"Let's take a look," Carol said. She searched the location and then looked up. "There are no serious hauntings recorded on that property, but the house is located above an Indian burial ground. You may see shadows or quick flashes like heat lightning, but nothing that will hurt you."

"Carol, we went to the town beach yesterday and a strange lady came to me telling me that I am in danger when next week's storm comes. I thought she was strange and I was ready to give her a bottle of water, and suddenly she was not there. My wife saw her in the ladies' room. My next-door neighbors said I was talking to a ghost. My wife heard a voice in her ear telling her a tornado is going to hit our house. My neighbors said I was talking to the beach ghost — they called her Maria Cooper, the town drifter. She identified herself with that name," Andy said.

"We have experienced several ghost sightings here in Mattapoisett. Strange things have even happened right here in this library," Carol said. "The Green Man is the worst one — he's a monster-looking devil that appears and disappears. When he's challenged, he's dangerous. This ghost may have burned down the boat marina during the pandemic with electric lightning-like energy. The Green Man has burned down homes and businesses, killed people and animals, and destroyed property over the years. As long as you live here, learn not to bother or harass the Green Man.

"We had a house on Sixth Street that was haunted by multiple ghosts for about fifty years before the house burned down — Ebenezer, a very powerful demonic ghost that's physical and can hurt you; then an unknown invisible dangerous ghost; then the Elmira ghost. People living in that house tried to get rid of the evil by inviting more powerful ghosts and practicing witchcraft, but it didn't work. The Deopola Debra ghost was invited in from the Alaska Triangle to get rid of the Ebenezer ghost, but Deopola Debra was a strong demon brought in through the Bridgewater Triangle to get rid of the Green Man. Instead, it made the Green Man stronger and it overpowered both Ebenezer and Deopola Debra. We have more strong demons here in Mattapoisett — a big black red-eyed wolf, a red-eyed deer, and big black red-eyed demon birds.

"We have a ghost inside this library that's invisible and may throw a book at your head. There's a book by author Richard Rezendes from Brown University called *A Haunting in Mattapoisett.* Talk to Gloria Stevens from the news — she will answer questions about the Mattapoisett ghosts," Carol finished.

Later, Andy and Alex talked with Gloria Stevens, then they went home.

At night, Andy and Alex were in bed when they suddenly heard wings flapping inside the house.

"Andy, do you hear that? It sounds like a bird is in our house."

"Yes, I did."

Andy grabbed his gun and checked every window and door, making sure they were locked and that the fireplace doors were closed. "The house is all locked up. It's impossible for a bird to be flying inside. The flapping sounds may be inside the walls or the eaves," he said.

The time of the flapping sounds was 11:02 p.m. An hour later they woke to a thumping noise at 12:02 a.m. Andy got up to check the house again; nothing was out of place. At 1:02 a.m. they woke to the sound of hard rain. At 2:02 a.m. they woke to thunder. At 3:02 a.m. a lightning strike flashed outside. Alex woke and looked at the alarm clock; the time was 3:02 a.m.

She saw lightning, then she heard thunder, and she saw lightning flashing again. Then it all stopped a minute later. They woke up hearing a strong wind; it was 4:02 a.m. The wind stopped a minute later. At 5:02 a.m., Alex woke up hearing a loud bang. She woke Andy.

"I think someone's in this house. Did you hear that bang?" she asked.

"Yes, I did! We have to get up for work in an hour, and it has not been a good night with all the noise!" Andy said.

He went looking around the house, trying to find where the noises were coming from, but found nothing. He stayed up until it was time to get ready for work. At 6:02 a.m. he heard an owl howling outside for about a minute; then it stopped. At 6:30, Alex got up to get ready for work.

"You're up already!" she said.

"Yeah. I got up about 5 a.m., hearing these strange noises and storms during the night."

"I heard them too! What would you like for breakfast?"

"You can make me sausage and eggs," he said.

At 7:02 a.m. a bird bounced off a window and Alex saw it; she screamed.

"What's the matter, Alex?"

"I just saw a big bird bounce off the kitchen window—two or three times!"

"Wow. That's not good. That usually means someone is going to die!"

"Really?" said Alex.

At 7:34 a.m. the couple left for work. At 8:02 a.m., a message came over their cell phones while they were driving: "Warning from the National Weather Service: Watch out for severe thunderstorms developing this afternoon for all of southern New England. Be ready to take cover."

When Andy and Alex arrived at work, Alex heard weather reports on the radio at the hospital where she worked as a nurse. She saw a black shadow moving along a wall; it was 9:02 a.m. Andy was at Durfee High School placing books in his classroom when he heard wind blowing outside strong enough to blow windows open; it was 10:02 a.m. An hour later the sun disappeared and it began raining. The rain stopped at 11:03 a.m.

At 12:02 p.m., Ruth and Debra—Andy and Alex's daughters—stopped at the house to drop off a package. They rang the doorbell, and no one answered, so they left. At 1:02 p.m. Alex finished her lunch and went out and bought a white pet rabbit to bring home after work. At 2:02 p.m., Andy was at a press conference at Durfee High School and would be coming home late.

At 3:02 p.m., Andy and Alex got alert warnings on their phones about a coming storm, "Tornado warning: Please get to a safe place in a hurry! Doppler radar reported a tornado touchdown in Dartmouth, Massachusetts. Please take cover right now! This is a life-threatening situation! Tornado warning for the following locations: Westport, Dartmouth, New Bedford, Fairhaven, Mattapoisett, Rochester, Marion, and all of Cape Cod, Massachusetts. August 8th, 2023."

The warnings kept repeating on everyone's phones and on TV and radio. Andy ran to the basement at the school; Alex ran to the basement at the hospital, holding her rabbit. The tornado struck homes in Dartmouth before exiting out to sea at a beach, becoming a stationary waterspout. It all lasted one minute and then it was gone.

Alex told one of the nurses, "Alice, my name is Alex Gillette, and my husband and I live in Mattapoisett. I had a dream about a week ago that a tornado hit our new house. My next-door neighbor had the same dream. A strange lady's voice at the town beach told me a tornado was going to hit our house; I clearly heard the voice in my right ear. I saw this strange lady in the restroom at the beach combing her hair. I turned to leave the restroom and when I looked back to say 'Goodbye,' she was gone! This lady came to my husband at the beach telling him he was in danger before next week's storm. My next-door neighbor said we were communicating with the beach ghost!"

"That's a cute rabbit you have," Alice said.

"Thank you," Alex answered.

At 4:02 p.m., a second tornado touched down in Mattapoisett and sliced through the Gillette's' home at 9 Milk Coffee Way.

Before the tornado struck, Sarah was working in her garden at 6 Milk Coffee Way. The sun was shining, then the wind picked up and dark clouds formed quickly. She heard thunder and then rain and hail started coming down. She went inside to close the windows because the rain and hail were coming down hard and blowing sideways. She saw a bright flash of lightning and heard a loud bang of thunder; then another crash, ten times louder than the thunder she had heard, and glass breaking—then another loud boom. Then it was over and the sun came back out.

Sarah screamed, "AHH!" Then she went outside when the wind and the loud noise were over. She saw what had happened to the Gillette's' home: the tornado had sliced through it, separating part of the house and the garage and carving a path through the backyard into the woods.

"Oh my dear God!" Sarah said to herself. She called Andy, but got no response because his phone was off—he was in a meeting. Then she called Alex.

"Alex, this is Sarah Smith. I have bad news: a tornado hit your house. There's a lot of damage!" she cried.

Alex left the hospital and went home. She called Andy. "Andy, a tornado hit our house. Please come home right away!" she begged.

"What? Are you busting my balls again?" he replied.

"No, Andy. Come home!"

By 5:02 p.m. the severe thunderstorm was over, the sky cleared, and the wind stopped. Alex arrived at the house and cried in Sarah's arms. Andy arrived and saw the damage; he couldn't believe it. Police cars, a fire truck, and a rescue unit arrived.

"Anyone injured?" a rescue worker asked.

"Not that I know of. My daughters were coming to drop off packages. I hope they weren't in the house," Andy said.

A fire had started in part of the house. The blaze began around 6:02 p.m., and the fire department quickly put it out. At 7:02 p.m., rescue workers went through the house looking for injured people or bodies, but they found no one. At 8:02 p.m., police closed off the area with yellow tape and put up no-trespassing signs.

Andy called the real estate office to report the tornado damage. The realtor heard about it and offered the Gillette's another place to stay.

"Hi, Andy and Alex. Sally Winters from Fall River Realtors. We saw the tornado on the news. I have keys to a room at The Inn of Shipyard Park (formerly the Mattapoisett Inn). Go there after you collect your belongings until the house gets repaired. If the home cannot be repaired, we'll find another one," the realtor said.

At 9:02 p.m. the Gillette's had dinner at their next-door neighbors' house. Lightning and more storms started again at that time. At 10:02 p.m., Andy and Alex went to their damaged home to get necessities, but police and firefighters chased them out.

"Excuse me, but you're crossing no-trespassing and closed-off police zones!" said a Mattapoisett police officer.

"This is our home, and we need to get our things before we evacuate," Andy argued.

"You people will have to leave. It's not safe here!" the officer said.

Andy and Alex argued at length before leaving to avoid arrest. It was what it was.

At 11:02 p.m., Andy and Alex watched a movie on Lifetime at Stanley and Sarah's home next door when suddenly a loud bang occurred: lightning struck the chimney at 6 Milk Coffee Way, and bricks fell into their fireplace, scaring the four of them and their dog. The dog barked nonstop. Lightning also struck a tree and a mailbox at 3 Milk Coffee Way; no one was home there. By 12:02 a.m., everything was quiet. The fire department was called to check out the lightning damage at 6 Milk Coffee Way.

The Smiths and the Gillette's were up all night cleaning storm damage. The next day the Gillette's' home was bulldozed because there was so much tornado damage. The Gillette's ended up moving back to Fall River.

That evening at the Mattapoisett Library, a man was reading a book around 7 p.m. when he heard a voice say, "Hey you!" The voice was clear. He looked around and said, "Who's that?" He got up to look and saw a lady at the front desk, but the voice wasn't hers. He sat back down to read. Suddenly a book flew off a shelf and hit him in the back of the head.

"Hey, motherfucker! Who's throwing books at my head? I'm going to strangle you, you cocksucker!" he yelled.

"Sir, watch your language, and you must be quiet—you're in a library," the receptionist said.

"Lady, who threw a book at my head?" he demanded.

"I don't know, sir," she said.

The man looked around the library searching for the thrower. He saw a black shadow slip by a shelf, then another book flew off and struck him; he blocked it with his arm. Another book missed his head, then another one hit him. He left the library in a hurry and went to Mike's Restaurant in Fairhaven to meet friends for dinner.

"Good evening, Derick, Lori, David, Doreen, Ron, and Linda. Don't go to the Mattapoisett Library—there's some kind of ghost there! I was reading when a book flew off a shelf and hit me in the back of the head. I got up yelling, screaming, and swearing. I saw a black shadow. I don't believe in ghosts, but then a bunch of books flew off the shelves at me! No one else was in the library except me and the receptionist. She didn't warn me—something didn't want me there!" he told them.

"Mike, what drugs are you taking?" Doreen asked. {Mike was the man from the library.

"Why don't you go find out for yourself?" he replied.

The seven of them watched the news about the tornado that hit 9 Milk Coffee Way before they had dinner. The following Tuesday, David and Doreen went to the Mattapoisett Library to look for the ghost. They saw nothing and left. A woman reading a book felt someone blow in her ear; she turned quickly and no one was there. She moved away from the windows and sat in a closed-off room surrounded by bookshelves. Suddenly she felt a chill and moved to sit somewhere else.

The woman, about sixty-five, returned to the main library where it was warm, but then felt the chill again and heard a voice call her name: "Nancy!" The voice called her name three times.

She stood and said, "Who's calling my name?" No one answered. Then she saw a bright mist come out of a heating vent and form into a black shadow that shaped a devilish human figure. It charged through her, disappeared into a row of books, passed through a wall, and was gone. She screamed:

"AHHH!"

She went to the front desk and said, "I don't want to take this book! Why didn't you tell me you have ghosts here?"

"You never asked me, Nancy," the receptionist replied.

"I'm not coming here anymore. You can have your ghosts!" she said.

The librarian was walking around the library before closing time, taking books off tables and placing them on shelves where they belonged. Then she checked all the doors and windows to make sure they were closed and locked. She went back to her desk to gather her pocketbook and keys, ready to leave.

She heard a voice, loud and clear: "Get out!" — about four times. The voices sounded like they were coming from behind a shelf of books. She called the Mattapoisett Police.

"Hi — I'm Dale Rogers calling from the library. Someone's in here because I hear voices behind my desk, but I can't find anybody. I checked the entire facility — no one is here. Somebody is hiding somewhere!" she said.

"Okay, Miss Rogers, we'll be right there," the police dispatcher replied.

While Dale waited for the police, strange things began to happen. She saw a white mist coming out of a heating duct; it quickly turned black and looked like the devil, with hands grabbing out of the black mass. It charged at Dale, passed through her, and then disappeared. Dale's hair stood straight up, as if blown in the wind, even though there was no wind inside the library. Her pocketbook flew off her desk onto the floor, dumping out money, credit cards, lipstick, and personal papers. Then books began flying off the shelves onto the floor, creating a big mess and setting off the alarm. It was 8:02 p.m., and all of this happened in only a minute — then it stopped.

The police arrived. "You have a big mess here," the officer said.

"Officer, you're not going to believe this, but some kind of evil is haunting this library," Dale said. "I saw what looked like the devil coming out from a heater/air-conditioning unit. It was a white and gray fog, then it turned black, forming into a demon with horns, red eyes, and pointy ears, with hands and grabbing arms coming out of it. It charged after me, went through me, and disappeared into the book gallery behind my desk. Then my pocketbook flew off the desk and emptied all over the floor. When I went to pick up what fell out, books started flying off the shelves and striking me. A woman earlier saw the same thing — it threw books at her and the temperature dropped. I'm new as the librarian here, and I was told we have a ghost in this library. I heard faint shadows and voices before, but today was the first time I saw the real ghost and was attacked. I never believed in ghosts until I started working here and hearing stories from customers. I heard voices from time to time, but I never paid them much attention."

"All right — I'll help you pick up your things so you can lock up. I'm new with the police department, and I've heard plenty of ghost stories in this town," the officer said. He helped Dale gather her belongings, locked up the library, and left for the evening. The officer looked at his watch; it was 8:51 p.m.

Dale had forgotten to set the alarm. At 9:02 p.m., books and papers flew off shelves, leaving a big mess for the day shift. The next morning, the library looked like it had been struck by a tornado. The morning shift staff were stunned. The police returned and searched the library for an intruder; they found a huge mess but no sign of anyone, and certainly no ghost.

The following day, the same police officer was driving his routine patrol down Wolves Den Road when he saw an Indian village with people dancing around a campfire, a field full of spider webs, and a boarded-up house that looked like Michael Myers's house from the movie *Halloween*. The area felt like Halloween in late August. Then he saw a deer with red eyes standing in the middle of the road; a fog formed around the deer. He drove his cruiser closer, and the deer ran off into the woods. The officer noted that a witch supposedly lived in the boarded-up house — the only house on that road. As it was getting dark he saw headlights coming up the road.

The headlights got close and then suddenly disappeared.

"That's strange," the cop muttered to himself as he continued driving down Wolves Den Road.

He soon entered a dense wooded area, and a green mist floated through the trees. *The Greenman was passing through,* he thought, and then it vanished into the darkness.

A bobcat with bright red eyes crossed the road. More red eyes flickered in and out of the forest as he drove. Suddenly, he encountered dead animals lying in the road—dozens of them. Some were torn open, their guts spilled across the pavement, others covered in blood. Giant black vultures feasted on the remains.

The officer turned on his lights, honking the horn and turning on the siren to scare the birds away.

"Officer George Kelly, Car #3, to headquarters, over!"

"Headquarters, Lieutenant Henry Lecter speaking."

"Lieutenant, I'm driving on Wolves Den Road and just came across a bunch of dead animals in the road. They're torn open, covered in blood—raccoons, rabbits, rats, foxes, bobcats, coyotes, deer... Some are so mangled I can't even identify them. It looks like something very big is killing these animals."

"Officer George, don't get out of your car. Just continue your routine patrol. You're going to see a lot out there. Make sure you check the only house on that road—the boarded-up one near the Indian camp. Keep your gun ready; strange things happen there."

"I'll be heading back that way soon," George said.

He drove further down the road. Fog appeared in his headlights, then cleared into darkness. He returned to the boarded-up house, driving over more dead animals. He exited his car, gun drawn, and rang the doorbell.

"Police! Anyone home?"

It was silent. He returned to his car and drove back into town.

Later, he stopped at the town beach. A lady approached his car.

"Hi, officer. Can you give me directions to the Wolves Indian Camp? My name is Maria Cooper, the town drifter."

"Sure, I can look it up for you," George said. He checked the map on his computer. "I have the Indian village located on Wolves Den Road."

When he printed out the directions to give to her, she was gone.

Later that evening, he saw her walking on the water along the beach, glowing in white. Her image dimmed and eventually vanished. George wiped the fog from his glasses, convinced he had seen what he saw.

Back at the station, he reported to Lieutenant Lecter:

"Lieutenant, who's Maria Cooper? She approached me on the beach after 10 p.m., asked for directions, and when I printed them out, she vanished. Then I saw her walking on the water in a bright white robe, and she disappeared right before my eyes! I even checked my foggy glasses!"

"Officer Kelly," Lecter said, "you were communicating with a ghost. Maria Cooper is the beach ghost. She appears like a real person and talks to you, sees into people, and somehow knows what you're doing, even if she doesn't know you. If she delivers a threatening message, pay attention—it's a warning. Mattapoisett is full of spooks; it's Halloween year-round here. Starting next week, you'll be on third shift from 11 p.m. to 7 a.m., assigned to Wolves Den Road, the library, the beach, and local parks."

A few days later, a group of teenagers from Fall River was roaming Wolves Den Road, causing trouble near the Indian village. The Indians were dancing around a campfire, roasting a pig, and calling on spirits. A car carrying five boys, ages 15 to 18, entered the camp. One boy got out and approached the boarded-up witch's house. He broke in, kicking down the front door with a karate move.

Minutes later, he didn't come out. The witch had killed him with a bow and arrow, then carried his body to a shadowy cave and dumped it in a dry well.

The other four boys fought with the Indians but were overwhelmed. They ran toward their car, only to be surrounded by a pack of Indians wielding bows, arrows, and sticks. They were killed, and their bodies taken away to unknown graves.

A passing driver saw the attack and a burning car near the village and called the police at 11:02 p.m. By the time officers arrived, the attack had lasted barely a minute.

"Officer Kelly, sorry to disturb you, but there's a serious situation on Wolves Den Road. A man saw a brawl and a burning car. Team up with Officer Rafael Punta and investigate. Fire, rescue, and additional help are on the way," Lieutenant Lecter instructed.

George Kelly and Rafael Punta arrived to find the burning car. Officer Punta exclaimed, "Oh my God! Is that a human head near the car?!"

"Car #3 to headquarters, over!" George called.

"Go ahead, Officer Kelly."

"There's a dead body! Officer Punta spotted a human head but no body!"

Minutes later, the area was swarming with police, rescue, and fire personnel. The coroner removed the human head using a shovel and placed it in a body bag. Only the head was found; the rest of the victims were missing.

"Officers, you need a search warrant! Otherwise, get out!" the Indians shouted.

The police presented the warrant and searched the camp and village. Help arrived from Marion, Rochester, Fairhaven, Wareham, New Bedford, and the Massachusetts State Police. Thirty-five Indians were taken into custody and questioned.

While the tribe was detained, their camp and village were destroyed. Bulldozers and armed vehicles arrived the next day, assisted by the National Guard. Human and animal bones were later found underground. The camp was closed off with police tape and a fence, with keep-out signs and military guards.

That night, Officer Kelly was driving past the camp when headlights appeared fast, aimed at him, then vanished before impact. Shaken, he got out of his car into total darkness.

As he drove further, a huge black wolf with menacing teeth crossed the road. Then a giant owl flew from a tree, bounced off his windshield, landed in the road flapping its wings, then flew away. Continuing down the road, he saw a strange animal, larger than a bear, with massive teeth and a wide jaw.

The strange animal disappeared just before Officer Kelly could drive close to it. The creature looked massive—big enough, he thought, to swallow his car.

"What more evil will I see driving down this road?" he muttered to himself.

He turned around, heading back toward town, and suddenly a deer with red eyes leapt onto his car. Before he could react, it vanished. The deer had moved at lightning speed.

Later, as Officer Kelly drove near the beach in a dark area, a lady dressed in white and black ran directly in front of his car. He hit her. The officer heard a thump—thump!—then stopped his car and got out to check. She was gone. He searched under the car and scanned the area with his flashlight. Nothing.

He radioed headquarters.

"Car #3 to headquarters, over."

"Headquarters, Lieutenant Lecter speaking."

"Lieutenant, I just hit a lady near the town beach! I got out to check, and she's nowhere to be found. I looked everywhere—she vanished!"

"What did she look like?" Lecter asked.

"I didn't get a good look, but she wore white and a black hat. It happened so fast—I didn't have time to react!"

"Officer Kelly, I think you hit the beach ghost," Lecter said calmly.

Kelly pulled into the police station to finish his shift. It was raining. He glanced at his watch: 6:52 a.m., eight minutes before his shift ended. As he parked near a large tree, a lady appeared from behind it, dressed in white and black.

"You hit me last night! You ran me over!" she said—and vanished before his eyes.

Kelly made the sign of the cross. "Holy shit!" he muttered.

Inside, he told Lieutenant Lecter what had just happened. Police had searched the beach and found no body.

"I told you, George," Lecter said. "This town is haunted by several powerful entities. You ran over the beach ghost—Maria Cooper. She's a ball buster. If she appears again, just say, 'Maria Cooper, go back to the beach.' Don't argue or joke with her. She and the Greenman are extremely dangerous. Do not challenge them; bad things will happen."

The next night, Officer Kelly was on his assignment on Wolves Den Road. He saw bodies being dug up and loaded onto flatbed trucks by National Guard troops. He stopped at the boarded-up witch's house and saw her cutting open a deer, pulling out the guts, and eating it raw. She drank blood straight from the deer's leg, then washed her hair in the bloody carcass, bathing in it like a grotesque ritual.

Kelly didn't get out of his car—he drove on, pulling over shortly after and vomiting violently. Branches of nearby trees seemed to move on their own, hurling apples at him. He got back in his car.

A giant owl swooped down from a tree, smashing into his windshield, showing its glowing red eyes before flying away.

"Jesus Christ! I'm not getting out of this fucking car!" he yelled.

The rain started, hammering down as Kelly checked the time: 3:02 a.m. Lightning struck a huge tree, trapping his car. The wind roared, blowing the tree aside and freeing the vehicle.

Finally, he came face-to-face with the Greenman in the middle of the road. Frozen with fear, he tried to drive through—but the ghost collided with his car. Kelly's vehicle crashed violently, and he was killed instantly.

FIVE

A HAUNTING IN EAST GREENWICH

A custodian was being hired at a school in East Greenwich, Rhode Island. At 1:02 p.m., a man was being interviewed at the town public schools office. The man went into the office.

"Good afternoon. I am looking for Mr. Bob Walmart, for a job interview."

"What's your name?" said the receptionist.

"David Leo."

"Follow me. Bob, you have a customer."

"Good afternoon. Have a seat. My name is Bob Walmart, the director for the custodians."

"Pleased to meet you. My name is David Leo, looking for work."

"David, we're looking for substitute custodians to work during the evenings at all the public schools in East Greenwich. I need one for the Eldridge School from 1 p.m. to 9:30 p.m., Monday through Friday. The night custodian there is out. If you do well, you can sub at the other schools when you're finished at Eldridge. You will be working at this school full-time for six weeks. Danny Rose will be your supervisor, and he will be here shortly to take you to the school and show you the job. Fill out some paperwork while you wait for him," said Bob Walmart.

Later, Danny arrived at the office.

"David. This is Danny Rose, your supervisor," said Bob Walmart.

"Pleased to meet you David. Come with me and I will take you to the school where you'll be working at."

"Nice to meet you sir: I look forward to working for the East Greenwich School Department."

Danny Rose took David in the school maintenance van to the Eldridge School. Then he showed him what to do.

"David, this is the school where you will be working beginning tomorrow from 1 p.m. till 9:30 p.m. You will be given a swipe card to enter the school, and when you leave at night, make sure the door is closed tight and it will lock itself.

"Come downstairs, this is the boiler room and the custodian closet is here and the next room is the custodian room and a restroom. All the supplies are stored in this room and equipment to work with. You have a microwave oven to warm up your food, a coffee pot, and a TV you can watch during your break periods. You have a timesheet to fill out the hours you work and supply slips to make orders.

"Come upstairs and I will show you your assignment. Let's meet the head building custodian. David, this is Gary Harry," said Danny Rose.

"Pleased to meet you," he said.

"This is John Newton, Gary's sub today. Tomorrow afternoon you will be taking his place," said Danny Rose.

"Pleased to meet you," said David.

"David, welcome to East Greenwich School Department. Gary will show you what to do each day. When you come in at 1 o'clock, you will help Gary clean up from the lunches, wash tables and sweep and wash the cafeteria and remove the trash/recyclables.

Then you remove the trash in the teachers' rooms and help Gary until he leaves at 2:30.

"Then you have to wait until all the school kids leave before you start cleaning at 3:30. From 3:30 until 6 p.m., you start cleaning the restrooms first—there's a boys' and girls' restroom on each floor. Then you remove trash, wash desks, sweep the floor, dust, and spot wash all the floors in the classrooms, starting on the fourth floor to the second floor. Gary cleans the first floor and the gym.

"After the classrooms are done, you sweep and wash both stairways. Last, you sweep the hallways and here we have a scrub machine to wash the halls. You fill it up with the cleaning solution and empty it at the end of the night, then you store it where you find it here on the fourth floor. Gary will show you how to operate the floor scrubber. The machine will fit in the elevator. You scrub all four floors. The custodian sinks are located in the middle of the hallway on each floor. There's a lot of work in this school, but you have enough time to do the work. I will bring you back to the key station to get your car."

"Yes, please."

"One more thing, make sure all windows are closed and doors are locked before you leave at night," said Danny Rose, supervisor.

The next day was David Leo's first day at work. After cleaning the cafeteria and kitchen, a kitchen worker gave David a meal and greeted him.

"You must be Mr. David Leo. My name is Sheila Dealer."

"Pleased to meet you," he said.

"Here's a meal you can have later. When we have extra food after all the lunches are done, we leave a plate for the custodians," said Sheila.

"Thank you!" said David.

Later, David and Gary were removing all the trash. They were in the teachers' room, and Gary was introducing David to the teachers in their break room. David said to Gary, "What's that, a storm shelter trap door on the floor?"

"Not exactly; it's a bomb shelter. It can be used for a storm shelter. Let me show you what's down there. Be careful: you have to climb down a ten-foot ladder ending up on a dirt floor. You have a long tunnel that never ends in the dark where soldiers used to hide from the enemy during World War Two. See all these barrels down here? There's hundreds of them scattered everywhere! They have food in them, and you can still eat them today. The surviving soldiers ate out of these barrels to stay alive in case of nuclear war," said Gary Harry, the head building custodian (HBC).

"Oh my God!" said David.

Then Gary left for the day, and David was on his own. David was doing a good job cleaning Eldridge School, following Gary, the HBC's instructions.

A few days later, on a Friday night about 8 p.m., an hour and a half before he was scheduled to leave for the evening, David decided to visit the bomb shelter again. He unlocked the deadbolt key on the floor door and climbed down the ladder into the bomb shelter. He turned on the flashlight on his phone and went on a journey, walking into the dark tunnel.

Minutes later, his phone rang.

"David, it's Danny. Make sure you reset the alarm tonight when you leave. You forgot to turn the alarm back on the last two nights; the police came to reset the alarm."

"Okay, Danny, I forgot."

Then David checked the time on his watch, and it was 8:15 p.m. He continued on his journey, walking in the bomb shelter tunnel. He saw water dripping down the walls. Then he came to a puddle of water and shined his phone flashlight down the tunnel, seeing lots of water on the ground. He decided to turn back, but suddenly he heard a crash and the trap door closed and locked on its own! Then his phone suddenly went dead, and his light went out!

He was in the dark, trying to get his phone to work. His phone fell out of his hands, and now he was feeling the dirt ground trying to find it, but with no luck. Now he had to find his way back to the ladder in the dark, feeling the rock and dirt walls to get back out.

Suddenly, he was attacked by vampires and piranha bats, biting and eating the flesh off his bones, killing him alive! He screamed hysterically, and no one could hear him getting eaten alive.

"AHHH! Help! Help! Help!! Help me please!"

Soon after, it was all over; David was dead. Water rats and tunnel rats joined the vampire creatures, finishing off David's flesh, leaving a skeleton. The rats drank the blood while the bats and piranhas chowed on the flesh and guts. David Leo was never heard from again.

A police officer drove up to the school and found a door propped open with a big stick and a rock. David had forgotten to close the door when he was throwing out the late-night trash. The police officer pulled up to the school. He looked at the clock in his car, and the time was 11:02 p.m. He went into the school, closing the door after removing the stick and kicking the rock out of the way so the door would close. Only one light was on in the teachers' room.

The cop started calling, "Anybody here! Hello!" He got no response. He checked the bomb shelter door to make sure it was locked. The light in the teachers' room started blinking on and off, and he shut the light off and closed the door. Then he went through the school, shining his flashlight, checking all the doors, and they were locked. Lights were off in the classrooms, and the building was dark except for emergency lights.

He heard thumping and banging on the second floor, and a window was swinging back and forth from the wind outside blowing in one of the classrooms. He closed and locked the window. Then he checked the gym, and everything was okay. A black shadow was flying along the ceiling in the gym, but the cop didn't see it! Then he set the alarm and left the school.

Bob Walmart, the director of the custodians, was working on his computer at home around midnight when he got a phone call. The time was 12:02 a.m., Saturday morning.

"Bob, this is Officer Charles Gate. Someone left a door wide open at the Eldridge School; I found it after 11 p.m."

"Thank you, officer, that God Damm David!"

The next day, Bob called Danny Rose, David's supervisor.

"Hi Danny, sorry to bother you on a Saturday morning, but David may have left an outside door open last night at the Eldridge School, and the alarm was off. It's the third time I got complaints from that school from the police. You need to talk with him, or I have to let him go; the substitute custodians can't be leaving doors open and not resetting the alarm at night before leaving."

"I will have a talk with him," said Danny Rose.

Danny called David on his cell phone, and it was ringing in the bomb shelter next to his skeleton body.

"Hi, this is David Reed Leo. Can't come to the phone right now, please leave a message after the tone. BEEEEP!"

"David, it's Danny Rose calling. You left an outside door open at Eldridge when you left, and you forgot to reset the alarm again. You can't be doing that. I will see you on Monday at 1 p.m. at Eldridge."

1 p.m., Monday afternoon, Danny Rose, David's boss, waited for him to arrive, and David never showed up. He looked at his watch, and the time was 1:11 p.m. Ten minutes later, he looked at his watch again. Then he went into the school, and Gary, the custodian, was washing tables in the cafeteria.

He said, "Gary, David's running late. Call me when he comes in?"

"Yes sir," said Gary.

Three days later, there was still no David. Bob Walmart said to Danny,

"David has not showed up for three days. When he comes in, fire him! I will call in another custodian for Eldridge."

Thursday, a new second-shift custodian came in to help Gary. Later that evening, the new custodian was filling up the floor scrubber machine on the fourth floor. He heard a faint voice:

"Get out!"

He looked around and saw nothing. He was all alone in the school at 8 p.m. At night, after scrubbing the floors, he started shutting lights off before he locked up. He saw two twin-like girls standing at the end of the hall on the third floor.

"Excuse me, girls, but you're not supposed to be here!"

The two girls vanished in front of his eyes and disappeared! The hallway went dark. Then the custodian went to the custodian room in the basement. Suddenly, he heard a loud growling in the boiler room that sounded like a mad junkyard dog! The time was 9:02 p.m.

He grabbed a snow shovel to whack the growling animal in the boiler room if it came after him. He reset the alarm and got out of the school as fast as he could! Suddenly, all the lights came back on in the school. He got in his car, locked the door, and called his boss on his cell phone.

"Danny: Rocky Hockey, the substitute custodian. I am sitting in my car before I go home because something strange is going on in this school. I was turning off the lights after scrubbing the floors, and I saw two little girls glowing in the dark, and when I said something to them, they vanished right in front of my eyes! I can't believe it! When I got to the custodian room,..."

I heard a mean dog growling in the boiler room. I set the alarm, locked the door, and got out of the school as fast as I could. When I got out, all the lights came back on in the school.

"I don't believe in ghosts. I experienced something I have never seen before!"

"Gary never told you that the Eldridge School is haunted?" said Danny.

"He said nothing about ghost here, he just showed me the job."

"Okay Rocky, just go home and I will come by to check on the school. See you at 1 p.m. tomorrow," said Danny Rose.

Rocky went home. Danny, his boss, came by to check the school. All the lights were out. He went into the school, turned the alarm off, and checked the boiler room. He went through the school, and everything was okay. He reset the alarm, locked up, and left.

Officer Charles Gate arrived at the school, parking his police car in the lot after 11 p.m. Everything was okay when he checked the school.

The next day, Rocky Hockey arrived with a gun hidden between his legs in case the mad growling dog came after him! He never experienced any more ghost's, but he was scared shitless working there!

12:02 a.m., Officer Charles Gate pulled out of the Eldridge School parking lot because he saw a group of people—maybe 20 or more—all dressed in black with their faces covered in the graveyard across the street. He drove into the graveyard, turned on his police lights, and got out of his car. The group all formed together, then vanished in front of Officer Charles Gate's eyes! He was stunned. He went over to where the group had been, and nothing was there. He searched, walking through the graveyard, but no one was there. He went back to the police station.

"Lieutenant Henry Hartford, something strange is going on in this town. Becoming a new night shift police officer, I was parked on Division Street across from Eldridge School, and I saw a bunch of people all grouped together in the graveyard, all dressed in black. I put my flashers on and got out of my car, and the group of people all vanished in the blink of an eye! I could not believe it! I am not a believer in ghost until I saw what I just saw! When I went through the graveyard, no one was there! When I saw the group all disappear at once, I thought I was beginning to have a stroke, but it was all real! I heard people talking about Eldridge School being haunted, and I got a good laugh because I didn't believe them, but what I saw tonight in the graveyard on Division Street—I'm a believer now! The group was about 20 people or more, all in black, with no face features and all looking alike, and then they all disappeared."

"Welcome to the haunted town of East Greenwich, Officer Gate. We have a lot of ghosts here! The town of East Greenwich is all built on top of an Indian burial ground; strange things happen here!" said the lieutenant.

Later, during the wee hours, Officer Gate got another call while on patrol. He had just finished stopping someone for speeding on Main Street.

"Officer Gate in car #3, there's a problem at the high school. Someone may have broken into the school, setting off the alarm."

"10-4, Lieutenant Henry. I will take a ride over there."

Officer Charles Gate arrived at the high school. He swiped his card to get into the school and looked at the alarm board. A blinking light was on, coming from the cafeteria and kitchen area. Officer Gate shined his flashlight, but no one was in the cafeteria. He went into the kitchen, shining his flashlight around, and saw a black formation that looked like some kind of bird stuck on the wall. He got closer to get a better look, shining his light at it. The bird-like figure flew off the wall, forming into a giant poltergeist, and it went after Officer Charles Gate as he watched in shock! He ran out of the kitchen, locking the kitchen door, but the poltergeist had already gotten to him, picking up the policeman and throwing him across the cafeteria floor, dragging him like he was sliding on ice!

And down the hallway from one end to the other, he was pinned up against a wall, and he could still see the black cloud chasing him, throwing him up against the wall. Finally, it dropped him on the floor and vanished! All this only lasted one minute! The time was 3:02 a.m.

Officer Gate got up and ran into the dark gym toward the exits and got out of the school. He closed the outside gym door, then went back to the main entrance to reset the alarm and left the school in a hurry. He contacted headquarters.

"Car #3 to Lieutenant Henry. Don't send me to the high school anymore. I was attacked by some kind of ghost or poltergeist! The activity was coming from the kitchen and looked like a big black bird, bigger than I have ever seen! On a wall near the ovens, and when I got close to it to get a better look, it jumped off the wall, forming into a monster chasing me out of the kitchen. Then it picked me up like a baseball pitcher throwing a ball, and it threw me across the cafeteria floor. It kept dragging me down the hallway, picking me up and throwing me against a wall, and finally dropped me on the floor. It was black, like the people that vanished in the Division Street Cemetery."

The lieutenant hung up. Officer Gate went back to the police station to fill out a report.

"Officer Gate, are you on drugs!?" said the lieutenant.

Another police officer went to the high school with a blow-torch to chase the poltergeist, but he saw nothing.

One day, a teacher at Eldridge School saw a mist coming up from the closed bomb shelter and called the fire department. The school was evacuated, and the firemen went in to investigate.

"There's smoke coming up from the bomb shelter, but it does not smell like there's a fire in the teachers' lounge," said a teacher.

The firemen unlocked the bomb shelter and went down, looking around, but nothing was there. They did not go down far enough to reach David Leo's skeleton.

"There's no problem down here, Mrs. Cousins. You may have seen fog from the humidity; it's a very humid morning after last night's rain," said the firemen, and they locked the bomb shelter.

"That fog was dark and strange!" said the teacher. The fire department went through the school to make sure it was safe for the students so they could go back inside. The teacher never saw the mist again. The mist was a warning because someone had died down there.

A custodian working late, cleaning up from a late-night event at the high school, suddenly saw two little girls running around in the hallway at 1 a.m.

"Hey girls, what are you doing here so late at night?" said the custodian.

The girls laughed and vanished! The custodian was shocked. He said to himself, "Did I just see a ghost!"

The next morning, maintenance workers were in the boiler room at the high school because there was no hot water, and they were interrupted by a poltergeist. The workers were checking the boilers and getting them ready for the coming winter. In late September and during October, you need the heat. The school was cold, there was no hot water, and the teachers were complaining. The workers were raising the heat levels in the boilers.

They heard a growling, like some animal down there. Then a black mass that looked like black smoke from a fire appeared, with red eyes, and it growled like a mad dog or a lion! One man saw the poltergeist form into an ape-like figure. He yelled,

"Hey fellas, something's happening near boiler #1! There's a lot of smoke coming out of it, and some animal may have gotten in from outside. I hear it growling!"

Another worker said, "Tom, go out and shut the outside door; something got in here!"

When Tom got to the outside door, an invisible force pushed

him down outside and held him on the ground for about a minute before releasing him. He got up and said to his workers,

"Something strange is going on here. I saw black smoke, and when I went to check the outside door, some kind of force I can't explain knocked me down, pinning me to the ground before I could get up to walk away! Something evil is in the boiler room."

"Tom, I saw something that looked like a devilish-looking mist with red eyes. Then it vanished, chasing you out," said another worker.

The growling continued, and all the workers left the boiler room.

Three workers grabbed weapons, looking for where the growling was hiding, and got out of there before someone got hurt. Tom grabbed a big stick from outside, another man grabbed an iron pipe, and the third man grabbed a shovel, ready for an attack.

"We have a ghost in the boiler room!" one worker called the police.

Around 8:30 in the morning, a group of students were practicing musical instruments in the band room at the high school when suddenly a dark black mist formed, and it stunk like the dead. The dark mist covered the room, chasing all the kids and teachers out! A teacher called the fire department.

"We have a fire in the high school somewhere!"

The police and the fire department arrived to check the school and the boiler room area and found nothing.

A teacher was talking to his students.

"It's not a fire. There are ghosts in this school. A police officer was attacked in the cafeteria the other day by a poltergeist! I saw that script in the East Greenwich newspaper."

Priests and paranormal investigators arrived at the high school to remove the evil there, saying prayers, but they saw nothing. The Catholic priest said to the high school principal,

"Mr. John Cooley, my name is Father Corey Hope. You do

have a dangerous poltergeist roaming this school that can hurt or kill people! According to the paranormal and clergy teams, we have not found or seen anything here, but the ghost boxes are going crazy like a pinball machine! The activity was found in the kitchen, cafeteria, main hallway, the old gym, the band room, and the boiler room. Make sure kids are not in these areas between midnight and 5 a.m., when these poltergeists are most active.

We have reports that maintenance workers saw something in the boiler room around 7 a.m., and one of them was attacked by an invisible force and was injured. A bunch of kids reported a black presence with red eyes in the music room just after 8 a.m. this morning. Teachers also witnessed the poltergeist sightings. It's rare for a poltergeist to be active at this time of day with a school full of kids. However, it wants to let you know it is here. You have more evil spirits roaming the hallways late at night. All activities must end before midnight until students arrive in the morning.

Our team will be here again on Friday night until Sunday, performing an exorcism to get rid of the evil here. If you see anything or any attacks, you send me an email and we will come back to remove it. My email is fathercoreyhope@gmail.com."

Later in the day, a substitute custodian arrived at 3 p.m., second shift. The new sub arrived at the back door of the high school, where the boiler room is located, and he met the HBC (Head Building Custodian).

"Good afternoon. I'm the new sub custodian working the high school tonight. My name is Robert Roberts."

"Pleased to meet you. Bob Basemen, the HBC. You can put your food in the refrigerator, and we have a microwave to warm it up. When you're ready, I will show you the assignment. First, we check in here each evening. This is the boiler room. You will be cleaning the second floor. From 3 p.m. to 4:30, you clean the restrooms first. Then you start cleaning the classrooms from 4:30 to 6:30 p.m.

Then you come back to the boiler room to have your dinner from 6:30 to 7 p.m., 30 minutes. Then you finish the classrooms. You sweep and wash two stairwells. Then you clean the ladies' locker room and the coaches' office. Then you take a 15-minute break. After that, you sweep all the halls on the second floor and wash them with the floor scrubber. Then you're done.

Up here, you have a boys' and girls' restroom and a unisex handicap restroom. The boys' and girls' restrooms have 10 toilets and 10 sinks—they're big! The small handicap restroom has one sink, toilet, and urinal. The boys' restroom has six urinals. You have 14 classrooms to clean. First, you remove the trash, wipe the blackboards, wash desktops, then sweep the floor. Tonight, on Monday, you wash four classrooms. You only have time to wash four rooms each night. Empty pencil sharpeners in all rooms.

Let's go to the locker rooms. Here we have a restroom. Move the trash, clean the coaches' room, and sweep and wash the floor. Do not touch the kids' stuff; if it's in the way of your cleaning, just leave it alone. Let me show you how to work the floor scrubber. First of all, you don't need to change the pads; the pads get changed once a week. You put this solution—two cups—in the tank and fill the rest with water up to the line. Then you get on it and drive it like a car. The key is already in the ignition. Here's the controls to drive back and forth, reverse, and drive. When you finish, you have buckets in the boiler room to empty the machine and put it back right here. I leave at 10:30. You will be all alone in the school until you leave at 11:30 p.m. Put all custodian equipment away in the boiler room when you're done. If you need supplies, everything you need is in the boiler room. When you leave, don't forget to reset the alarm, shown here, and lock the door.

By the way, we have a poltergeist here in the high school. People have been hurt here, so be careful. If you see it, keep your distance and don't go near it."

"What is a poltergeist?" said Robert Roberts, the sub custodian.

"A poltergeist is a demonic ghost."

"Mr. Bob, go home!"

"You don't believe!" said Bob. "If you believe in ghosts, you must be on drugs!"

"Well, you'll find out working here, Robert. A policeman was hurt last week late at night, being dragged along the hallways before he was thrown up against a wall. Just be careful. Good night."

The HBC left. Robert swept and washed the halls. When he finished, he was emptying the floor scrubber and saw a black mist roll along the floor. As he watched, it vanished. He said to himself, "Holy shit! Maybe Mr. Bob was right; something strange is here, and it doesn't look nice!"

Robert looked at his watch, and the time was 11:02 p.m. The black mist vanished a minute later. Then he put equipment away in the boiler room. Then he heard a growl like some kind of animal. Robert backed up slowly and grabbed a stick, ready to strike! Then he saw a black mist coming from one of the boilers, form into a creature with big ears/horns, red eyes, and sharp white shark-like teeth. It looked like the devil!

Then he heard a voice: "Get out!"

Robert stood his ground with a big stick and said, "Come on, motherfucker! You want to play!"

Then the poltergeist opened its mouth, showing teeth, and it charged at Robert. It went right through him, knocking him down, and then vanished! The boiler room stank like the dead.

Robert got up, put the alarm back on, ready to lock up and leave. Then he saw the black mist reform and left the school in a hurry. He started his truck, but it stalled. He couldn't get his truck started and was stuck there. He called his wife.

"Sara, it's Robert. I am still at East Greenwich High School. My truck will not start. Can you come and pick me up?"

Then his truck started on its own, and he drove away. He called his wife again to tell her not to come; they live in East Greenwich.

He made it home, but the poltergeist may still be with him. He said to his wife,

"I am not going to the high school again if I want to keep working for the East Greenwich School Department. There's a poltergeist ghost in that school, and it came after me, and it went through me! I just hope I'm not bringing it home! Mr. Bob, the HBC, told me to be careful because of the ghosts there. I didn't believe him until I saw it myself. It began as black smoke—I thought it was coming from the boiler in the boiler room where I check in and out. I saw it in the hallway earlier. Then it formed into a monster about 8 or 9 feet tall, and it looked like the devil! It came after me with a big stick, then it charged at me, went through me, and vanished!"

"Oh my God!" said his wife.

Then Robert and his wife were in bed around 3 a.m. and they heard noises in the house but saw nothing. Sara Roberts, his wife, works during the day as a nurse's aide from 8 a.m. to 4 p.m. Robert works the 3 p.m. to 11:30 p.m. shift at East Greenwich schools.

He went into the main office to tell his boss about what happened at the high school last night.

"Well, the only opening I have is second shift at the high school. Follow me, and I will have you work the rest of the week at Cole Middle School. Next week you will be at the high school," said Danny Rose.

Robert followed his boss to Cole Middle School.

"Robert, this is Bob Arvidson, the HBC. He will give you instructions on what to do here," said Danny Rose, his boss.

"Pleased to meet you, Robert," said Bob Arvidson.

"Robert was chased out of the high school because of the poltergeist and ghosts there," said Danny Rose.

"We have ghosts in this school too!" said Bob Arvidson.

Later, Sara, Robert's wife, arrived home around 4:30 p.m. The house smelled like the dead—it stunk so bad she could not go inside! She called the police. The police and the fire department arrived, went into her house, and it smelled like roses.

"Mrs. Roberts, your house smells nice, like flowers, now!" said the firemen.

"Oh wow! It didn't smell like this earlier," said Sara.

"We had a problem with the town sewer drain system earlier today, but it's all cleared up now. It may take a while for the bad smell to go away," said the firemen.

Then she went in to take a shower, but the water came out black, and the house was dark even with the lights on and the bright sun shining outside. Sara called the fire department again.

"East Greenwich Fire Department, good afternoon."

"Hi, this is Sara Roberts calling again at 135 Center Street. Black mud is coming out of my shower and sink, and the rotten smell is back."

"We have a sewer problem in that area. Just let the water run for a few minutes, and it will clear. The town is working on the issue."

Sara ran the water in the shower and sink and flushed the toilet in the bathroom. Minutes later, it all cleared up, and she was able to take a shower. The time was 5:06 p.m. While she was washing her hair, the house filled with a strong smell of flowers!

Then, when she was done with her shower, she saw a quick glimpse of a dark shadow go by and was frightened.

"Ahhh! What was that!"

She got out of the shower to grab her towel and noticed the bathroom door was open. She said to herself,

"What the hell is going on in this house? I closed that door so the cat wouldn't come in."

She dried off, put on her housecoat, and went to the bedroom to get dressed. Then she went to the kitchen to start cooking. She put a roast in the oven, boiled potatoes, and cooked mixed vegetables on the stove. She had the oven set to 375 degrees.

When dinner was ready, the potatoes and vegetables were hot, but the oven was not working and the roast was cold. She was so mad she took the roast out of the oven, slammed the oven door shut, put the roast back in the refrigerator, and boiled some hot dogs to finish her dinner. The time was 6:02 p.m. when the oven went out.

After dinner, she was doing the laundry in the basement, and it suddenly got cold. She looked at her watch; the time was 7:02 p.m. A big black demonic poltergeist was standing right behind her while she was starting the washing machine, but she did not see it.

She went upstairs to do some house cleaning. She heard stomping noises, and the house was getting warm. She went to the kitchen and saw the roast she had put away lying on the kitchen floor. The refrigerator door was wide open, the oven door was open and set to 375 degrees, and the kitchen was getting pretty warm!

She shut the oven door and turned it off. Then she picked up the roast, put it back in the refrigerator, and closed the door. She screamed:

"AHHH!"

"Whatever is in my house, get the fuck out right now!" Then the hauntings stopped a minute later! She called the police and told him what was happening.

"Mrs. Roberts, you might have a ghost here; there's no sign of a break-in," said the police. Then he left.

The kitchen haunting happened at 8:02 p.m. Then she went downstairs to put the clothes in the dryer, and the hauntings stopped. When Mrs. Roberts told it to leave, it went to visit her husband at Cole Middle School.

Robert was cleaning the library—wiping down tables, dusting furniture, and vacuuming the floor on the second floor. Suddenly he saw a white fog passing above the tables, and the library was so cold he had to leave. The time was 9:02 p.m.

At the same time, Mrs. Roberts was at home, placing rosary beads and crosses of Jesus and the Virgin Mary in every room.

At 10:02 p.m., Robert was emptying trash, throwing it into the dumpster, when suddenly five raccoons jumped out of the dumpster. One landed on Robert's shoulder, another on his shirt, a third on his head, and a fifth curled around his neck, its yellow eyes staring at him. A minute later, they all jumped off and ran away!

Robert Roberts was practically having a heart attack, crying, "Help! Help! Help! Help!"

Then the raccoons were gone. He left the barrels there and ran back into the school and closed the door. He said, "Bob, the HBC, you empty the trash from now on! A bunch of raccoons jumped on me and hung on to me until I was ready to have a heart attack!"

Bob laughed. "Are you hurt?"

"No, just a few scratches. I should be okay."

"Good, Robert. We need to set up about 200 chairs in the cafeteria because there's a function here tomorrow. I need your help and our work will be done!" said Bob Arvidson, the Head Building Custodian (HBC).

"Okay!" said Robert Roberts.

They were setting up chairs in front of a stage. The cafeteria has a stage like an auditorium in Cole Middle School. Just when they finished, the movie screen came down, showing a black poltergeist devil-looking monster. It roared like a mean bear, then sprayed a fireball out of its mouth into the cafeteria, but the flame vanished before hitting the ground! Then the power went out! The time was 11:02 p.m. when the hauntings were happening.

"Robert, sit down and stay put until I go back to the office and grab a flashlight," said Bob, the HBC.

The lights came back on a minute later.

"Robert, start locking up the school, and I will get the flashlight in case the lights go out again!" said Bob. Then he helped Robert close up the school and they left together. When the lights went out, the movie screen lifted back up on the stage. The poltergeist followed Robert back to his house.

His wife was taking a shower when Robert came home before midnight. When she got out, she erupted, yelling at Robert.

"What the hell did you bring into this house!?" She told him about the strange things going on in the house.

"Oh my God. I hope the ghosts didn't follow me home from the high school. Tonight at work, I was cleaning the library and saw what looked like a white mist flowing over all the tables after I finished washing them. Then I was taking out the trash, and about five or six raccoons jumped on me, hanging on to me and staring at me, ready to attack. I started pushing them off, and luckily they jumped off and ran away! I got nothing more than a few scratches; I didn't get hurt.

Then Bob Arvidson, the HBC, and I were setting up chairs in the cafeteria-auditorium when suddenly the movie screen dropped by itself, and a devilish dragon appeared, spraying fire where we were working. It vanished before hitting the floor near us. Bob and I were shitting our pants; we were so scared! On top of all that, the lights went out for a few minutes, then came back on. We shut the school down and got the hell out of there alive!!" said Robert.

"We must pray before we go to bed. If any more hauntings happen tonight, you better get out and go sleep in a hotel somewhere until we get a priest," said his wife.

After they said their prayers, Robert took his shower before going to bed. While saying prayers and watching Thursday night football in the living room, the house darkened because the poltergeist was in the house; the time was 12:02 a.m. Then the house brightened a minute later. The Roberts were in bed sleeping before 1 a.m.

Sara woke up because something was blowing in her ears. She moved away from Robert, facing him in bed. She looked at the alarm clock, and the time was 1:02 a.m.

One hour later, Robert woke up to a loud roar and saw the same devilish poltergeist he had seen on the movie screen at Cole

Middle School and in the boiler room at the high school. Sara woke too, and they saw the poltergeist standing behind their bed, pulling the blanket and bedsheets off, grabbed both of them, and threw them on the floor together, banging both of their heads!

They screamed hysterically.

"AHHH!"

Then it was gone at 2:03 a.m.!

They got up, grabbed what they could, and got out of the house as quickly as possible. Sara said,

"Robert, you better stay away from me until I see a priest, and quit your job at the East Greenwich School Department. If this evil thing you brought into our house comes again, we're getting a divorce!"

The couple went their separate ways.

At 3:02 a.m., the dagger struck—their home burned to the ground!

The next morning, at Cole Middle School, a group of kids were going to class in Room 302. Around 10 a.m., the teacher came in, coughed, and nearly fainted. Blood came out of her mouth. Suddenly, a black mist came out of her mouth as she started coughing again, forming into the devil with grabbing hands and red eyes, covering the classroom in dark mist!

The kids ran out of the classroom like a bat out of hell! The teacher opened a window, and the poltergeist devil flew out and was gone. The room looked normal again.

Priests and a paranormal team had to come in to perform an exorcism to remove this demonic poltergeist from all the schools in East Greenwich.

Sara got a call at work. Ring, ring, ring, ring, ring—five or six times.

"Robert and Sara Roberts, please leave a message."

"Hi Sara, East Greenwich Fire Department. Your house at 135

Center Street burned to the ground. When you get this message, please call the fire department."

Later, the couple learned their home lay in a pile of ashes and bricks. The couple ended up getting a divorce.

Around mid-October of 2023, the poltergeist decided to visit the rest of the schools in East Greenwich before returning to the Division Street Graveyard.

The same teacher from Cole Middle School was working in the library at Hannaford School, and the windows were open. The demonic poltergeist came into the school from outside, flying around the library at 8 a.m., before the kids arrived. The black mist flew in circles.

The teacher yelled at it,

"Get the hell out of here in the name of Jesus Christ!"

She grabbed a cross out of her pocketbook and held it in front of the poltergeist, and it flew out of the library into the hallway and disappeared. She reported the ghost to the school principal.

"I saw it too! I'll call the Catholic priest!" said the principal.

The poltergeist would continue to visit Robert Roberts until he left East Greenwich.

The evening custodian, Mr. Bob, was cleaning the classrooms at Frenchtown School when the poltergeist visited that school, roaming the hallway. The custodian saw a big black rolling mist in the main hallway; it went into the gym and vanished. A function was going on at the school, and a lot of people were there, but they saw nothing. Only the custodian saw it.

Mr. Bob at Frenchtown School called the police.

"You saw a ghost, Mr. Bob," said the police.

The next day, around 10 a.m., the poltergeist visited Meadow-brook School, flying around in the gym like the Wicked Witch in *The Wizard of Oz*, but no one saw it.

SIX

A HAUNTING OF THE BLACK MASS DEVIL IN A MAINE TOWN

Onset, Maine, A quiet bedroom community. It was about a week before Halloween in 2023, and a couple were looking for a quiet place to live in the Maine forest with beautiful lakes, a view of the mountains, and a cabin located deep in the woods. There was a little bit of snow on the ground. The couple had a four-by-four truck, good for driving in the snow, a snowmobile, and a seaplane located at a nearby lake. They had drones to fly in case of emergencies, a snowblower, and finally a camping trailer home hooked up to the couple's truck.

The couple pulled up to the log cabin with the truck and camper, waiting for the realtor. The realtor arrived in a Mercedes.

"Nice car. My name is Michael Powers, and this is my wife, Michelle Powers."

"Pleased to meet you. Michelle Manhandle from Bennington Realtors, out of Vermont. Welcome to Onset, Maine, Bangcock County. We are a major real estate company servicing all of Northern New England, Upstate New York, and properties in Canada."

"We're from Suffolk, New York, in the White Plains area. I am a retired military police officer in the National Guard, 71 years old. My wife Michelle is a retired nurse, 69 years old. We have luxuries to bring here if we like what you have. We want to live in a quiet place like this so we can enjoy the wildlife, forest hiking, and the lakes," said Michael.

"We get a lot of snow here during the winter. Don't you like the snow?" said the realtor.

"Yes, we do! And we like the lakes!" said Michael.

"Come inside and I'll show you the cabin. It's a cold late October day. The fireplace and wood stove are going, and it's nice and warm in here. This cabin is all in one. You have the kitchen with a cooking and heating wood stove, refrigerator, deep freezer, a large microwave oven, double sink, and plenty of cabinets. You have a five-by-five fireplace living room, dining room, and a closed-off bedroom with a shower, Jacuzzi, sink, and toilet. The bedroom has plenty of closet space and two windows. All floors are hardwood, so don't carry anything out of the fireplace and burn the house down!" The couple laughed.

The realtor continued showing them the property.

"You have gas heating during the winter, hooked up to a propane tank outside, or you can go into town and buy wood pellets for the stove to save money. Outside, you have a big shed for storage. There's no garage; everything is wide open out here. You have nothing but woods, water pools, and lakes in Bangcock County. About a quarter mile down the road is Bangcock Lake, overlooking the Maine mountains. There's no police or fire department here until you go into downtown Bangcock. You do have a country store and gas station about half a mile away. If you want to buy booze, go to a supermarket—Market Basket in downtown Bangcock. You have needs here, but you may have to drive a bit. I suggest you have a big gun because you have a lot of moose and black bears!" said the realtor.

"Do you have ghosts here?" said Michelle Powers.

"Not that I know of, unless you go looking for them!" The realtor laughed.

She continued, "Come inside and sign the lease and you can start moving in. This cabin is rented monthly; there's no mortgage. The rent is $1,475 a month, not including utilities. The security deposit is $1,000. Your mail will go to the US Post Office in downtown Bangcock. Make checks payable to 'Bennington Realtors of Vermont.' Your utilities are propane gas heat, as I mentioned. You can get refills at the Onset Country Store. You have well water, and your bill will come from 'Water Works of Maine.' Your electric bill will come from 'US Maine Electric.' The address is One Donna Road. Good luck, and I hope you enjoy living cabin-style in Maine."

Later, Michael and Michelle Powers began moving in. A moving company from New York, Suffolk County Movers, arrived in a big truck in the pouring rain to bring the furniture for the cabin. Michael hooked the camping trailer to the big propane tank outside the cabin and a generator. He put the snowmobile in the shed along with the lawn mower, drones, garden and working tools, a shotgun, shovels, rakes, and other items.

Later, Michael went into town to rent a space for a seaplane in downtown Bangcock. Then they went back to New York to get the seaplane. Michael flew the plane back to Bangcock Lake, where he had a spot for the plane and a boat. Michelle drove the truck back with the boat and placed it at the seaplane dock location. Michael put a motorcycle in the shed and stored handguns and a shotgun in the bedroom closet in the cabin.

For furniture, they had an eight-foot solid oak table with ten chairs, a twelve-piece pit group for the living room with solid oak tables to put lamps on, a king-size bed, two tables with lamps, and a large bureau with a French mirror and drawers to put clothes in around the bed.

Then they finished moving in. Michael went deer hunting, killed two deer, dragged them to the cabin, cut them up for hamburgers and steaks, and put them in the deep freezer. The couple cleaned and stuffed the deer heads, hanging one over the fireplace and another above the cabin entrance, with solar panel lights to illuminate them at night. Michael built a fire pit outside while Michelle put the deer steaks in the deep freezer. They would have enough steaks and hamburger for more than a year.

One night before Halloween, Michael saw a dark figure that looked like a bigfoot with big horns, long arms, and red eyes. He went into the woods with a flashlight and a shotgun, but the beast was gone.

"Whoever is out there, I have a big gun. You're on private property," said Michael before going into the house. He told his wife what he saw.

"What could it be? Was it a bear? A moose? Or a bigfoot? What was out there?"

"I can't describe what I saw," said Michelle. "It was black and hairy with big horns and red eyes. It could be some kind of bigfoot. But don't worry, I have a big gun ready in case we get threatened. There's a lot of wildlife out here, that's why I chose to move to Maine."

Later, around 3 a.m., Michael and Michelle were in bed. Michelle had a dream of a devilish-looking monster with big horns, red eyes, pointy ears, and a wolf-like jaw with sharp teeth standing in the bedroom. She woke up screaming:

"AHHH!" The time was 3:02 a.m.

"What's wrong, Michelle? Did you have a bad dream?"

"I just had a dream that the devil was in our bedroom!"

"What did the devil look like?" said Michael.

"It was black and hairy like a bear with big horns, red eyes, big ears, and a jaw with sharp teeth, standing near the bed. It was about eight feet tall, floor to ceiling, looking at me! I thought I was having a heart attack! It was the scariest dream I've ever had. I never believed in the devil, but this dream was terrifying."

"Michelle, there is a devil as well as a God, but not here in Maine. You had a dream like the black creature I saw out in the woods yesterday. Don't fear; I have my gun right here beside the bed. Nothing's coming in this house."

Then the couple went back to sleep.

Michael woke up hearing a banging noise against the house. He looked at the alarm clock: 4:02 a.m. He lifted the window shade and saw a tree branch banging against the house because of the wind. He went outside, broke the branch, then went back inside and returned to bed.

At 5:02 a.m., a deer defecated outside near the cabin. At 6:02 a.m., wild turkeys passed through.

At 7:02 a.m., it started raining, and a bunch of robins were running around outside. One hour later, snow was falling.

At 8:30 a.m., Michelle got up to make breakfast. After breakfast, Michael and Michelle went into town to get gas, buy a few things, and get wood pellets for the stove and wood for the fireplace.

Michael asked the store clerk, "Excuse me, sir: do we have bigfoot creatures here in Maine? Last night I was outside my cabin and saw a creature that looked like the devil. It stood tall with red eyes, big horns, and black fur like a bear. When I told my wife what I saw, she had a dream it was in our bedroom."

The clerk laughed. "You saw the Maine Devil. It's a cross between a black bear and a bigfoot. It's a forest creature known as the East Coast Bigfoot. This creature is rarely seen in this part of Maine; it's usually seen in the Arctic regions of Greenland and Iceland, but they're migrating into the Maine forest from the far north. They're harmless; they keep bears and moose away. It's a good thing to have roaming around here."

"Will this creature bother us?" said Michael.

"No, it will protect your property. The Maine Devil feeds on bears and moose—anything big! It will attack a horse, so if you have a barn, keep it inside at night unless you're riding it. Don't keep a horse out in the open at night. Where do you people live?"

"We live in a cabin at One Donna Road," said Michelle.

"You have a lot of wildlife there! The Maine Devil hunts bears before they hibernate in late October-November. When they come out in spring, they can be aggressive. It might be related to the New Jersey Devil," said the clerk.

"It might be in the same family as the NJ Devil and the Mothman. All these unknown forest creatures are related to bigfoot," said the clerk.

"If we see it again, what do we do?" said Michael.

"Keep your distance, don't get close, and let it do its thing. It hunts bears when it starts snowing. It's more afraid of you than you are of it because it knows humans have guns!"

"I shot the thing last night and it disappeared right in front of my eyes!" said Michael.

"Don't do that; now it may never come around again. Now watch out for black bears and moose," said the clerk.

Then Michael and Michelle bought what they needed and left the store. On the way to their truck, Michelle asked a woman going into the store, "Did you see the big black Maine Devil?"

The woman looked at her strangely, said no, and went inside.

Tomorrow was Halloween, 2023. During the day, Michael installed a fence around the cabin to keep all the critters and wild animals out. Michelle was inside doing laundry and cooking. Later, Michael took Michelle for a seaplane ride at Bangcock Lake. Then they went shopping in town and visited a bar in downtown Bangcock to celebrate Halloween, the *Spook House Café*.

Michael was dressed as a clown, and Michelle was dressed as a witch. Michelle was socializing with women, playing pool and card games. Michael was at the bar drinking beer. He said to the bartender, "Have you ever heard of the Maine Devil creature?"

"Yes, it's a bigfoot with a big head and red and yellow eyes. Why? Did you see it?"

"Yes, it was on my property. It was a black hairy creature with big horns and red eyes, and it looked like the devil," said Michael.

"Keep your distance because this creature will have sex with anything that's alive. If it's a male, it will buck you like a bull and ram you, potentially ripping you apart! Don't turn your back, or it will ram you from behind like a goat, ram, or bull," said the bartender.

Michael got a good laugh with a few men drinking beer. Later, Michael and Michelle got something to eat—burgers, fries, and salad—before going home.

The next day was November 1, 2023. Michael and Michelle drove around town to see what was going on in downtown Bangcock. The town had only one bar, a restaurant, some homes, a church, a liquor store, a Market Basket supermarket, a Cumberland Farms store, and a gas station. There was also a small mini-mall. The rest of the town was all woods. The lake had a beach, a few cabins, and woods surrounding it. Michael and Michelle had a boat dock and a place for the seaplane. The Bangcock Police and Fire Station were located near the lake.

Later, they went hiking and walking through the forest near their cabin. Michelle watched TV and enjoyed the fire in the fireplace while cooking dinner on the wood stove. Michael was outside cutting and chopping wood for the fireplace. He briefly saw the devil-like creature in the woods and its red eyes, then it faded away into the forest and vanished. He went to get a better look, but the creature was gone. He went inside to have dinner, bringing wood in to store near the fireplace.

"What are we having for dinner, honey?"

"We're having cheeseburgers, sweet fries, and salad, with a glass of wine," said Michelle.

"I saw that creature again way out in the woods while cutting wood. I went out for a better look, and it was gone! I have an electric fence, and nothing will bother us, so don't worry," said Michael.

A few nights later, light snow was falling, and they went to bed around midnight. At 3:02 a.m., Michelle woke and saw a black fog forming over the night light. She turned on a lamp and saw a black figure, looking like the devil, right near the bed—the same devil from her dream! She screamed:

"AHHH!"

The devil-like creature roared like a mean grizzly. Michael woke and saw it too. The devil blew the bed sheets off the bed. Michael was naked because they had had sex before going to sleep. Michael grabbed his shotgun, fired one shot, and the devil-like creature disappeared.

PHRASE: The devil-like creature was not a bigfoot or devil creature; it was a poltergeist, a demonic ghost.

"Michael, take me back to New York! I am not staying here!" Michelle got dressed as fast as she could and went out to the camping trailer.

The poltergeist reappeared in the bedroom while Michael was getting dressed, blowing hot wind that knocked him down. The ghost flipped the bed over on top of him, but he managed to free himself, grabbed his shotgun, fired a few shots, and the poltergeist vanished. He even broke out a window while shooting at the demonic entity.

Then he finished dressing and drove Michelle back to New York. On the way, he said, "Michelle, the devil we saw is not a bigfoot; it was some kind of demonic poltergeist force. When I was getting dressed, the poltergeist reappeared, blowing hot air on me strong enough to knock me down and flipped the bed upside down on top of me. I was able to free myself, grabbed my gun, and started shooting at it, breaking a window. I next saw a gray mist and heard a puffing noise like wood cracking in a fireplace, then it vanished! When we got here, I had a funny feeling this place was haunted!"

"The devil appeared again! Oh my God!" Michelle cried.

At 4:02 a.m., the Powers couple arrived back in New York.

"Michelle, we'll go to the lake and spend the rest of the night in the trailer. Then you drive the truck to New York, and I'll fly the seaplane to Suffolk Pines Seaport and see if we can stay at your Aunt Jacky's condo until we find another place. In the morning, we go," said Michael.

"Just suppose this devil ghost follows us back to New York," Michelle cried.

"I think it has something to do with the cabin, not us. It does not want us there! I will call the realtor in the morning."

The ghost did not follow them to the lake. Around 10 a.m., Michael and Michelle slept in the camper, then left for New York. Michelle drove the truck with the camper hooked up, and Michael flew the seaplane.

When they arrived at Aunt Jacky's condo, Michelle unhooked the camper and parked it in the backyard, then picked up Michael at the seaplane. Aunt Jacky was not home; she was away. Michael called the realtor.

"Bennington Real Estate of Vermont. Sandra Busch, speaking."

"Sandra, Michael and Michelle Powers just rented the cabin at One Donna Road in Onset, Maine. We just left because we were attacked by a devil poltergeist. You owe us a refund, or you'll be hearing from my lawyer, Avery Point, in New York. You have to tell people the property was haunted; this is not right!"

"Oh my God, Michael. Why don't I send you an email to fill out so you can get your refund?"

A truck arrived a few days later to remove all the furniture from the cabin and shed. Michael drove back to Onset to help the movers get the furniture and follow it back to New York to unload it into storage until they found a place to live. The Powers stayed in the camper until Aunt Jacky returned.

{Is Aunt Jacky on vacation, or is she in Florida for the winter? Who gives a shit—they're out of that haunted cabin in Onset, Maine!}

{Michelle continued to have bad dreams about the Black Mass Devil from Maine. She woke up screaming!}

Back in Onset, Maine, around Thanksgiving 2023, Sandra Busch from Bennington Realtors arrived at the empty cabin at One Donna Road on a snowmobile. She went in with her pass key, looked around, and said, "There are no ghosts here!" She waited for the next renters. She put some wood in the fireplace and lit a fire to warm the place, then added wood pellets to the stove so the cabin would be nice and warm when the new guests arrived.

Four people arrived, and Sandra showed them the property, sitting near the fireplace to complete the paperwork. Suddenly, a popping sound came from the fireplace, followed by jet-black smoke.

"Everyone, move back!" said Sandra, the realtor.

Black smoke started coming from the wood stove. Suddenly, a standing poltergeist devil with big horns and red eyes emerged from the burning fireplace. A fireball shot out, striking Sandra and setting her fur coat on fire. She ran out of the cabin, jumping into the snow to put out the flames. The other four guests ran to their cars and snowmobiles and left in a hurry.

Burning wood flew out of the fireplace from a strong gust of wind caused by the poltergeist devil, and the cabin burned to the ground within minutes. Sandra stayed at the Hilton Hotel in downtown Bangcock and contacted the main office to report what happened.

The Bangcock Fire Department arrived to put out the fire, leaving the cabin in a pile of ashes. Days later, Bennington Realtors hired a priest to bless the property before rebuilding. Priests and a paranormal team arrived to rid the property of the so-called 'Black Mass Devil Poltergeist.'

"Father Donald Dame from Notre Dame Church in Bangcock, Maine. My name is Harry South Bend, a paranormal management investigator supervisor. We have a demonic devil poltergeist haunting this town, and it's going to be hard to get rid of it. This thing was last seen in 1910 haunting Bangcock Lake, and somehow it has resurfaced. We do not know if it was brought back by a large animal, such as a bear or moose, or if it rose from hell under the ground through a cave or an erupting volcano somewhere. This poltergeist was also seen in the Arctic region."

PART TWO

HAUNTINGS
AND TERROR

SEVEN

TERROR ON THE

BRYANT UNIVERSITY CAMPUS

Fall in 2025. A young girl was on her way to field hockey practice, walking along a path near the woods, and she had her hockey stick with her about 5 a.m. when suddenly a big black wolf with red eyes attacked the girl and tore her apart, coming out of the woods!

The girl's legs were torn off, and her stomach was torn open, and her guts were hanging out, laying in the path in a pool of blood. Her head was half bitten off, and there were several bite marks on her.

Two more girls were on their way to field hockey practice, and they were attacked too: one girl's head was bitten off, and the second one was dragged into the woods and eaten by the big black wolf! The girls never saw it coming; a head got bitten off, then the wolf grabbed the second girl, taking her away!

A group of girls heard screams, and then it was quiet. The group of girls were walking up the path on their way to the indoor sports facility, and the group of eight female Bryant field hockey players saw the dead girls laying in the path. They screamed hysterically! They called police. The rest of the group had their field hockey sticks ready to attack.

"It looks like a bear attack here!" said campus police. Rescuers arrived to remove the dead bodies. One girl was missing.

"Ladies, get inside as soon as possible until the bear or bears are found," said the police.

A search with police and animal control searched the Bryant campus and surrounding woods but found nothing. Fences were installed near campus buildings to keep bears from attacking and killing more people!

The crying ladies were escorted to the Chase Center, where Bryant plays their basketball games. The field hockey coaches met them there.

"Good afternoon, ladies. Michelle Wise and Katrina Brown were killed on the path going to the baseball and soccer fields. They were attacked and torn apart by what I believe would be a bear bigger than a black bear! Jennifer Pinstripe is missing; it is not known if she was attacked. She's not on campus, and no more bodies were found.

Everyone here will be given a can of bear mace every time you're out of your dorm. Even just going to class, I want you to have it with you until this bear is captured; there could be more than one. The campus groundskeepers, staff, and police are installing electric fences around all woods surrounding the Bryant University campus. Do not go near or touch them. I don't know if these fences are going to stop bears from breaking through!

Everyone grab a can. Our games and practice are canceled this week because of this tragedy. Please be careful out there," said the coaches.

Later in the middle of the night, the Smithfield Animal Control Unit, with big guns, were riding around in college shuttles through the campus. SWAT teams patrolled the woods behind the fences with big guns, looking for any bears due to the attack.

"Look here, officers. Here are parts of a human body. Teeth, a titty nipple, and an eyeball laying in a pool of blood! Scoop it up in a bag, and watch your back for the attacking bear or whatever animal out here doing the attacks!" said a police officer.

No bear was found day or night. The SWAT team and Smithfield Police had the dead body parts identified at the town coroner's office and notified Bryant University.

"Claire Walters, medical team at Bryant University, speaking."

"Claire, this is Robert Gray from the Smithfield Coroner's Office. Smithfield Police found body parts from the third Bryant missing lady in the woods, and her field hockey stick and a Bryant T-shirt were found in the woods behind the indoor sports facility. She's identified as Jennifer Pinstripe."

"Thank you, Robert."

Everyone on campus got an email to attend a meeting at the Student Union the next morning. The Rhode Island National Guard surrounded the Bryant University campus to protect the students walking through campus.

The dorm leaders instructed the students where to go. {MEETING}

"Good morning, ladies and gentlemen. Welcome to the Student Union Dome. My name is Colon Cockhound, Dean of Students here at Bryant University. If you notice, there are several police, news reporters, and military present on campus the last couple of days searching for an attacking bear or unknown animal on campus.

We lost three women from the field hockey team: Michelle Wise, Katrina Brown, and Jennifer Pinstripe were killed and brutally attacked by a bear or some kind of animal. All evening classes and activities on campus are canceled from dusk to dawn until the animal is captured," said the Dean of Students.

As the meeting continued, a few days later no bear or wild animal was seen, and the military and police set up guard stations to keep students safe so activities and sporting events could go on, on campus.

The big black wolf was hiding in the woods, even climbing

trees to blend in with the leaves, because it knew the police and the National Guard were ready for action if it was caught!

The Bryant football team had a game against Brown. The Brown team took the field first; the crowd went, "BOO!"

Then a banner was set up introducing the Bryant team busting through to take the field; the crowd went, "Yeah!"

"Ladies and gentlemen! Your Bryant University Bulldogs!" said the announcer.

"Bryant won the toss, and they will be kicking off and receive in the second half," said the head referee, and the game went on!

Bryant led 21 to 14 at halftime. The Brown band took the field first when suddenly a big black wolf came crashing through the scoreboard onto the field at Beirne Stadium when the Bryant football team was coming out for the second half! The scoreboard showed the Bryant bulldog.

The wolf charged after the Bryant football team at a high rate of speed, biting arms and legs off! People started running out of the stadium like a bat out of hell! The football players were throwing things at the big bad black wolf: coolers, helmets, chairs, benches, and everything they could get their hands on to take down this wolf!

The wolf kept charging and chased the cheerleaders, the dance team, and the Bryant University Band out of the stadium, biting more limbs off people and scratching the shit out of spectators like a mean big cat! There was blood everywhere!

Finally, the National Guard and police shot the wolf dead! The wolf was shattered in a million pieces after it was blown apart with hundreds of bullet holes! Blood flowed out of the stadium into the parking lot like a red river! Rescuers arrived to take the injured to hospitals. The rest of the game was canceled. Arms and legs were flowing in the river of blood!

The campus police and the National Guard troops helped students and spectators to their cars and led the students in groups back to campus. One man's head was bitten off, and he was dead!

News reporters, TV, and radio people arrived. Helicopters flew over the Bryant campus and the nearby woods looking for more black wolves.

The animal unit arrived describing this animal.

"Mr. Campbell from the Bryant University Police and the United States National Guard. My name is Jay Boil, from the Smithfield Animal Control Unit. The wolf was identified as a big black mega wolf that has the strength of a grizzly bear, and they're known to live in the northern region of the UK, Russia, and the Arctic regions. These kinds of animals are known to keep polar bears and sea lions at bay from attacking neighborhood villages.

These wolves are not known to be aggressive, and they feed on sea lions and seals like the polar bears. However, these wolves will attack and eat a polar bear. It is very unusual to see them here unless they're very hungry, looking for any living things to eat. It could have been someone's pet and let it loose, or it could have come here off a boat.

It is rare to see mega black wolves in Rhode Island. The last one seen here was in the 1700s. The only time these animals will eat humans is if they are very hungry!" said Jay Boil, Smithfield Animal Control.

THE NEWS: "Good evening. We have breaking news from Bryant University. Four people are dead and several injured from a rare monster animal attack at the Bryant and Brown football game today.

Witnesses saw a flying huge black wild dog wolf with red eyes crashing through the Beirne Stadium scoreboard and landing on the field, charging after people! One man from the Brown band was attacked first by the wolf, biting his head off and eating it. He was killed! Then it charged after the Bryant football team and the crowd, biting limbs off people. One cheerleader was eaten alive until the wolf was shot dead by police and National Guard troops.

Four dead and 32 spectators, cheerleaders, and football players lost arms, legs, hands, and fingers! Last week three more Bryant students were attacked and killed!

This is Anna Maria reporting on WJAR News Watch 10, Providence."

The animal control personnel were going over the autopsy of the wolf.

"May I have your attention, please. My name is Greg Bowling from the National Animal Alliance Company in Edmonton, Alberta, Canada.

The autopsy shows that this animal was a Devil Wolf! These wolves are seen in the northern territory; places like Siberia, the north region of the United Kingdom, Greenland, and the Arctic woodlands! This animal is one of the deadliest killers on earth; it has the ability to kill polar bears and grizzlies. These wolves have the strength to torture lions and tigers; they feed on tigers or animals in the cat family. They even eat each other!

How a creature like this got on the Bryant University campus and killed all these people, I don't know! The only possible way that this animal got here: it had to be brought here from somewhere; by boat or a truck from Canada, the Arctic, or flown in from somewhere and let loose! This animal could be something from outer space, we don't know!

It's a wild dog in the cat family, and it's very deadly! It could be in the chupacabra family. God help us if more of these wolves are here, or a lot of people may die because they will eat everything that's alive! They've been known to eat rocks and small trees!

Thank you very much," said Greg Bowling, Animal Alliance patrol officer.

About three weeks later, it was quiet on the Bryant University campus. One day another giant black Devil Wolf, bigger than the last killer, crashed into the library, smashing through a big window, attacking people, biting legs and arms, and eating one girl who was chopped in half and eaten in two bites!

Another wolf broke into a fraternity house, Delta Chi Omega, attacking students. Two of them were eaten alive when the wolf bit their heads off, and the victims disappeared in four bites! Fraternity members beat the wolf with baseball bats, sprayed it with fire extinguishers, and one man had a shotgun to kill the fucking thing!!!!!!!

People were running for cover, running out of the library. Don't help the poor girl being eaten alive, or more people are going to die!!!!!!!

The wolf ran into the food court and ate all the food—cakes, muffins—and broke into a refrigerator to eat all the food. Then it tipped over a deep freezer, ripping it open and eating all the frozen foods! Finally, it was trapped by the Smithfield SWAT Team and gunned down until it was dead! All the food in the food court was gone! The library was covered in blood, and the injured and the dead were removed. The girl who was eaten was never found.

While the massacre was happening at the library and the fraternity house, a third giant wolf broke into the Chase Center where a basketball practice was being held. The wolf broke through an open door to get in, chasing basketball players, and they threw basketballs at the wolf, throwing chairs at it!

The wolf was eating the basketballs being thrown at it. The players were able to escape and run for cover before getting eaten. The wolf swallowed several basketballs until it choked on them and dropped dead. Then the SWAT team shot the wolf to make sure it was dead!

The dead and injured were all over the news. It was so bad students left campus and went home, finishing their college careers at home. Helicopters flew over campus looking for more wolves to kill.

Newspapers read: *"25 dead and 77 injured from Devil Wolf attacks at Bryant University."*

EIGHT

A HAUNTING AT THE

MT. WASHINGTON HOTEL

A couple planning a retirement vacation from North Smithfield, Rhode Island, was at home booking a vacation trip to New Hampshire, staying at the Mount Washington Hotel, from their computer. It was late November 2025, and the couple, both 65 years old, had just retired from their jobs and they went on a bus trip from Providence, Rhode Island. They boarded the bus at the Bonanza bus station. It was a tour to the Mt. Washington Hotel.

"Good morning, ladies and gentlemen, welcome aboard Conway Tours. My name is Paul Damon, your tour guide, and we will be going to the Mt. Washington Hotel and viewpoints in New Hampshire. The trip will take about 6 to 7 hours and we will be making two stops before we get to the Mt. Washington Hotel. Our tour leaves Providence at 11:02 a.m., and we should be at our destination, the Mt. Washington region, at about 6:00 p.m., depending on weather and traffic during our travel. The bus will travel up Route 95 north to Route 128 north through Boston, going over the Tobin Bridge, Route 93, then Route 16 all the way to the

White Mountains in New Hampshire. We will stop for lunch after passing through Boston, about 1:00 p.m. We will stop again for a rest break at 4:00 p.m. before we get to the White Mountains. The weather is sunny, and the temperature is 45 degrees. It's zero on top of Mt. Washington in New Hampshire. Please sit back and enjoy your trip. Once again, my name is Paul Damon and your bus driver is Bob Chelsea."

The bus arrived at 6:14 p.m., and snow flurries were falling. The couple got off the bus and went into the hotel to check in.

"Good evening," said the receptionist at the check-in desk.

"Hi, my name is Alan Johnson and my wife Pam, from North Smithfield, Rhode Island, checking in with Conway Tours."

"May I see your itinerary, please?" said the receptionist.

"You will be in room 413 with one king bed overlooking Mt. Washington. The bellboy — his name is Daniel Davis. You will have room service for dinner for your first night. Prime rib, oven-baked potatoes and green beans and a garden salad will be served, and carrot cake and coffee will be served for dessert. Tomorrow morning we have continental breakfast in the dining room where you will meet your tour guide. Her name is Debra Debreuil. She will give you a tour up Mt. Washington after breakfast," said the receptionist.

"Look at this big woman," said Alan Johnson. The woman was a big black lady with big tits; she's 6 foot 6 and weighs about 350 pounds!

"She's Debra Debreuil, your Mt. Washington tour guide," said the receptionist.

"Oh my God, we better not mess with her!" Alan joked. "She sits on you she'll kill you!" Pam laughed.

Later the bellboy took their luggage to their room. Alan tipped the guy, then settled in the room. The couple went to the lounge to sit in front of the fireplace, then went for a walk to see the dining room, and they went to the indoor pool for a while before returning to their room.

"This hotel is beautiful, expensive but very nice!" said Pam.

"Our trip cost $3,000; it should be a nice place," said Alan.

Later they took their shower, watched Thursday Night Football before going to bed. Pam heard a loud noise; the time was 11:02 p.m.

"Alan, did you hear that noise?"

"What noise?"

"It sounded like a big crash in the bathroom!"

Alan checked and nothing was out of place. "You didn't hear that noise, Alan!"

"I did not hear nothing, but whatever you heard may be from another room."

After the game they went to bed. At 12:02 a.m., Alan woke up because air was blowing in his ears. He got up and a heat was blowing on him, so he turned the fan off. Then he went to bed. The room was dark; only a night light was on. At 1:02 a.m., Pam heard a voice, "Hello!!!!" The voice was not from Alan.

She woke Alan: "Wake up! Someone's in here!"

Alan got up to check, and he said, "You might be hearing some-one from another room. There's nobody here, just go to sleep."

Alan felt like someone was hanging over him, heavy breathing! He woke up and looked at the alarm clock, and the time was 2:02 a.m. He got up to go to the bathroom and check the room, and no one was there. Then he went back to sleep.

Pam woke up, and she saw a little boy that looked like he was crying in a bright green glow with a brown trim standing inside the bedroom. She screamed, "AHHH!"

She quickly turned on the light, and the little boy ghost was gone! The time was 3:02 a.m. Alan woke up out of a sound sleep wondering what's going on!

"Alan, we have a ghost in our room! We need to get out of here!"

"Pam, you're dreaming, you must have had a bad dream!"

"Alan, it's not a dream, I saw a little sad-looking boy glowing in the dark; it's not a dream!"

"Let's sleep with the lamp on until we get up in the morning. I felt something breathing on me earlier, almost like blowing in my ears, but the heater was blowing in my ears, so I shut the fan off in the heater."

"Alan, I'm going downstairs to sleep in the lounge. I am too afraid I'll see something again!"

"Why don't we get another room, Pam?"

"Okay!" she said.

Then the covers flew off the bed, and the pillows flew off the bed across the room. The lights were blinking on and off, and the bathroom door was opening and slamming shut. Then an ashtray and a flower vase flew across the room, almost hitting Pam in the head as she was screaming hysterically!

They both ran out of that room half-naked before they got killed and went to the main desk—and no one was there!

"Just fucking great! No one at the front desk to get another room!" said Alan.

Then a security guard in the hotel lobby came by. The couple told him about the ghost in their room.

"Can you take us to our room so we can finish getting dressed and check out of there?" said Pam.

"We're staying in room 413," said Alan.

The room was a mess, and it smelled like the dead! The time was 4:02 a.m.; the smell went away a minute later. The couple finished getting dressed, packed up, and got the fuck out of there!

The couple and the security guard went to the lounge to bull-shit for the rest of the night!

"We paid more than $3000 for this trip, and the hotel clerk never told us this hotel is haunted, can you believe it!" said Alan.

"How long are you here for?" said the security guard.

"We're here until Saturday, November 29th, 2025. It's our retirement Thanksgiving vacation," said Pam.

"The clerk should be there all night in case emergencies like this happen; that's rude for a high-class place like this," said Alan.

"Usually they're here all night long on weekends, because not many check-ins during the week," said the security guard.

"It's too late to get another room now, it's after 5:30 in the morning," said Pam.

The couple slept on a couch with a blanket over them in front of the fireplace until breakfast. The security guard left to do his job walking through the hotel. He left a message with the clerk receptionist about the couple's haunting in room 413.

About 7 a.m. Alan and Pam woke up and went to the dining room for continental breakfast, sharing their horror story during the night.

One man said, "This hotel is haunted, a lot of things happen here; you people are not the only ones! We've been here since last week, but we haven't seen anything yet. But we're waiting to see something before we leave on Saturday."

Said a man getting food: pancakes with Vermont honey maple syrup, sausage, eggs, ham, hash browns, omelets, bagels, donuts, muffins, fruit bowls, orange juice, coffee, and milk were served in the continental breakfast.

Then Alan and Pam and the other man they were talking with in the food line sat together with his wife.

"My name is Alan Johnson and my wife Pam, celebrating a retirement vacation. We're from Rhode Island."

"Pleased to meet you, Mr. and Mrs. Johnson. My name is Richard Ford and my wife Diane. We're from White Plains, New York. We are lawyers, and we're here for a conference today."

"I think we are going to need a lawyer before we leave this hotel full of ghosts!" Alan laughed.

"I worked 27 years at Rhode Island Hospital as a nurse, and my husband had a contractor business building condos and resort hotels in Miami, Florida, West Palm Beach, Bermuda, and some of the Caribbean Islands, and he finished his work in Aruba. So for vacation, we want to stay in a hotel that tops them all; a world classic overlooking Mt. Washington, and so far the view of ghosts in our room instead! Hopefully, it gets better today!" said Pam.

The couple kept chatting, enjoying breakfast, before Pam and Alan went to the front desk before Debra Dubreuil arrived. Alan was pissed.

"Excuse me, Mrs. Fitzgerald, but I have a bone to pick with you people. We arrived last night staying in room 413. The room was full of ghosts and strange things happened to me and Pam all night! It was a sleepless night for both of us! Pam saw a ghost of a little crying boy glowing in the dark, wind blowing in my ears, glass flying off shelves nearly hitting me and Pam in the head, doors opening and closing and slamming shut, then the bed sheets and blankets flew off the bed, pillows and feathers flying all over the room; the room looks like a tornado struck! We are high-class retired people looking for a historic vacation in one of the world-famous hotels, and we get a room with the devil! We were not informed that there are ghosts here, Mrs. Margret Fitzgerald! I am sorry to put the pressure on you this morning, but the receptionist last night was wrong! I want a room overlooking Mount Washington, and if we get spooked again I want my $3,135 dollars we spent for this vacation, and you will be shipping us back to North Smithfield, Rhode Island!" said Alan. He was pissed.

"I am so sorry, Mr. & Mrs. Johnson. I will give you a suite. You were supposed to be in a suite according to your vacation package. I will speak to Nancy when she comes in tonight. You will be staying in room 531 beginning tonight; there shouldn't be any ghosts in that room. The suites are not haunted!" the receptionist joked.

"Thank you," said Alan & Pam.

Then the shuttle arrived to take the couple up Mt. Washington. The big fat black lady arrived and got off the shuttle bus and walked into the lobby, pounding her feet side by side, shaking the lobby floor because she was so heavy.

"Good morning, everyone! My name is Debra Dubreuil, the tour guide going to Mt. Washington. The shuttle is here and you may board."

While the tour was boarding the shuttle, the receptionist clerk told one of the workers, "Marie, can you go to room 413, clean and remake the room? There was an incident there last night and the room might be a mess. If anything is broken, take pictures with your phone and bring it back to me."

"Yes, Mrs. Fitzgerald."

The girl Marie, a new hotel housekeeper just hired, went to the room and it was a mess. The bed was torn open, sliced right down the middle; the mattress was torn open, and pillows with feathers pulled out of them, pillowcases hanging on lamps, and the bed sheets and blankets were laying on the floor with broken glass on them. A light fixture was broken and drapes torn off the windows and ripped, and the room smelled like something was dead in there. She went looking for where the bad smell was coming from.

She looked under the bed and around the bed and room all over but she could not find where the bad smell was coming from. She went in the bathroom and towels were hanging over a light, dripping water on the floor, and a coffee cup stuck to the mirror over the sink. The shower curtain was torn and hanging down. Marie looked in the shower and she flushed the toilet.

Then she took pictures of the damage with her cell phone and went back to the front desk to show the receptionist. She said,

"Whoever stayed in this room must have been very angry! The damage is out of control, and it stinks like someone died there!"

"Marie, let's go to this room and see what's going on. Alfred, can you watch the check-in desk?" the receptionist, Margret Fitzgerald, said to the security guard.

The housekeeper Marie and the hotel clerk went to that room. The clerk swiped her card to get into room 413, and everything was normal! The room was clean, the bed was made up, and the room looked like no one had slept in there. Nothing was out of place! Everything was set up ready for the next customer.

She said, "Marie, did you go to the correct room? There's no problem here!"

"That's strange, Mrs. Fitzgerald, this is the same room, 413! Is there another 413 somewhere else in this hotel? See, on my phone, this is the same room!"

"There's no other 413, but the damage you have on your phone shows much different than what the room looks like now! If damage like this really happened, the front desk would have known about it a long time ago. I want you to strip all the linen off the beds and clean and remake the room to be on the safe side."

"Mrs. Fitzgerald, this room is clean like nothing happened and it smells nice, but this is the room, 413! I can't believe it; another housekeeper must have cleaned up the mess in 15 minutes!"

Later, Marie came back to strip and clean the room. *(When Marie took the pictures of the damage and left the room when she was done, the room fixed back to normal from the power of the ghost in there!)*

After Marie finished cleaning and re-setting the room, she was playing games on her phone. The sun was shining brightly through the windows, and suddenly the room was getting dark. She heard a voice as loud as day:

"Get Out!"

She jumped up quickly from sitting in a chair playing with her phone. Then she saw a black humanoid form coming out of the heating unit. It looked like the devil and was a hairy poltergeist black moving mist with horns and red eyes! Then it went over the bed and vanished!

Marie, the housekeeper, screamed hysterically:

"AHHH!"

She ran out of the room, and a strong gust of wind blew her down the hall about 50 feet, bouncing her off the walls. Suddenly she came to a stop! She was not seriously hurt and came to rest in front of the elevators.

She went down to the check-in desk, crying and screaming, and told the clerk what happened.

"I saw the devil in room 413! I quit! I am out of here!"

Mrs. Fitzgerald went back to that room with a big stick. Everything was normal.

The clerk said to the security guard, "That lady must be crazy. I went to that room three times, and nothing was there!"

"Mrs. Fitzgerald, I was talking to Alan and Pam Johnson, staying in that room last night, and they had a horrifying experience with ghosts and demonic happenings in room 413," said the security guard.

"The housekeeper Marie showed me pictures about what happened in that room, and when she and I went back there, the room was normal, clean, smelled nice, and all made up like no one's been in there! I found that strange. I heard a lot of horror stories about that room from guests staying there! I have been working in this hotel for three and a half years, and I never saw anything paranormal, just heard a lot of stories," said Mrs. Fitzgerald, the clerk receptionist.

The tour shuttle bus with Debra Debreuil was late leaving the hotel, waiting for more people to board.

"Good morning, ladies and gentlemen, welcome aboard Mt. Washington Shuttle Tours. Today's Friday, November 21st, 2025. My name is Debra Debreuil, and we will be departing shortly.

We're 45 minutes late waiting for more people to board. I am looking for one couple: Alan and Pam Johnson. Are you here?"

"Here!" they said.

Debra Debreuil continued calling names until the bus was filled.

"Everyone is here, and we are ready to go! Our first stop will be at the gift shop at the bottom of Mt. Washington for coffee and snacks and to take pictures. Then we will go to the Summit Depot and take the cog rail train up the mountain to the top of Mt. Washington. The weather is sunny and 39 degrees at the base of the mountain, and it's 9 degrees below zero at the summit. It's snowing up there with 70-mile-per-hour winds and gusts as high as 85! So when we get up there, you need to hold on to things and each other because you do not want to get blown off the mountain! Take plenty of pictures! When we get to the summit, there are gift shops and a cafeteria to get lunch, and you will see a movie about the history of Mt. Washington. Then you will have a tour of the summit. Once again, I am your tour guide, Debra Debreuil."

"May I have your attention, please! Please make sure all windows are closed because it's very cold and windy! Avoid frostbite!" said the train conductor.

The view was horrible; you could not see anything because it was a whiteout all the way up the mountain! The wind was so bad that it was blowing snow onto the windows of the cog rail train, freezing on contact.

Just before the train got to the summit, the sky cleared for a short time. Alan and Pam saw a black figure with no facial features standing on the side of the mountain with a big drop behind the figure! Then the clouds passed by, and everything turned white again.

Minutes later, the cog rail arrived at the summit.

"Ladies and gentlemen, welcome to the top of the world! Make sure you are bundled up, wearing hats and gloves because it's bitter cold, well below zero up here! When we get off the train, I want everyone to grab the railings and hold on to each other because the wind is strong enough to blow you off the mountain! Hang on until we get inside and meet tour guide Robert Evans," said Debra Debreuil.

The Mt. Washington crew came on the train to rope and chain 16 passengers together, holding on to the railings and following each other until they got inside.

"Be careful, there's blowing snow and ice, and it's very slippery!" said the mountain crew.

"Good afternoon, ladies and gentlemen, welcome to the top of Mt. Washington. My name is Bob Evans, and I will be giving you a tour of the top of the world! We will not be going outside because of the dangerous conditions. How does 60 below zero wind chill feel with 101-mile-per-hour wind gusts? Look out there, you can't see anything! You will be here for about two hours before we go back down the mountain. Do not wander off alone or go outside because if you do, you may not come back! Everyone, grab lunch in here, go to the gift shops, and in 45 minutes we will see a movie about the history of Mt. Washington. Then we will go on a brief tour," said Bob Evans.

"Ladies and gentlemen, the highest wind on Mt. Washington ever recorded was 231 miles per hour in 1934. There were unconfirmed wind gusts as high as 260 miles per hour in 2022. The highest temperature ever was 72 degrees, and the lowest was 68 degrees below zero in February of 1973. In February of 2023, we had minus 108 degrees wind chill. Take off your clothes and run around naked in that kind of cold—you'll freeze to death in five seconds! You'll disintegrate!" said Bob Evans.

Everyone laughed. Then he finished the tour.

The Mt. Washington tour saw a movie, and tour guides showed what they do on Mt. Washington all day, getting weather reports. Then Debra Debreuil's tour was escorted back on the cog rail going down the mountain.

It was raining when the tour got to the shuttle to go back to the hotel. When the shuttle got back to the Mt. Washington Hotel, Alan and Pam got their new room overlooking the White Mountains.

When the couple finished checking in, room 531 was a big suite. They later went to dinner in the dining room. Family chicken was served for dinner on Friday evening, along with fish. First came the chicken soup, then the salad, then pasta fries, followed by the chicken and fish. Ice cream and Boston cream pie were served for dessert, along with tea and coffee.

It was Friday night, and a band was playing. Alan and Pam joined the couple of lawyers they had met earlier that day. They were dancing and drinking until 2 a.m., then Alan and Pam went to their room. They went to bed around 3 a.m.

Pam looked at the alarm clock, and the time was 3:02 a.m. She stared at the alarm clock until 3:03 a.m., then put the blanket over her and went to sleep.

One hour later, Alan got up to go to the bathroom. He looked at the alarm clock, and the time was 4:01 a.m. He sat on the bed until the time was 4:03 a.m. Nothing happened. He walked around the room for a while, hoping not to see anything paranormal. Everything was quiet. He went to pee, then went back to bed and fell asleep.

At 9:02 a.m., there was a knock at the door. Then again. Pam woke up and heard a voice.

"Hello! Housekeeping!"

She woke Alan because she was still half asleep.

"Alan, someone's here!"

"Housekeeping! Please come back later, we're not up yet!" said Alan.

The housekeeper left. Alan put the sign on the outside door: *Please Do Not Disturb.*

Around 10 a.m., Alan and Pam got up and got dressed. Alan

looked out the window and said, "Pam, come look at this: a perfect view of Mt. Washington. It looks so close you could walk to it!"

While they were looking out the window, the black devil-like poltergeist was standing right behind them — the same one that had been in room 413, with red eyes. Alan opened the drapes on the window to let the daylight brightness in the room. The poltergeist vanished, but they did not see it. It was still in the room, but Alan and Pam could not see it.

They went down to the dining room to get breakfast. One man saw a ghost in his room of a man with no head. The new guest who stayed in room 413 last night was spared from the evil.

Another couple saw people dressed like they were from the 1600s, talking and loading shotguns — about five people who were not supposed to be there. The couple woke up screaming and telling them to get out, and the apparitions vanished.

Another couple saw a princess in their room. When they woke, the man said to her, "Excuse me, little miss, but you're in the wrong room. You have to leave." He turned on the lamp, and the princess vanished.

Guests were calling the office, complaining about ghosts in their rooms. About six people in a suite saw a group of people standing and talking in their room. The group looked like soldiers from the Civil War, holding big guns and talking to each other.

"Mommy! Mommy! We have ghosts in our room!" said a little boy.

All six saw the apparitions of the men, and as soon as someone turned on a light, the visions vanished.

"Son of a bitch! We have ghosts in our room!" said a man.

One girl sleeping alone woke up and saw a man in old dirty clothes holding a big gun to her head. The room stank like the dead. She was held down on the bed by a mysterious force. She couldn't scream or move, just watch the horror in shock. The time was 3:02 a.m. She was released a minute later, and the spirit vanished. She turned on the lamp, and the room was quiet; the bad smell went away. She got dressed and left the room. She ran to the front desk crying.

"Help! There's a fucking ghost in my room!"

She slept in the lounge for the rest of the night.

The night before Thanksgiving, a couple was sleeping in room 413. The man woke up hearing a gunshot. He saw a vision of a man who looked like Clint Eastwood, pointing a gun at them. The man had a gun by his bed and pointed back. As soon as the vision man was ready to pull the trigger, the man in the room fired his gun. The bullet shattered a mirror in the room. The vision vanished. When he turned on the light, nothing was there.

Many people staying at the Mt. Washington Hotel had plenty of stories to tell Alan and Pam at the dinner table about the ghosts there while having Thanksgiving dinner.

NINE

BLOOD CEMETERY IN
HOLLIS, NEW HAMPSHIRE

People come to the Blood Cemetery to see if the stories there are true. Two girls — high school girls, it seemed — broke into the cemetery late at night around 3 a.m., climbing over a 7-foot gate to get in. They decided to go for a walk through the cemetery looking for the blood pool. There was about 10 inches of snow on the ground. The girls heard something bubbling like boiling water, and they found the mysterious blood pool in the cemetery, but they disappeared. Their bodies were never found; they fell into a sinkhole full of blood and drowned.

At 4:04 a.m., Hollis Police pulled over to check out a vacant car parked near the cemetery. The car was from Massachusetts. The officer ran the license plate, checked the locked car, then left. Two hours later, the same officer checked the car again, shined his flashlight into the cemetery, and found no one there. Three nights later, the same car was still there. The officer put a ticket on the windshield, then left. A few days later, the same officer returned with a partner during the day, and the car was still parked there.

"Miss Pam Elliot, welcome to the Hollis, New Hampshire Police Department. It's your first day on the job training, and this will be your new assignment on the 11 p.m. to 7 a.m. evening shift. The first week you will be my partner before going on your own next week. I've been training you for three hours, and I haven't introduced myself yet. I am Captain James Dubreuil, and I work all three shifts. I usually work the graveyard shift, 11 to 7, most nights, and during the day when I'm training new officers. Please to meet you.

This car has been here for a week now with three tickets on the windshield. I hope nothing happened to the driver or possible passengers — though that is possible. This cemetery is called Blood Cemetery. Here we have a blood pool that appears and disappears occasionally. When we get heavy rain or snow, a blood pool appears — why, I don't know.

A priest from St. Mary's Church near the police station says there's something evil here. We have a 7-foot picket iron gate surrounding Blood Cemetery. Some areas of the gate reach 9 feet high. It's unlikely people are going to scale these gates to get in because the town sprays a slippery substance on them so nobody can climb and get in.

In the last 39 years, 11 people went missing in this graveyard, and I hope it's not #12. The only way people can get in here is when the graveyard is open for visitors and they hide somewhere when the gates close at 4 p.m. When it rains or snows, the graveyard does not open. We have a problem with sinkholes in this graveyard during bad weather. When the missing — or animals — get caught in them, they drown, and the blood from the victims or animals gets sucked out in the sinkholes and rises to the surface somehow. The native Indians from Bennington, Vermont, believe the devil rises from Hell to get the victims or animals.

Try to climb the gate, Pam," said Captain Dubreuil. Pam couldn't grab it. Captain Dubreuil laughed.

"It's a nice day today, and the graveyard is open till 4 p.m. and closes during bad weather. The driver of this car is identified as Wendy Watson, a student at UMASS Lowell," he added.

About a week later, during Christmas vacation, about five UMASS Lowell students came to Hollis, NH, looking for two girls missing since Thanksgiving 2025. One girl went to the Hollis Police Department looking for Wendy.

"Good afternoon, officers. My name is Lea Levers, a student at UMASS Lowell. Have you heard from Wendy Watson and Linda Lamb? They were last heard from weeks ago here in Hollis. They said they were going to the Blood Cemetery. They're missing!" the girl cried.

"We have identified her car and wrote up a missing person report, but no bodies were found. Who's the second person?" said the police.

"Her name is Linda Lamb," Lea cried.

"Okay, I will file a second missing person's report. Let me get your information, and if we find them, we will get back to you. They might be somewhere else in New Hampshire, but her car was found parked near the Blood Cemetery. Don't go there — it's a dangerous place," said the police.

{Phase — do you think a bunch of college kids exploring a new journey is going to listen?}

The girl and four of her friends went to the Blood Cemetery anyway. It was 2:49 a.m. on a snowy night, and the five girls had scheduled a plan to break into the cemetery. It was snowing heavily, and no one was around. The same girl, Lea Levers, who had been at the police station earlier looking for the two missing girls, was the ringleader for the plan.

"Ladies, there's no chance we can climb this fence because it's very slippery unless we set up a ladder to climb and jump over. Then, once we are in, we have to put a rope to pull the ladder over the gate so we can jump back out. I have a ladder that can reach 8 feet in my car and a shovel to dig a hole in the ground and make a tunnel to get into the graveyard. The problem is the ground is frozen! Let's go with Plan #1!"

Lea Levers' plan worked.

She had a fold-up ladder and opened it, placing it against the gate. She jumped over first and landed feet-first in 18 inches of snow on the ground. The rest of the college girls followed, jumping over one by one. The last girl was able to sit on the pickets at the top of the gate and pull the ladder over inside the graveyard.

Once inside, the five UMASS Lowell female students began their journey, finding the blood pool and taking pictures. Suddenly, a sinkhole opened quickly and swallowed all five of them. They all drowned in the blood pool and disappeared.

A security policeman was in a booth near the gates, sleeping in the cemetery. Video cameras showed the girls breaking in. The booth alarm rang, waking the sleeping security officer at 6:50 a.m. The cop never checked the camera footage and left for home.

The next day, the graveyard did not open because it was still snowing. By evening, after the snowplows cleared the streets, Captain James Debreuil stopped by the cemetery to check on a van from Massachusetts. He saw a ladder standing against the gate inside the closed graveyard.

The next morning was sunny, and the graveyard opened. A SWAT team went in looking for the five girls who had broken in. Officers reviewed the camera footage, which showed the five girls climbing the ladder to enter the graveyard but never coming out. The SWAT team searched the entire cemetery, but no girls were found. The blood pool was fenced off.

"Officers, these five girls must have exited somewhere or climbed out, because the entire area was searched and no girls were here. Two things had to happen: either they all fell into the blood pool and disappeared, since no one came out when the graveyard opened this morning, or they got out from under the ground somewhere. There's no footage showing the girls exiting the graveyard after breaking in. They were seen breaking in from somewhere, then vanished!" said the SWAT team investigators.

"Fellers, and the graveyard caretakers and coroners: we need to close the graveyard for a week to see if anything surfaces. In fact, shut it down until the snow goes away. If it takes until spring or summer, I want this place closed. We have too many missing persons reports dealing with the Hollis town Blood Cemetery. Now it's possible five more kids are lost here. In the last 36 years, we have had 11 missing persons reports, and this week has grown to 13. I hope the number does not rise to 18!"

"It makes this town look bad!" said Capt. James Debreuil.

"Captain sir: A lot more than five or more people have died here during the day; never mind breaking in at night! We have several sinkholes in this graveyard, and anyone can be a victim at any time, including you, me, and anyone else visiting here! Most of the sinkholes are filled in, except the restricted areas. Seekers come in here looking for them, and that's when they get into trouble because they're not supposed to be in the restricted areas!" said the cemetery caretakers and workers.

A bunch of policemen and Capt. James Debreuil were shitting their pants right now and left the cemetery!

Later, Captain Debreuil went to the security guard's office, and he said, "Good evening, Officer Mitchell Curry. Did you by chance see the footage on the cameras before you went home early this morning?"

"No, I didn't, but I heard about it from a police officer."

"What the fuck are you doing all night! There's an empty fifth bottle of vodka in the trash; drinking on the job! You smell like booze right now, and your shift's just starting! What were you doing, sleeping all night! I warned you before about your drinking and sleeping on the job! I can't have this! I know you have been working in this booth for ten years with no issues until now! Five people broke into the graveyard and were never seen again! Now I have seven victims! I have to let you go if you don't do your job! I want no more sleeping or drinking on the job. I like you, Mr. Curry; you have done a good job here, and I have caught you several times sleeping. You need to be awake and stop your God damn drinking!"

"Yes sir, Capt. Debreuil."

Then Captain Debreuil ran the license plate on the van, and the car was towed.

"Ellen J. Jennings; Jesus H. Christ: another UMASS Lowell student!" Capt. Debreuil said to a police officer.

The next morning, Capt. Debreuil contacted UMASS Lowell about the missing seven persons report.

"Good morning: Marion Douglas, dean of students at UMASS Lowell."

"Hi, this is Captain James Debreuil from the Hollis, New Hampshire Police Department. Three students from UMASS Lowell have been reported missing after breaking into the Hollis Blood Cemetery, identified as Wendy Watson, Linda Lamb, and Ellen J. Jennings. Wendy Watson's car and Ellen J. Jennings' van were spotted at the cemetery before breaking in. Five more girls reported breaking into the cemetery coming from the van parked there! I don't know if these women are alive or dead, but they have been reported missing."

"Thank you, Captain Debreuil," said the UMASS Lowell dean of students.

UMASS Lowell students got emails about the missing students in the Blood Cemetery.

The new night officer, Pam Elliot, was policing the Blood Cemetery, and she saw a helicopter land there; the helicopter disappeared and sank into a sinkhole of blood, and it was gone before it could take back off again! The rotor went: wop, wop, wop, wop,

wop! And the propeller in the back went: ginny, ginny, ginny, ginny, ginny! Splattering blood all over the snow!

Pam Elliot was screaming, watching the horror unfold! Birds and other animals got into the graveyard, eating the dead as the bodies resurfaced, and animals were swallowed up in the blood pool!

The town and the police department sent drones flying over the blood pool, and they saw dead animals, humans, and gravestones washing in a whirlpool, like in a washing machine.

Days later, a town meeting took place at the Hollis High School. Hollis residents got emails, and the police and the fire department went riding around, calling with loudspeakers for everyone in town to attend this meeting.

"May I have your attention please: all residents of Hollis, NH, must attend the town meeting at the high school tonight!" said the police and fire department.

"Good evening: My name is Robin Mason, the mayor of the town of Hollis. The Blood Cemetery is now closed indefinitely as of today! Last evening, a helicopter landed there and disappeared, and several persons have been reported missing, and police drones spotted dead humans and animals washing in the blood."

TEN

CHASE HOUSE HORRORS

Portsmouth, New Hampshire. A basketball team arrived at the Chase House one Friday afternoon.

"Good afternoon, I called Tuesday about booking rooms for 20 basketball players and staff. My name is Jason Freddy, the coach of the Providence Pirates ABA semi-pro basketball team, and we are playing a pair of games Saturday evening and Sunday afternoon with the New Hampshire KINGZ, playing at the new Portsmouth Forum. This hotel is the closest place to stay. I booked the first night, but I will need Saturday night too because the New Hampshire KINGZ want to play the weekend instead of just one game."

"Freddy, let me see what I have. You're good for tonight, and tomorrow I do have rooms for 20 people, but you may be moved around a little if that's okay with you. My name is Greg Cookingham, the Chase House owner."

"Pleased to meet you, Jason Freddy."

"Sorry, sir: I called your name in reverse. I have two to a room all on the second floor. We have 15 players and five coaches and staff. Head coach, you will be alone staying in room 201. Two others in room 202 and 203. Then two players will stay in each room from 204 to 210. The bellboy, Barrows Dana, will bring all luggage to your rooms. Dinner will be served in the Ghost Dining Room, up the hall on the first floor after 5 pm. Good luck and enjoy your stay here at the Chase House Bed & Breakfast."

The players went to the elevators up to their rooms. They saw what looked like a young girl hanging from a rope wrapped around a light in the hallway. The young girl had a short skirt with no undies, and her bush was visible! They could barely see the apparition because it was barely visible.

"I swear I just saw a ghost hanging from a rope in the hall with no panties on!" one of the players laughed. Several players saw it too. When they got close to what they saw before getting to the elevators, it vanished! The players and coaches were looking around, and nothing was there.

The players were cleaning up and getting ready to go to dinner. Coach Jason Freddy was washing up and taking a shower in his room, staying alone. The hot shower suddenly went ice cold, then shut off; the time was 4:02 pm. He tried to figure out why the shower shut off, and it came back on a minute later, hot the way Coach Freddy likes it.

Then he was shaving, and the water in the sink shut off, came back on, went off again, then came back on again and stayed on until he finished shaving. He turned the water off in the sink, but it would not shut off! He tried again, but the water would not shut off. He called the front desk.

"Hi, it's Coach Jason Freddy in room 201. The faucet in the sink will not turn off! The shower was acting funny, turning on and off!"

"Maybe you have a ghost in your room!" the front desk clerk laughed.

"I will send maintenance up to check it." Then the water in the sink shut off on its own.

A maintenance man came to check the bathroom, and he said,

"Everything is alright in here. Make sure you turn the faucet fixtures tight when you turn them off because they may run due to the cold outside."

"It's not that, sir. Before you came here, the water turned off on its own," said Coach Jason Freddy.

"That's strange, but everything is okay!" said the maintenance worker, and he left.

The coach was putting on his tie, looking in the bathroom mirror, when he heard a noise in the room. He looked around, checking under the bed, and saw nothing. Then he heard water running in the bathroom. He went to check it out, but there was no running water. He looked up at the ceiling in the shower and saw a big water stain. Then he saw a drawer open and closed it.

Finally, he went and joined the players for dinner.

After dinner, the coaches and players sat in the lounge in front of the fireplace, telling ghost stories.

One of the players went to his room and saw two people sleeping in each bed. He went down to the front desk and said, "Excuse me, miss, four people are sleeping in my room."

"What room are you staying in?" said the lady.

"I am in room 205. My name is Stan Dee, and my roommate is Kevin Bentley."

"Come with me, and we'll see what's going on. Only two people to a room," said the lady at the front desk.

"The room is fine; there's no one in here. You may have gone to the wrong room," she said.

"That's strange, but it's possible because everything looks the same here!" Then Stan stayed in his room, and his roommate Kevin arrived.

After a night of eating, drinking, and partying, the players and coaches called it a night.

The lady at the desk looked down the hallway and saw the girl hanging from a light. She went to get a better look, and the apparition vanished! She looked at her watch, and the time was 3:02 am.

One of the players was getting into bed when the TV came on by itself. He got up to turn it off and then went back to bed. Minutes later, a window opened, and the room got cold. He got up and saw the open window behind a floor-to-ceiling curtain. He closed the window, locked it, turned the heat up, and went back to bed.

In another room, players were sleeping when a basketball popped out of a bag and bounced on the floor. The red, white, and blue ABA ball came to rest between the beds where they were sleeping. Then both players heard a loud scream, waking them up from a sound sleep. The basketball started bouncing again on its own.

The players woke up yelling, "Who's in here?"

"Hey!"

They got up and turned on a light, but no one was in the room.

"Gary, something's going on in here. Did you hear that loud scream? I think we have a ghost in here! How does a basketball bounce around on its own? Something is happening in this room!"

"I heard it too! Arron! Let's pack up and get the fuck out of here!"

The time was 4:02 am, and the strange happenings stopped a minute later. The two players went to the check-in desk to get another room. It was a sleepless night for the Providence Pirates basketball team staying at the Chase House.

Coach Jason Freddy felt something pinching his foot while he was in bed, waking him up from a sound sleep! He quickly got up and threw the covers off the bed, and nothing was there. The coach felt his foot and was okay. Then he saw what looked like a fox with a long tail run across the floor and vanish.

"I swear this room is haunted!" he said to himself.

He went to the bathroom, and something pinched his foot again! He grabbed his foot and started kicking until the pinching stopped. He rubbed his leg and foot and was okay. Then, while he was sitting on the toilet, he saw the water turn on in the sink and the shower at the same time—and turn off at the same time!

He didn't bother wiping himself. He got dressed in a hurry, and while he was getting dressed, a mysterious force pushed him, knocking him down! He grabbed his suitcase and belongings and got out of the room before 5 am.

The coach went to the front desk and told the lady what had happened in his room. Then he sat in the lounge in front of the fireplace, talking to his haunted players and reading a newspaper.

Two players were thrown out of their beds by an invisible force, banging their heads together and dragging their bodies across the room! Other players were told to get out of their rooms, and nobody was there.

The assistant coaches staying in room 202 woke up to see a lady in the bathroom. When they confronted her, they said, "Hey, miss, you're in the wrong room!" The lady vanished.

"Did I just see a ghost?" one of the coaches said.

Other players saw the bed blankets and sheets fly off the bed. They saw a ghost appear and vanish! The same players were pinned down in their beds until the hauntings vanished one minute later before they were let go. The two players left their room.

Another player in a different room was taking a shower when the shower curtain wrapped around him, pulling him down into the tub. He pulled the shower curtain down, and the haunting stopped.

Two players in another room were haunted, being thrown out of bed and swept into the middle of the room together. Then a bald-headed eagle crashed through a window and landed on the bed, looking at them. It then took off and flew back out the window it came through.

The two players got dressed, grabbed their luggage, and left the room in a hurry. The entire basketball team was haunted during the night and forced to gather together in the beautiful lounge in front of a warm fireplace before 5:30 in the morning, telling their horror stories.

"May I have your attention, please. This hotel, bed & breakfast, or whatever it is, we have to stay another night because it's a non-refundable environment. I just spoke to the owner on the phone after I was forced out of my room. He will have a meeting with us after our game. He said a lot of strange things have happened here for years. However, according to the state law in New Hampshire, hotels or homes do not have to tell you that their property is haunted. Luckily, no one was seriously hurt, but I am going to file a report of injuries anyway, because we do have injuries from flying debris! He said he will set up the convention room with bedding so we can all be together," said the coach.

Later, the game was played. When the players got back to the hotel, the owner held the meeting.

"Good evening, how did the game go?" said the Chase House owner.

"We lost to the NH Kingz 118 to 114 in overtime," said the coach.

"Come down to the conference room in the basement. I have 20 bunk beds set up military-style to sleep 40 people! We need to have a meeting about the history of the Chase House, and it's not very good. I am sorry I didn't inform you about the hauntings here. The New Hampshire State Law does not have to tell guests that the properties are haunted unless injuries happen. I do have injury reports, and I am sorry these strange things happened to you. It has been a while since the Chase House ghosts have been acting up. My name is Greg Cookingham. We met when your group checked in Friday night. You will be safe down here; there have been no hauntings."

Bullshit, the whole place is haunted!

Greg Cookingham continued, "In the 1600s, the Chase House

was a slaughterhouse! People were murdered, tortured, hung, and chopped up for human sacrifice. The KKK burned people here, *Mark of the Devil* was filmed here. People were tortured here like in that movie. When you walk around late at night, you may see a girl hanging from a rope in the hallways. Young girls were raped, murdered, and hung in several locations on this property. This bed & breakfast resort is built over unrest spirits, and priests and paranormal teams cannot get rid of them. Exorcisms were performed here, but they will not go! I have not heard of any serious injuries from the hauntings here.

"Before I bought this property, it was a boarding house, a mental hospital, and a church. The previous owner back in the old days was named Katrina Chase, along with many owners after her. I can't explain the horrors these unrest spirits caused. If you sleep together down here, you will be okay. The spirits seem to pick on one person at a time, and when two people are staying in one room, the spirits will haunt one person and then bother the second one later. The activity usually happens between 2:30 am and 5 am, then it stops. But you can see something in this building anytime during the day and night. Sorry for the inconvenience," said the owner, Greg Cookingham.

The team slept in the convention room for the night with no hauntings. They then had continental breakfast and headed off to their second game against the NH Kingz. The Providence Pirates dominated and then bused their way back to Providence.

The Chase House never got much business because of the hauntings there!

ELEVEN

A HAUNTED HOUSE IN NEW HAMPSHIRE

A man working at the Admirals Gold & Silver plant in Connecticut was preparing for the company's move to New Hampshire. Bridgeport, Connecticut. A meeting at the plant was being held.

"Good morning to all physical plant operations. The Admirals Gold & Silver company here in Bridgeport and New York City will be moving to Meredith, New Hampshire, as of Monday, January 5th, 2026. My name is John Porter, director of plant operations in Connecticut and New York. The company will pay for your transportation and help you find a home, apartment, etc., in Meredith, less than ten miles from the company. The company will move all your belongings from where you live and place you in a home like the one you left. If you're married with kids and animals, we will pay for you. During Christmas week before the New Year, I need documents from where you live and what you have, and the company will help you with the rest. Sorry for the unexpected inconvenience. Merry Christmas and Happy New Year!" said company director John Porter.

In January 2026, it was a zero-degree day, and a couple at the new site waited for a real estate person to come and show them a home. Real estate shuttles arrived at the new Admirals Gold & Silver to take people to a hotel until they could move into their new homes, staying at the Meredith Country Inn.

One agent called out names. "Mr. and Mrs. Jason Green."

"Right here, miss. Jason and my wife, Gerry."

"Come with me and I will take you to your new home. My name is Ellen Jones, from Sarah Elizabeth Realtors. It's a pleasure to meet you. Admirals Gold & Silver Company will be bringing your furniture later today and helping you set it up. The address is One Town Road in Meredith, New Hampshire, seven and a half miles from the Admirals Gold & Silver Company. The drive is two and a half miles from the hotel to where you will be living. Follow me to the location," said the realtor.

The house was a colonial home between two lakes in a nice area.

"Here we are! The truck is already here to get you moved in!"

"Wow! This house is nice. It's bigger than we lived in before in Connecticut," said Jason.

"You have a long driveway to get to the house. This home is a colonial home built in the late 1880s. It has been renovated, and it's a nice home between two lakes. You get a lot of snow and wind during the winter. We have two feet of snow on the ground right now, and the driveway and crosswalks were plowed and shoveled about an hour ago so you can start moving in. Benny Realtors in Connecticut will transfer your mortgage over to Sarah Elizabeth's. Come in and let's see the house.

"First, you have a two-car garage. You enter in the center of the house from the front door, and the back door exits the kitchen out onto the deck and patio. The first room on the right is a family room, and the second room is the dining room. Then you have the living room with a gas-powered fireplace. You also have a big kitchen with a black-and-white checkered floor, and the rest of the rooms have wood vinyl floors and brand-new windows.

"The other side of this home on the first floor has a full bath with a walk-in shower and plenty of closet space throughout. The next room is the den, where you can set up a workplace or computer. The next room on the front left side is a playroom or an extra bedroom. The last room on the first floor is a gathering room or a second living room.

"You will love upstairs! The room on the right is the master bedroom; it's huge! You have five windows and a gas-powered fireplace. There is a mega bathroom in the master bedroom with two sinks, a toilet, a bathtub, a Jacuzzi, and a large French window looking out at the lake and the mountains in the background."

You have two more bedrooms on the left side, front of the house, and you have another small bath, toilet, and sink. Then the last room up here is a guest room or storage area. You have a lot of room in this home; it's beautiful! Come down to the first floor and I will show you the garage and basement.

The garage is big; you have a workbench and room for two cars. The basement door is here near the dining room. Down here you have a lot of open space, big enough to put a bowling alley down here! You have two washer and dryer hookups, hookups for a basement kitchen, and a spot for a built-in freezer; I would have one if I were you because we get a lot of snow here during the winter, enough snow to bury your home under until the springtime! You better get a lot of food to freeze living out here! To get out of the basement you have a bulkhead to exit the backyard. The backyard is on a hill, so you're not in a flood zone. The water and snow fall flows into the Kunt's Brook at the end of your backyard and flows into Kunt's Lake in the next town. The brook and the lake and nearby town do not have a very nice name, but it's the name of a famous woman Indian.

"Good luck, and I hope you two enjoy your new home. Your company will plow your driveway for free until the end of March; after that, you're on your own. Welcome to Meredith, New

Hampshire! You can stay at the Meredith Inn until you get moved in," said the realtor. Then she left.

It's a big house for two people, and they have a dog and a cat. Three days later, Jason and Gerry Green were all moved in, putting things away, moving furniture, hanging pictures, and organizing things until the house was all set up. It was snowing, and it was really coming down! The cat and the dog were acting a little strange, running around the house. Jason and Gerry opened up a bottle of wine, watching the snow falling outside and kids ice skating on the lake and eating sausage and pepper sandwiches.

During the evening, the couple sat in front of the fireplace wrapped up in a blanket. The cat hid under the couch where they were sitting.

"Are you okay, Blackie?" Gerry said to her cat. The cat went: Meow!!!

Suddenly the dog saw something at the bottom of the stairs and started barking like a storm!

"Brownie! What are you barking at?" said Gerry, and she went to investigate. The dog kept barking, looking upstairs. Gerry looked up and saw nothing.

"Come on, Brownie, come and keep me and Jason company." The dog saw a ghostly figure with a straw face and snake-like tentacles coming out of this strange figure! The dog kept barking, and Gerry said, "It's okay, Brownie, we're in an old house."

Bark! Bark!! Bark!

The dog would not stop barking. Finally, at dinner time, the dog stopped barking. Jason and Gerry had hot dogs and beans for supper. Gerry fed the dog, and Jason took the dog for a walk. Gerry saw the cat hissing at something and said, "What are you hissing at, Blackie? There's nothing there."

Then Gerry felt a cold draft, and she checked the front door and windows in the house; they were closed and locked. The cold draft stopped. The cat started hissing again! Gerry checked the fireplace and looked around the room, trying to find out what the cat was hissing at! She saw nothing.

Jason came in with the dog, and the dog started barking again.

"Jason, the cat is hissing at something, and the dog keeps barking! I don't know if something's here because I don't see anything. Maybe they see something we can't see, or do we have a ghost here?"

"Gerry, a ghost? Be real, there's no such thing! It's an old colonial house in the middle of nowhere, and it's going to take time for Brownie and Blackie to get used to it. The pets are in a different environment. When they are with us, they're quiet, and when we separate, they act up!" he said.

A few minutes later, Brownie started growling and ran over to the bottom of the stairs, growling and barking like a bad dog!

"You might be right, Gerry. Brownie is barking for a reason! The dog and cat have been staring at the staircase going upstairs since we moved into this house."

Jason grabbed his gun and went upstairs. Brownie followed, and he checked every room, closet, and looked under the beds and furniture. He found nothing. The dog stood in an attack stance, looking at a window, barking and growling like a mean junkyard dog! Then Brownie leaped off his hind legs up at the window, attacking it, and fell on the floor crying, "Yelp! Yelp!"

Jason said, "Brownie! That's enough! There's nothing here!!"

Finally, around bedtime, Jason and Gerry managed to calm the animals down before going to bed. They had a king-size bed. The cat slept with Gerry, and the dog lay at the foot of the bed. Whatever the cat and dog were seeing vanished. The couple went to bed before 10 p.m. because they had to go to work in the morning.

At 11:02 p.m., the dog died, lying at the foot of the bed. The cat jumped off the bed and wandered through the house, and about an hour later, it dropped dead on the kitchen floor.

At 12:03 a.m., Blackie took its last breath.

At 1:02 a.m., Jason woke up and saw the dog at the bottom of the bed. Then he rolled over and went back to sleep.

At 2:02 a.m., Gerry woke up, went to the bathroom, and returned to bed.

At 3:02 a.m., the straw ghost Brownie had seen earlier was standing behind the bed. Then it vanished.

At 4:02 a.m., Jason woke up to a chill, covered himself with the bed blankets, and went back to sleep. One hour later, Gerry woke up feeling a chill and then went back to sleep.

At 6:02 a.m., the alarm clock rang. It was time to get up! They got up, cleaned up, and went downstairs to the kitchen to make breakfast. Gerry saw Blackie lying on its back on the kitchen floor, with all four paws pointing upward, tail straight out, and tongue hanging out—dead!

She screamed, "AHHH! Blackie's dead!"

Jason saw the dead cat and was shocked. "Oh my fucking God! Maybe it's carbon dioxide poisoning! Let me check on the dog."

Jason called, "Brownie! Brownie! Brownie!" No answer. He went upstairs and saw the dead dog lying on the bed. He started crying, "Oh no!" Then he carried the dog downstairs and said, "The dog's dead too!"

He buried the animals in the snow in the backyard for now. Later, the gas company came to check the carbon dioxide levels.

"Mr. and Mrs. Green, the carbon dioxide levels were very high; you're lucky to survive the night. Open one window in each room for the day, and I will put in new carbon dioxide detectors, change all batteries, and check the fire alarms. You should be okay by tonight," said the gas man.

The Greens stayed home from work and called animal control to pick up the dead dog and cat.

"The animals are buried in the backyard. They died from carbon dioxide poisoning. My wife and I are lucky to be alive!" said Jason.

Animal control removed the dead animals and took them away

on a snowmobile. The rest of the day and evening was quiet. The Greens worked together at Admirals Gold & Silver and had their story to tell at work about the dead dog and cat.

The next night was okay. The rest of the week, the house was quiet. The next day was Saturday, and they had the weekend off.

Suddenly—crash, bang, bang, bang! A bear broke into the kitchen, opening cupboards and tossing pots, pans, plates, glasses, and silverware all over the kitchen! The floor was covered in glass. The bear broke into the refrigerator, ate a whole ham, and knocked milk, juice, and eggs all over the kitchen floor! What a fucking mess!

Jason heard the crash, grabbed his shotgun, and went downstairs to the kitchen. He saw a big brown bear licking and sucking up the milk, juice, and eggs on the floor. He shot the bear in the head several times until it was dead. Now there was a lot of blood to clean up!

Gerry screamed when she saw what the bear did to the house. The back door was busted right through where the bear had crashed in! When she saw the giant brown bear lying dead in the kitchen, she was horrified!

Animal control came again to remove the dead bear.

It was a job to clean up the kitchen and fix the broken-down back door!

"Our dog and cat died from carbon dioxide poisoning, a bear breaks in to eat our food, damages our house, what else is going to happen here! The kitchen table is busted, and chairs are broken!" Gerry cried.

"The back door going to the kitchen is now going to be a wall so no other bears can break through!" said Jason.

A week later, the work was being done, and the house was quiet. One day, Gerry was home sick from work. She heard voices in the basement while she was doing laundry. She heard what sounded like a rumbling noise, something that didn't make sense. She couldn't make out what the soft voice was saying.

She checked Jason's workbench area and his tools. Then she checked the wine cellar. She looked up at the ceiling, turning lights on and off. She checked the bulkhead to make sure it was locked. She sat in a chair in the laundry room until the wash was done. Then she put the clothes in the dryer.

She went upstairs to the kitchen, made herself an egg salad sandwich, had a cup of tea, and smoked. Suddenly, she saw a black shadow zip by, then she heard a voice: "Get Out!"

Then the kitchen cupboards started opening and closing, and dinner plates, coffee mugs, and glasses flew out, smashing on the kitchen floor and breaking. A mug or drinking glass flew out, striking Gerry in the head!

The time was 1:02 p.m., and the activity stopped a minute later. Then she heard a big bang! She screamed her brains out. She called Jason at work, crying.

"Jason, please come home right away! Strange things are happening in the house!" She told him what was happening, and he left work to go home.

When he got home, Gerry cried, "We have a ghost in our house!"

Jason saw the mess in the kitchen and said, "I know what happened here! We were attacked by a solar flare from the sun, causing a magnetic field effect. We're surrounded by cell towers, electric towers, and in the middle of two lakes, causing a power surge! It's rare something like this happens; it's not a ghost!"

"Jason, I heard strange noises in the basement when I was doing laundry. I couldn't make out what the voices were saying. Then I heard what sounded like a voice telling me to get out! Then I saw a black shadow in the kitchen go by! How do you explain that?"

"Gerry, a magnetic field power surge plays tricks with your mind. Did you hear a noise that sounded like a buzzing sort of electric charge?" said Jason.

"Yes, I did! It sounded like an electric zapping," she said.

"That's the sign of a magnetic field power surge. Look outside right now! You can see the Northern Lights! That explains what's happening in this house. Until I see something not relating to what's happening in this house, you can't convince me that we have a ghost!"

"Tomorrow, Jason, why don't you stay home, and I will go to work? Maybe you'll see for yourself what's happening here!" Gerry went downstairs to put the wash in the dryer.

Later, the clothes did not dry; they were still soaking wet.

"Jason, something's wrong with the dryer. The clothes are not drying, and it's a small load."

Jason checked the dryer. He pulled out the lint tray, and it looked like a fluffy animal. He said, "Gerry, when was the last time you cleaned the lint tray? You're lucky we didn't have a fire. Look at this!"

"Oh my God! I never cleaned the lint tray since we brought this dryer. I thought when we hooked it up, the lint would blow outside through the pipe hookup!" she said.

Then she cleaned the lint tray and slipped it under the dryer where it belongs. She put the dryer back on, and the clothes dried this time.

A fog formed in the basement when Gerry went down to remove the clothes from the dryer, and it vanished. Then she could smell mold. She brought the clothes upstairs to fold them before she cooked dinner.

They were eating a prime roast dinner and drinking a bottle of wine in the dining room. Later, the quiet evening got noisy! Suddenly, a bright flash of lightning and a loud bang followed, and it was snowing with a whiteout, thunder snow, and a lot of lightning! Four feet of snow had fallen during the night. I guess this couple was not going to work tomorrow morning, so the ghosts could haunt them while they were snowed in!

At bedtime, the thunder and lightning stopped, but it was still snowing hard outside, blowing and drifting over the house. The wind howled all night long! I hope this couple's ready! Because it may be a sleepless night!

At 10:17 p.m., Jason went in to take a shower, and the water was lukewarm. After the quick shower, he went to bed to have sex with his wife. After they were done, Jason felt a cold draft and saw a blue mist forming near a night light, expanding and getting brighter. He got up, waving his hands through the mist, and the heat was off, so he turned the heat back on and turned it up high. The mist vanished a minute later. The time was 11:02 p.m.

When Jason raised the heat in the master bedroom, the boiler came on, making a big noise in the basement. Suddenly, a black mist formed into a demonic ghostly figure coming out of the boiler, then it vanished! No one was in the basement at the time.

Gerry woke up feeling cold. She looked at the alarm clock, and the time was 12:02 a.m. She got up to check the heat; the room was 83 degrees! Why was she cold and shivering? She went to the bathroom and looked out a window at the falling snow. The straw-creature ghost her dog Brownie had seen was right behind her, but she did not see it. Her hair stood up on her arms and legs as she walked through the ghost she couldn't see. She drank a glass of water at the sink, then went back to bed. The room was nice and warm now, and she went to sleep.

Jason felt like a hand was choking him and holding him down on the bed. He woke, coughing and struggling to breathe! Then it was over. The time was 1:02 a.m.

Gerry woke and said, "Are you okay?"

"I felt like a hand was choking me in bed, holding me down, and I had trouble breathing. Then it went away! I don't like eating late at night before going to bed. I must have choked on a piece of meat, and it felt like it was stuck in my throat. First, I could feel something in my stomach from getting heartburn, then it stuck in my throat, making it feel like someone was choking me. I feel okay now!" said Jason.

Then he lay down to go to sleep. Gerry wanted to have more nookie before they went back to sleep.

At 2:02 a.m., Gerry woke up, hearing her own voice calling her. She looked at the alarm clock; the time was 2:02 a.m. She looked at the foot of her bed and saw her own self talking to her in a funny voice! She screamed hysterically.

"AHHH!"

Jason woke up.

She said, "Jason! We have a ghost imitating me! I just saw myself at the foot of the bed, looking at me, calling me, and saying strange voices!"

"Gerry, you just had a bad dream; there's no such thing as ghosts!"

"It's not a dream, Jason! I'm going to get up and watch TV for a while. I can't sleep anymore!"

Jason went back to sleep. Gerry went down to watch TV. She was watching *NCIS* on TV.

At 3:02 a.m., Jason woke up smelling something burning, and he saw smoke. He got up quickly and went through the house, and the burning smell and smoke vanished a minute later.

He said, "Gerry, were you cooking something? I could smell something burning and saw smoke."

"No, I didn't see anything, just watching TV."

"We will not be going to work; there's more than three feet of snow on the ground—we're snowed in!"

Then Jason went to the basement to check the boiler, and everything was okay. He went upstairs and went back to bed.

At 4:02 a.m., the power went out.

"Oh! Fuck!!" Gerry said to herself, and she stayed put.

At 5:02 a.m., Jason woke up to a loud growl! He saw the straw-faced ghost with red eyes at the foot of the bed, and the room stunk like the dead! He was a believer now!

TWELVE

THE DANVERS STATE HOSPITAL IN DANVERS, MASSACHUSETTS

March 2026. The Danvers State Hospital was a nut house for the mentally challenged, like the Boardmen Institute in Connecticut. The building had been vacated for years, and because of the crime and crazy people lately, the mental hospital was reopening for lunatics and the homeless.

Several job openings were available before the ghostly facility reopened. Many people showed up for a job fair on the weekend. A lady met them at the main entrance. She was letting people inside to form a group, sitting in a hall with pews like a church, and she gave a speech about job openings and the history of the hospital.

"Good morning, ladies and gentlemen. Welcome to the Danvers State Psychiatric Hospital. My name is Ashley Ashole, Director of Facilities Management of the workplace. We have several openings in all work-related areas. I want to give a brief speech about this facility before you start filling applications for work.

We have crazy people here with all kinds of defects. We have humanoid possible victims—I mean people with viruses deforming into an animal-like state. We have demonic patients that look like some kind of deformed werewolf. If you don't believe in werewolves, you might want to think again. We have patients who transferred from the University of Connecticut Psychiatric Hospital, formerly known as the Boardmen Institute of Mental Health, that closed, and now they are here.

In 1890, the Danvers State Hospital opened to 2,500 lunatics and was renamed the Lunatic Hospital, increasing to 74,000 patients, before the town of Danvers took the name back. A lot of bad things happened here: we had witches, human sacrifices, devil worship, hangings, murders—the hospital of the dead in the late 1800s—and they all lay beneath this hospital and throughout the grounds. The hospital has its own graveyard.

Things were so bad here that the hospital had to close, and the buildings were vacant for years. Part of the property had to be knocked down. Later, the facility opened up an apartment complex, which still exists today in the wing branch on each side of the main building.

The main building is now opening back up into a lunatic and mentally challenged psychiatric hospital because of all the crimes, shootings, and special-needs people that need help! We have a school, a church, and Danvers University is now here. We have athletic facilities for all sports: basketball courts, tennis courts, baseball and softball fields. We have walking and hiking trails and a swimming pool.

I am hiring for all shifts. All jobs will be filled on the graveyard shift first, 11 PM to 7 AM, then the mid-day/evening shift, 3 PM to 11 PM, and finally the first shift, 7 AM to 3 PM. All shifts will be filled before the hospital reopens.

You may experience strange things, such as seeing shadows or ghosts from the past. I have seen ghosts in this building, but I haven't seen anything like that in a while. We have had exorcisms, private paranormal investigators, and priests and pastors from all churches remove all the evil spirits and bless the dead. This hospital is built on top of a burial ground. I just wanted to let you know what was here. You may start filling out applications, and I will start calling people or sending emails tonight," said Ashley Asshole, Facilities Management.

A week later, a nurse was hired on the graveyard shift. She parked her car in front of the building in the main building parking lot. She looked at the building before going inside. The hospital looked scary at night, like a haunted mansion.

She checked in for work, meeting a security guard/policeman to check her in.

"Good evening, sir. My name is Valerie Mucus, a nurse. It's my first night on the job."

"Pleased to meet you. I'm Officer Joseph Wales. See the head nurse supervisor, Amanda Amen, in room 307."

"Thank you, officer. Nice meeting you."

The girl met her boss. On the way, she could hear voices in the hallway until she got to the elevators. She looked around, but she didn't see anything.

Valerie met her boss.

"Are you Amanda Amen?"

"Yes."

"Pleased to meet you, my name is Valerie Mucus, the new nurse."

"Pleased to meet you. Come with me and I'll show you your assignment. You will be working in the ozone from 11 PM until 7 AM. You will work alone, taking care of patients in rooms 001 to 026. Down here we have 10 patients, but no more than 15 or 20. If rooms get busy, there are no more than two patients to a room. Down here you have storage rooms where you get your supplies.

Room 001 here is the hospital morgue. When a patient dies, you bring them in here and assist doctors and coroners with autopsies. Room 003 is the crematorium, where the dead are cremated or for burning human waste. Keep the room closed because it stinks in here when dead bodies/flesh are being burned. I have a cremation scheduled at midnight tonight.

The next room, 002, is the laundry room. You have 10 washers and 10 dryers. Room 002A is the laundry storage area. The laundry room is right between the morgue and the crematorium. Across from the laundry room is room 004, the main hospital storage facility.

The next room, 005, is your office. This is where you check in nightly. Some nights you will meet another nurse, and her name is Vicki Valentino. When a patient needs help, lights will come on with her room number and location. Across from your office, rooms 005A & B are restrooms. Rooms 006 to 026 are the patients' rooms.

When you come in each night, a lot of these patients are sleeping, and all you do is check on them. Some patients are high-strung and are strapped to the bed. When they have to get up to go to the bathroom, make sure you put a straitjacket on them before moving them so they don't fight with you or bite you. You need to put muzzles on them before removing them. Vicki will show you when she comes in tomorrow night.

You and Vicki have it easy on the graveyard shift. The patients are given their medicines after dinner and bathed in the morning. The only thing you have to do is check on them during the night to make sure they are okay. Any questions?"

Said Amanda, the head nurse.

"Yes, do I have to go in that room with all the ovens?"

"No, Valerie. All you have to do is make sure the door is closed at all times."

"Amanda, what are all these people coming for?"

"They're here for the cremation."

A body was brought down. It was a dead man with his eyeballs popping out of his head, his mouth wide open, buck teeth sticking out, pointy ears like the devil, and a bald head with stitches all over. He was dressed in a three-piece suit. The coroners covered the body in a body bag, and a priest was there saying prayers. The family of the dead man was playing classical music on an iPad while the body was being put in the oven to be cremated.

After the cremation was over, smoke came from the closed oven, and the family celebrated, dancing around the room and playing "Another One Bites the Dust" on the iPad.

"I hope I enjoy working here in this hospital because it's scary and spooky down here," said Valerie.

Later, when the cremation was over, Valerie was on her own in the ozone checking on her patients. One man was laughing, another man was crying, another man was jerking off while watching TV. One girl was strapped to her bed, sleeping with a straw up her nose. Another woman looked like she was dead, lying in her bed. One man was sleeping and snoring like a bear! Valerie covered him with a blanket.

After checking on the patients, she checked all the rooms and went to her office to play gambling games on the computer after filling out paperwork. She set the alarm on her phone in case she fell asleep.

At 7 AM, she left her shift and went out for breakfast at Denny's in town. She had a Western with home fries, orange juice, and coffee. Then she went home to sleep.

She had a dream about a black mist with red eyes that looked like a dragon ghost circling her in the hallway and pulling her down to the floor, dragging her to the morgue. All the dead bodies started getting up from the morgue tables, walking like the walking dead, and crowded her so she couldn't move. She woke up screaming. Her mother came into her bedroom to make sure she was all right.

She told her mother about the frightening dream.

"Don't worry, Valerie. The stories you hear at work are all fake! The dead are not going to come alive; there's no such thing as ghosts. The Danvers Hospital has a haunted history, meaning all the people who died here, and when people see things, there must be something wrong with them. I would just ignore the stories you hear and do your job," said her mother.

The next evening, she came into work. She saw a big eagle flying around in front of the building, flying lower and lower until it landed in the trees. She checked in with the security guard and went to work. She met the other nurse helping her tonight.

"Good evening, my name is Valerie Mucus."

"Hey, Mucus McCain! Nice meeting you. I'm Vicki Valentine! Pleased to meet you!"

The other nurse was a hotshot, and Valerie made friends with her. She told Vicki about the dream she had and said it was spooky down here.

"Valerie, you're in for a rude awakening; there's a lot of shit going on in this hospital, and there is such a thing as ghosts and the walking dead. You will see them when you least expect it. With me here, you may not see them, but when you're alone and it's quiet, something may surprise you some night. I have been here for three weeks now working the night shift, and I saw spirits walking in the hallway, walking through walls, and black shadows flying by! I saw a spirit rise from a dead body in one of the rooms. I heard voices. These spirits will not hurt you, but once in a while, you may see them.

One night I went to the elevator, and when the elevator door opened, I saw a man hanging from a rope around his neck. The door closed. I pressed the button, the door opened, and nothing was there! Valerie, do you hear that?"

"It sounds like a baby crying."

"We have no babies here, and the crying sounds are coming from the crematorium! Did the head nurse, Amanda Amen, show you the crematorium and the morgue?" said Vicki.

"Yes, she did. It's scary in there."

"The patients' rooms are that way, and the baby cries are coming from this end of the hall. I can't hear them now," said Vicki.

Vicki and Valerie checked the patients to make sure everyone was sleeping at 1 a.m., then they hung out for the rest of the night telling ghost stories.

A few days later, while working with Vicki, there were no hauntings—just patients acting up during the night. Vicki had to restrain one patient with a needle, and Valerie had to put a straitjacket and a muzzle on another! These patients are crazy down in the ozone.

Then, one night, Valerie was alone because it was Vicki's night off. Things went haywire. Valerie was in the medical storage room getting supplies for the patients. She saw a big black rolling mist/fog coming from a heating vent, with jet-black tentacles covering the room and crawling all over Valerie. The mist had red eyes, hands trying to grab her, and arms coming out of the mist. She couldn't move or get away!

The tentacles were pricking her until blood was dripping from the stings, and a waterfall of blood flowed from her as she felt like her insides were coming out. She was screaming hysterically! The ghost was worse than the one she had in her dream! She was pulled down to the floor, attacked by this thing, and the tentacles covered her completely. She was swimming in the blood flowing on the floor, trying to escape!

The horror show lasted only 60 seconds, and it was over. Valerie was soaking wet, covered in blood and attacking tentacles. The attack happened at 3:02 AM and was over a minute later.

Finally, the room was clear, like nothing had happened, and she was able to get up and get out of that room. A doctor heard her screams and met her in the hallway.

"I was attacked by some kind of poltergeist in that room! It was uglier than the devil! I had a dream the other night about this black poltergeist, and now I saw it for real!" Valerie cried, telling the doctor what she saw.

"Valerie, never go in that room alone."

"You must be Valerie Mucus. My name is Dr. Anthony Depression."

"Pleased to meet you!" she said.

The doctor was rolling a wheelbarrow with human waste from dead patients in the hallway, going to the crematorium to burn the waste. On the way, the wheelbarrow tipped over, and human organs covered in blood fell from a bag in the wheelbarrow: hearts, livers, blood and guts, fingers and hands cut off, a cut-off leg, a human skull, and bones splattered all over the floor!

Valerie started puking her brains out because she had to clean this mess up!

The doctor said, "You motherfucker! God damn it!" when the wheelbarrow tipped over!

Valerie left and quit her job.

A few nights later, Vicki had her turn. Five patients died that night. She went into the medical storage room to get supplies; she did not see anything because she was not in there at two minutes after three! She went to one room, and a man had just died. She could see the spirit lift out of him up to the ceiling, then vanish! Vicki kept her distance and called Amanda Amen and Dr. Depression on her phone to report the dead body and what she saw.

Amanda and the doctor removed the dead body and took it to the morgue, putting it in a freezer until the coroners came to do the autopsy. Vicki went to her office only to find out another patient had passed away! She went to room 007 and saw a woman lying dead in her bed, in a pool of blood dripping on the floor, and three big black rats were sucking up the blood. Then Vicki saw a black shadow hanging over her! She yelled, "Hey! Get out of here!"

The ugly demonic spirit vanished! She called Amanda and Dr. Depression again from her phone, and a second body was taken to the morgue. The time was 1:02 a.m.

About an hour later, Valerie was in her office and reported

a third person had died. Amanda and the doctor went to room 011. A man was in his bed, dead! He was a big man, his stomach expanding and bloating until it burst and exploded; blood and guts filled the room, splattering all over the walls and floor. Then a green iguana came out of the man's stomach, crawling in the blood and guts and eating it! Vicki puked her brains out and left the room.

The doctor struck the iguana with one of the dead man's crutches, put it in a bag, and took it to the incinerator in the crematorium. Vicki had to clean this mess up!

Later, a fourth man was found dead in his room. A few minutes later, a woman was found dead in her bed, and a white rat was crawling on her; it went in her mouth and vanished! Poor Vicki was sick to her stomach!

After the five dead bodies were taken to the morgue, Vicki went to wash the room where dead man #3 had exploded. She saw a man struggling in the hallway and he threw up! Snake-like tentacles, worms, black flies, cockroaches, mice, maggots, black crawling spiders, black blood poured out of his mouth, finally throwing up a big rat! Then it all disappeared in 60 seconds, and the hallway was normal, except for Vicki's puking. She cleaned up her mess and quit her job. She told Amanda what she saw and said,

"Amanda! I've had enough! I can't take it anymore! The ozone is the gate to hell!"

Then Vicki walked out, puking one more time outside before she got to her car, leaving her mark in the parking lot of the Danvers State Hospital. The man throwing up in the hallway was a poltergeist ghost; it wasn't real. The time was 4:02 AM when Vicki saw the struggling man poltergeist.

Amanda Amen was down in the basement ozone checking on Vicki's work, and a mysterious force picked her up, threw her down the hall from one end to the other, pinned her against a wall, and dropped her to the floor, hitting her head. She quit her job! Many people were hurt and killed in this haunted hospital.

Now, let's meet the crazy people! New people come and go, meeting the hauntings in this hospital. The hiring continued because of the turnover from the hauntings here. A group of people were given instructions during a meeting.

"My name is Ashley Ashole, facilities management instructor."

The group was in a lounge area sitting next to a fireplace when suddenly a black fog poltergeist came out of the burning fireplace, raised up to the ceiling, attached to a heating pipe, and formed into a person figure hanging from a rope, swinging back and forth. Then it vanished right in front of several witnesses' eyes! When the poltergeist vanished, it made a sound like a loud balloon popping. Several job interviewers ran out of the building screaming! The fire in the fireplace went out when the poltergeist vanished; the time was 3:02 PM. A minute later, the fire re-lit in the fireplace. Ashley Ashole and the rest of the people left the room.

The employees that remained had a rude awakening waiting for them.

"Good afternoon, ladies and gentlemen. Welcome to the ozone at the Danvers State Hospital of Mental Health. Did anyone see the poltergeist in the lounge earlier today during the job interviews? My name is Doctor Anthony Depression. Today, we are going to see some freaky people and humanoids.

Here in room 026 is the only normal man, suffering from over-sexed orgasms. This is why he's strapped to the bed—because if he gets loose, he will run wild through the hospital, raping all the nurses. He's under police custody and he's a sex offender.

The next patient, in room 024, is a humanoid. He's half man and half deer. He has the head and ears of a deer and animal fur across his back. He's also strapped to the bed.

The next patient, in room 019, is Lady Lilly, who is possessed by the devil, brought here from Connecticut. She looks like the devil. She's also strapped to the bed so she can't get out. Most of these deformed patients have muzzles on them so they don't bite or attack people.

Next, room 017: We have a young man, humanoid, part man and part wolf, also brought here from Connecticut. He's a confirmed werewolf. We call him the Mass Wolf!

The next room, 016: This man just passed away. He died from spontaneous human combustion, where his body caught fire from the inside out, leaving the bedclothes untouched! He was possessed by the devil and looked like the devil! He was also a drug dealer, and he put acid and cocaine in his food and drank deer blood. I swear some of these freaks rose from the gates of hell or came from another planet! Most of these deformed humans were brought here from The University of Connecticut nut house!

The next room, 014, is Alice Mann. She's half man and half woman, with ears like a rabbit and a nose like Pinocchio. She's a nice lady/man. She did a lot of drugs, she is 35 years old, and she can go fuck herself!

Room 013 has two demonic men, possessed and connected together, deformed and looking like some kind of animal. It's not known if these men could be he-she.

The next room, 013: We have two more nut cases! In the first bed is a woman, half human and half ape, with elephant ears, and her nose looks like the trunk of an elephant. The second bed is her husband, Freddy. He looks like a monkey with lots of hair.

These nine humanoids and freaks never get out of their beds, tied down all the time because they're dangerous. Down here in the ozone is the most haunted area in this hospital. We have a lot of nuts here and a lot of ghosts because thousands of people have died in this hospital since the mid-1800s," said Dr. Depression to a crew of job seekers.

Teenagers breaking into the hospital grounds, going to the graveyard, all disappeared, being overtaken by a devil-like creature coming up from a well underground, taking the victims to hell!

THIRTEEN

THE OLSEN HOUSE IN MAINE

The Olsen House is a bed & breakfast place with a ghost in Cushing, Maine. A church tour went to the Olsen House for a weekend retreat. A bus shuttle with ten people aboard pulled up to the house. The ghost, Christine Olsen, would make her presence known. The tour was coming from Boston.

"Ladies and gentlemen, welcome to the Olsen House of Maine. First, let's check in, then we will visit the art gallery to see the Olsen House's fabulous paintings and the history of this house. Later, dinner will be served in the dining room. Chicken, baked potato, and corn will be served, and apple and vanilla ice cream for dessert, along with tea and coffee. Then our retreat begins with prayers before evening bedtime. The Olsen House is a bed & breakfast and serves a free continental full breakfast. Let's go inside and check in," said the tour guide.

The tour guide and guests began checking in.

"Good afternoon. My name is Gloria Gobble, the tour guide with Chelsea Congregational Church Tours. We are here for a Christian retreat from tonight, departing Sunday afternoon. We're all from Chelsea, Massachusetts."

"Pleased to meet you, Gloria. My name is Linda Lincoln Cumberland, the house receptionist. Welcome to the Olsen House. We have you here, and you will be staying on the second floor. Dinner is served at 5:15 p.m., and a free breakfast is in the morning beginning at 6:30. This is Joey Zoe, the bus boy. He will take your luggage to your rooms. Enjoy your stay!"

When the church group checked into their rooms, they noticed a fog forming in the hallway and in their rooms. It was a foggy, cool mid-May day with a light mist outside. The pavement and the road were wet when they arrived, and a light rain fell later in the day.

Room 201 had one couple staying; another couple was staying across the hall in Room 202. The next six guests were in Rooms 203, 204, and 205, all single, with two guests in each room.

The couple checking into Room 201 saw water running in the sink in the bathroom, and the mirror was fogged up. The woman shut the water off in the sink, and then the toilet started flushing three times before it stopped.

"Gary, I think we have a ghost in our room," the woman joked.

"Cathy, I'm not surprised. This place looks spooky!"

The couple staying in Room 202 were the minister and his wife, Gloria Gobble, the tour guide. They saw the lights blinking on and off in the room; the time was 3:02 p.m. The lights stopped blinking a minute later, and the room was normal; the fog disappeared too.

Two women staying in Room 203 started opening all the windows because it was too hot, and they had to take some clothes off until the room cooled down. They turned the heat off to cool the room.

Two more women staying in Room 204 saw the windows wide open, and the drapes were blowing wildly. It was not very windy outside, and the room was very cold. The women closed the windows, fixed the drapes, and turned up the heat.

A young boy and his mother were staying in Room 205.

Mommy, Lori Bell, and Joey Bell, the boy, found their luggage open, pulled out, and spread all over the floor, and the bed was unmade. The room had a funny smell.

Mommy Lori went to the front desk and said, "Excuse me, Lincoln Cumberland, whoever you are. My son and I are staying in Room 205. The bus boy threw my luggage on the floor, the bed's not made, and the room stinks like the Charles River!"

"Oh my dear, that can't be true. That room was just cleaned. I'll send maintenance up there. I am so sorry."

"Thank you, Miss Cumberland."

When Lori and Joey went back to the room, everything was normal. The beds were made, and the suitcase was still locked and placed near the door where it was supposed to be.

"Something strange is going on in this room because it was not neat like this a few minutes ago! We do not believe in the paranormal in our church, but something's weird in this room. To be on the safe side, Miss Cumberland, can you give Joey and me another room, please?"

"Yes, you will be in Room 208."

Mommy Lori checked into Room 208 with her son Joey. The bell boy brought the luggage over to them. They heard a squeaking noise in that room.

"Joey, did you hear that? What's that squeaking sound?"

"Mommy! You can't hear a dump truck crashing into a Nitro-glycerin Plant!" the boy joked.

Later, the group got together and went to the lounge for a prayer meeting before dinner. After dinner, they had a church service.

At bedtime the couple staying in Room 201 felt electric energy, like the hair on their arms and legs rising a few times during the night. It was thundering and lightning outside, and when the storm passed, the electric energy stopped.

The minister and his wife, Gloria Gobble, were taking a bath in

Room 202. A woman walked into the bathroom while they were in the tub and stood there.

The minister said to her, "Excuse me, but don't you knock before entering a room? You're in the wrong room. Please leave!"

The woman said, "Good evening. I'm Lady Christine!" Then she vanished right in front of the minister and Gloria Gobble's eyes.

Gloria screamed, "Ahhh!"

"We have a ghost in here, Gloria. Let's get dressed and get out of here!"

They went down to the check-out desk.

"Excuse me, but we have a ghost in our room! My wife and I were taking a bath, and a lady walked into the bathroom. She said she was Lady Christine, and then she vanished right in front of our eyes! I, as a church minister, never believed in ghosts until we saw this lady just appear, say her name, then disappear! I have never experienced anything like this in my 44 years in the church!"

"I am sorry, Pastor John. You saw the lady of the house. She was the first owner in 1769. She usually appears when we get a bad storm. Her name is Christine, and she's harmless. Sometimes she appears, says her name, and goes away. Her body lies beneath this house. She died in 1817. I will give you another room. Go to Room 105 here on the first floor," said the receptionist at the main desk.

The women staying in Room 203 heard someone crying in the bathroom. One of them got out of bed and saw a naked lady, about fifty years old, standing in the tub, crying, "Help me please! Help me please!!" Then she went *puff!* and vanished. The woman who saw her was stunned. Before she could say something, the naked lady disappeared. They left their room, complaining at the front desk.

"We have a naked ghost in our room!" the women cried.

One woman in Room 204 woke up and looked at the time on the alarm clock. It was 3:02 a.m. She got up to go to the bathroom and saw a light was on. Then she saw what looked like someone in the shower because the curtain was closed. She pulled back the shower curtain and saw a lady in a white house coat hanging from a rope wrapped around the shower head, with water dripping on her.

The woman screamed, "Ahhh!" Then the lady hanging in the shower vanished when the woman started screaming. They left the room, complaining. Christine had died from hanging in 1817.

Lori Bell and Joey were staying in Room 208 next. Little Joey woke up to go to the bathroom at 4:02 a.m. He turned the light on and saw a naked lady sitting on the toilet, douching herself. He yelled,

"Mommy! Mommy! A naked girl is in the bathroom with a white thing between her legs!"

Then Lori woke up and saw the lady in a white house robe standing over the bed, looking at her. She went *puff!* and vanished. Lori screamed.

The next morning, everyone had their story to tell during breakfast.

"Ladies and gentlemen, this place is haunted. I don't know if it's evil or a spirit wanting to make its presence known. We need to get out of here!" said the minister.

FOURTEEN

THE CAPTAIN FAIRFIELD INN

KENNEBUNKPORT, MAINE. A colonial bed & breakfast that's haunted by an invisible ghost that appears anytime, 24/7, and has the ability to move things, not haunting the guests with evil but as a ball-busting ghost. The name of the ghost is Captain Jack Fairfield Junior, who haunts the inn, the harbor, and the beach.

It was Memorial Day weekend 2026. A boat pulling into the harbor and a shuttle waiting at the beach were going to the Fairfield Inn with tourists.

"Good afternoon, ladies and gentlemen. This is your Captain Jack speaking, and welcome to Goosebumps Beach. Everyone will board the shuttle when the boat pulls into the pier, and a shuttle will take you to the Fairfield Inn. Hope you will see President Donald Trump. He will be here this weekend."

The power went out, and the tour boat was stuck 200 feet offshore. The tour guide, Captain Jack, couldn't finish his instructions. He called on his cell phone, but there was no service. He had to address the tour on the boat by mouth because the boat lost power.

"Ladies and gentlemen, the boat lost power, and I can't get to the dock until another boat comes to get help. We have no cell service, so we're stuck here for a while. You have two choices: stay on board, or if you're in a hurry, you may swim to shore; the water is 53 degrees!" Captain Jack joked.

About an hour later, a second boat arrived to get the guests to the dock. They had to get off and board the second boat to reach shore. Captain Jack put the anchor down and left his boat out at sea. The tour guests boarded the shuttle to go to the Fairfield Inn, an hour and a half later.

The next day, an Air Force One helicopter landed in the courtyard to drop off President Donald Trump. A bunch of bodyguards and military officers were with the president during his stay. Police and security kept people away. The president and the bodyguards and military police stayed in the suites, protecting President Trump.

The president was sitting outside on the porch when a seagull flew by and shit on his head! Then President Trump saw a chair move on its own. He got up and went inside. People were outside taking pictures, hoping to see the president. Air Force One helicopter took off and would return after the president finished his stay. The president shampooed his hair to get the bird shit out.

Later, during the president's speech about world power and getting rid of illegal aliens, he had a bottle of water at his speech podium. He went to grab the bottle, and it flew out of his hands and landed on the floor.

"We have spooks here!" he said. Then Donald Trump continued his speech.

The lights flickered in the conference room, and a door slammed shut. Empty chairs started moving, and drinks fell off the table onto the floor. Then a window opened and closed on its own. A bird crashed into a window, bouncing off until the window cracked, and the bird suddenly flew away!

The president was quite surprised about all the strange things happening during his speech at the Fairfield in Maine. He said, "I have done speeches like this all over the world, but I have never seen anything like what's happening in this room. I was told that the Fairfield Inn was haunted when I got here, and I laughed it off! I have been told many stories before at places I've been, but today, I am seeing it for myself with everyone here! First, a seagull pooped on my head, and I saw a chair move on its own outside my room. What's going to happen when I go to bed tonight?" President Trump laughed.

While he was continuing his speech, strange things continued to happen in the conference room! A book flew off a bookshelf and knocked water bottles off the conference table onto the floor. A shade suddenly closed on two windows, then flapped open and fell off both windows, landing on the floor.

Then snacks were being served—crackers, cookies, cheese, fruit, chips, and bottles of wine. Suddenly, the snacks started flying off dishes like missiles all over the room, striking the walls and windows and making a mess! Then the corks popped from the wine bottles, and the bottles tipped over, spilling wine all over the table and floor; the bottles rolled off the table, breaking into pieces.

None of the several people attending the president's speech were hurt or attacked by the invisible hauntings; only the walls, windows, and floor took the beatings. The president had to cut his speech short before people got hurt. Donald Trump's eyes were wide open, standing in shock, watching the strange happenings unfold. He said, "Whatever is happening here does not want me here! I will send emails to finish my Fairfield Inn speech because I need to get out of here while I'm still alive!"

All the windows closed, and the doors closed on their own, but everyone was able to exit the conference room. There was a big delay before guests could check in until President Trump was done saying his speech.

"Mr. Trump, I am so sorry about what happened in that room. My name is Mrs. Tulip Organ, the owner here at the Fairfield Inn."

Later, the president went to dinner in the dining room, being guarded by security and bodyguards. The president had family chicken for dinner: chicken soup, salad, pasta, fries, and chicken—all you can eat. Ice cream, coffee, and tea were served.

Then the tourists were checking in.

"Good evening, my name is Mrs. Tulip Organ, the owner here at the Fairfield Inn bed & breakfast. Sorry about the late check-ins; President Trump is here today and leaving tomorrow. The Maine National Guard will guide you where to go on the property until the president leaves. Just be patient. Don't try to find him because they will not let you see him. Just check into your rooms, and dinner will be late tonight, served at 7:30 p.m., until the president has his meal first. Thank you for your cooperation."

Dinner was okay for the president and the guests throughout the evening, but the guests had the same experiences in their rooms during the evening that the president went through during his speech. The guests saw lights flickering, windows opening and closing, water turning on and off in sinks and showers, and bedsheets pulling off the bed on their own. No one saw any ghost because they were invisible! Drinks and food fell off tables and counters in their rooms.

President Trump and his wife were taking a bubble bath when the water in the tub emptied, and all the bubbles disappeared, so they had to take a shower instead. The president was shaving, and the shaver flew off the sink, bounced off the bathroom mirror, and landed on the floor. Trump picked up the shaver, holding it with a tight grip to finish shaving. His wife/girlfriend, whoever she is, was saying prayers to make the strange happenings go away.

President Trump looked at the alarm clock; the time was 11:02 p.m. Then they went to bed. While he slept, bodyguards, security, and the National Guard stood by his room all night in the hallway of the suite he was sleeping in.

Later, the bedsheets were slipping off the president's bed, and he grabbed the sheets to keep them from getting away. The time was 12:02 a.m. Did the president experience any more hauntings during the night in his room? Who knows.

At 1:02 a.m., something was blowing in Trump's ears, waking him up. At 2:02 a.m., the lamps and the lights came on in the room, and he had to shut them all off. An hour later, the president woke up to a bad smell, then it went away.

At 4:02 a.m., the president woke up hearing a thunderstorm and heavy rain. At 5:02 a.m., the hauntings stopped because it was starting to get bright outside. At 6:02 a.m., the president got up and had breakfast at 7:02 a.m. Then Air Force One helicopter arrived to pick him up at 8:02 a.m., and the president was gone a minute later.

All the guests were spooked during their stay.

FIFTEEN

THE SALEM INN, SALEM, MASSACHUSETTS

Another inn that's haunted with the witch and many ghosts of all kinds. The town of Salem, Massachusetts, is built over a burial ground of the slaughtered and the witches, and no, it's not Halloween—it's June 2nd, 2026.

A young couple who had just gotten married were going on their honeymoon after leaving the Red Sox game at Fenway Park. The couple took a bus ride to the Salem Inn bed & breakfast in Salem, Massachusetts. The bus pulled into the Salem Bus Station, and they took a cab to the Salem Inn. It was Tuesday night, June 2nd, 2026.

"Good evening. I'm Tanya Tango, and my husband is Ted Tango from North Attleborough, Massachusetts. We just got married May 30th at the Golden Arch in Plainville, Mass., and I won a trip for five nights and six days here at the Salem Inn."

"Welcome. You will be staying in room 307. My name is Olga Bartley, the check-in supervisor. Dinner will be served in the dining room at 5 p.m., and we are a bed & breakfast resort with a full breakfast served beginning at 6 a.m. tomorrow morning. We have an indoor pool and a lounge to enjoy. Your room has a queen-size bed with a curtain canopy over it and a gas fireplace. The rooms are very nice—enjoy your stay."

Ted and Tanya went to their room before dinner.

"This room is really nice, and the bed is soft. We have a jacuzzi to enjoy later. Central air, and the room smells nice." said Tanya.

A black shadow appeared, crossing from one wall to another, but Ted and Tanya didn't see it; they were checking out the bathroom. Later, leaving the room, they met a girl in the hallway.

"Hi, my name is Sheila. Welcome to the Salem Inn."

"Pleased to meet you," said Ted and Tanya on their way to dinner downstairs. Tanya looked behind her after passing the girl in the hallway, and she was gone.

The couple went to dinner, and pasta with meatballs and salad was served.

"The food's good here!" said Tanya.

"Little Tina's Dining Room. This place is Italian," said Ted. Not many people were in the dining room on a Tuesday evening.

Then Ted and Tanya went to the pool to go swimming and later went for a walk outside. The couple saw the same girl, Sheila, in the hallway sitting on a bench, and they said, "Hi." Ted and Tanya got no response. Ted looked behind him, and the girl Sheila was not there. They continued walking and saw a black cloud in the sky as it started thundering. Then they walked back to the hotel.

Later, Ted and Tanya took a bath, sitting in the jacuzzi. They heard noises in the room. When they got out of the jacuzzi, they looked around to see where the noises were coming from and found nothing. The air conditioner was making loud noises, and Ted shut it off. The strange noises stopped.

"Ted, the noises sound like a baby crying, a grinding sound, and the noise of a barking dog."

"Tanya, it sounds like the noises are coming from another room, or it was coming from the air conditioner. That might explain the noises, since I turned the unit off. I don't hear the noises anymore."

Later, Ted was watching the Red Sox game on TV, and Tanya was reading a book in bed. At 10:03 p.m., they shut the lights out and went to sleep. The Red Sox were losing 11 to 2 in the fourth inning, and Ted shut the TV off. The TV came back on at 11:02 p.m., waking Ted to turn it off; it came back on, then went off again. Ted made sure the TV was turned off and went back to sleep.

At 12:02 a.m., Tanya woke up to a thumping noise. She got up to look around the room and found nothing, then went back to bed. One hour later, Ted woke up because he was cold.

"Jesus Christ—it's freezing in here!" he said, turning on the heat. Then he went back to bed.

At 2:02 a.m., Tanya woke up because she was hot. She shut the heat off and went back to bed.

At 3:02 a.m., Ted woke up because his hair was standing straight up on his head, arms, and legs. Then he saw a flash of lightning; the hair friction went away a minute later. He got up to go pee, then went back to bed.

Tanya woke up and looked at the alarm clock; the time was 4:02 a.m. She heard a faint voice—"Get out!"—but she couldn't make out for sure if that's what she heard. Then she heard it again, then it stopped. Then she heard someone talking outside the bedroom door in the hall. She looked around the room and had to go pee before going back to bed.

At 5:02 a.m., Ted woke up and felt like someone was sitting on the bed. He looked at the foot of the bed and saw nothing, then went back to sleep.

At 6:02 a.m., Tanya woke up hearing a noise. She sat on the edge of the bed and looked toward the window, still half asleep, and saw a lady hanging from a rope behind the drapes covering the window, even with the morning sun shining on the shade! She was shocked, covering her mouth, then turned her head away, rubbing her eyes to wake up. She looked back at the window, and nothing was there! She turned her head away, rubbed her eyes again, and looked back at the window—still nothing!

She got up to go to the bathroom and saw an apparition of herself coming out of the bathroom, which vanished in front of her eyes after a popping sound! She screamed:

"Ahhh!"

Tanya had blue PJs on and a white house coat. The apparition looked the same as Tanya coming from the bathroom.

Ted said, "What's the matter, Tanya?"

"I saw a ghost of myself coming out of the bathroom, and it vanished right in front of me! I saw a lady hanging in the window a few minutes ago! This room is haunted; we have to get out of here!"

"That's strange. I heard noises but didn't see anything. Let's get another room. It smells like a dead mouse or something; it stinks in here," said Ted.

The time was 7:02 a.m., and the bad smell went away a minute later. They got dressed and went to the check-out counter to get another room, then went for breakfast. Later, they went for a walk and saw Sheila again walking toward them, then she vanished into thin air.

"Tanya, did you just see that?"

"Yes, I did! This hotel is haunted, and the outside too!"

"The girl was Sheila—the girl we met in the hallway and the same girl sitting on the bench last night," said Ted.

"Ted, if we see more spirits in our next room, we have to leave here before something happens," said Tanya.

Later that night, Ted and Tanya were staying in room 204 on the second floor. The room was just as nice as the last one but quieter. Ted looked at the alarm clock; the time was 11:02 p.m. Then they went to bed.

Ted woke up hearing a loud scream and felt like someone was

sitting on the bed. He looked at the foot of the bed, and that girl Sheila was sitting there! He said, "Excuse me, lady, you're in the wrong room!"

She let out a loud scream and said, "My name is Sheila, please help me! The darkness is covered in black!" Then she vanished right in front of Ted's eyes. He heard a popping sound, and she was gone. The time of the haunting was 3:02 a.m.

He woke up Tanya.

"We need to get out of here! I had a visit from that girl Sheila sitting on the edge of the bed, right there! The girl we met in the hallway, sitting on a bench, and the same girl who vanished during our walk earlier today. I'm freaking out right now," said Ted.

They got dressed and left the room at 3:30 a.m. They heard a voice in the hallway while going to the elevator:

"Get out!"

Ted and Tanya went to the check-out counter and told the clerk about the ghosts.

"You saw the house witch, who was murdered in the 1600s, haunt this hotel from time to time. Her name is Sheila Hartford. You see, this hotel was built in the 1600s and was a slaughterhouse. The bodies were fed to the witches, being chopped up, crucified, hung, and burned. There's a burial ground below this hotel. Spirits of tortured humans and animal sacrifices haunt this hotel and property because they are not at rest. It does not matter what room you're staying in because these spirits will come to visit at any time. Sometimes you never see them, and sometimes they will haunt you. I will give you another room, but whatever you saw will follow you.

Most of the hauntings here: you may see a witch hanging in the window. She's Sheila Hartford, who was hung by a tight rope until her head popped off and the body fell into a burning pit below. Her head was saved for human sacrifices, then fed to crows and vultures. The human and animal sacrifices were performed by the witches.

Sheila Hartford was a prostitute and was hung in her shame by the witches of Salem. She was the head witch during those times before becoming a prostitute, and that's why she was tortured and burned. She appears as a well-dressed red-haired woman in several areas of the hotel and property, or you will see her being hung in a window, and her appearance is black," said the clerk.

"How about the spirit I saw of myself coming out of the bathroom while I was going in?" asked Tanya.

"You saw yourself, modified by Sheila Hartford, after you saw her hanging spirit in the window. She can make you look the same or different. She can do something to make you uncomfortable and can hurt you if you challenge her. Sheila was evil! We have had exorcisms and paranormal help, and Sheila Hartford will not leave; nothing can get rid of her. If you see her again, don't talk to her—just ignore her, walk away, and keep your distance. If you hold a conversation with her, she will lead you to evil. Sheila was once the owner of this hotel before being overtaken by the Salem witches. She was the instructor for all the killings and witchcraft sacrifices. She will always be here, and the guests who stay here have to deal with her and put up with her hauntings.

We have other ghost sightings here, but most of the time you may have a visit from Sheila. Sheila's hangings are seen anywhere in this hotel at any time, 24 hours a day. Many guests come here to see the ghosts of the Salem witches and end up disappointed because they know what they're thinking, and they will not manifest themselves because you know about them while staying here. When you check in and you do not know the hotel is haunted, that's when they come around. I will give you another room, but if you see any ghosts, do not use a cross or preach the word of God or religion at it because it will not work. That's when the entity can hurt you—something could be thrown at you or get into your body and take over your soul. They can kill you if you challenge or aggravate them! If you see them, just go along with your business, act like they're not there, and they will leave you alone. My name is Rita Rochester, the check-in receptionist."

"I'm Ted Tango, and my newlywed wife is Tanya. We just got married and were celebrating our honeymoon here at the Salem Inn, but we are scared shitless of all the ghosts here. We were not believers in ghosts until the experiences we've had staying here. I heard about the Salem witches, but I never expected to see them!" said Ted.

The couple got another room.

"Go to room 17 in the basement; it's quiet down there," said the receptionist, Rita Rochester.

Ted and Tanya went to room 17, the most haunted room in the hotel, but they had no issues sleeping in that room because they knew what was going on after their lecture with the desk clerk. Ted looked at the alarm clock; the time was 4:35 a.m., and he went to bed.

Around 9 a.m., a group of people were in the dining room eating breakfast, and the hanging lady dropped down from the ceiling, hung from a light. All the guests started screaming!

SIXTEEN

THE BRIDGEWATER TRIANGLE

June 2026. The Bridgewater Triangle is a dangerous place. The area is haunted. A group of Bridgewater State University students were studying for a summer science project class. School was out, and this science project group was in for a rude awakening. A mini bus left campus with about twelve students and a doctor of environmental science studying paranormal activity in the Bridgewater Triangle. They would be staying in an old military fort near the Hockomock Swamp. The number of the fort was 1420, set up military style—one side for men and the other side for women.

Before the bus left campus, the instructor, the doctor, gave instructions:

"Good morning, ladies and gentlemen. My name is Doctor Ray Fry. Very easy name to remember—just call me Dr. Fry. We will be going to building 1420, a military apartment building located in Freetown—Hockomock Swamp and the Taunton River. We will be investigating the following paranormal sites in the Bridgewater Triangle. You will be treated like being in a military boot camp, and everyone must stick together and not wander off on your own, because you may not come back. Many people have died visiting the Bermuda Triangle—I mean the Bridgewater Triangle! This place is haunted, and we are here to find out for ourselves what is here. You may see ghosts, poltergeists, deformed creatures/animals, intersex humanoids, spacecraft, and possible aliens from out of space. The Bridgewater Triangle is a secret place of the unknown! The bus will stop for lunch at McDonald's, and dinner will be served in a military mess hall connected to building 1420. When we get there, we will figure out what we're going to do. Tonight will be a social night getting to know each other, and bedtime is 9:30 p.m. We will rise at 6 a.m. tomorrow morning, have breakfast, and then go on our search," said Dr. Fry.

Late that evening, several UFO reports were coming into police stations in local towns in the Bridgewater Triangle. The sky was full of lights. Freetown Police were following lights in the sky, getting lower and ready to land in a forest area heading toward Taunton. One cop said to another, "What are they? UFOs!"

"I doubt that. I believe it's a bunch of illegal drones. We have to follow them to find out where they're going."

"Officer Downing, I think we're following UFOs because they look a lot bigger than a bunch of drones," said the other cop.

The police drove down a quiet road through the Bridgewater Triangle, and they saw a spaceship UFO land in the woods. A ladder came down, and two humanoid aliens came out of the spaceship. The Freetown Police drove as close as they could to the flying saucer. The humanoids were holding what looked like big guns, standing outside the spaceship. The police flashed their lights. Suddenly, the aliens shot at the police with a very powerful laser, blowing up the police car. Officer Downing was killed instantly.

The other police officer started shooting at the aliens; the aliens shot back with another laser and missed the officer. The aliens got back in the spaceship and took off, leaving a fire and burn marks in the forest, alerting area fire departments from Freetown, Fall River, and Taunton.

The officer who witnessed what happened called back to headquarters:

"Lieutenant Robert Colon, this is Officer Shane Brady, location Taunton River Forest, just outside Freetown. Officer David Downing is dead! You're not going to believe what happened! David and I were following a UFO, not a bunch of drones. A spaceship landed about 100 feet away from the police cruiser, and when David put the flashers on, two aliens shot a laser gun, blowing up the police car and killing Officer Downing. I shot back with my revolver, and the aliens got back in the spaceship and took off, leaving a fire. A big fire is brewing, and I need the fire department and lots of help because more UFOs are circling around me."

"Okay, Officer Brady. I'll send help! Police headquarters to the fire department: there's a big fire in the forest heading toward Taunton. Location: Freetown/Taunton River. Over!" said Lieutenant Robert Colon.

"10/4, Lieutenant. We'll be on our way and will call Fall River and Taunton Fire Departments," said the Freetown Fire Department.

"Officer Jerry Perry, I need you to follow the fire trucks out to the Freetown Hockomock Swamp location near the Taunton River. Officer Downing was killed in the big fire. His partner Shane Brady claims he was shot by aliens coming from a UFO he followed landing in the forest. Please see what drugs Officer Brady is taking! We've been getting several reports of UFO sightings all night long! I believe they may be a bunch of drones," Lieutenant Robert Colon reported to his officers.

Officer James Perry went to the location to meet Officer Shane Brady. Several police and fire trucks arrived at the scene. The flying objects disappeared when all the police and fire trucks arrived. Officer Perry saw the burnt police car, and Officer Downing's body was removed and placed in a rescue vehicle to be taken to a hospital.

The news at 11 p.m. said:

"Several Massachusetts towns reported UFOs flying over the Bridgewater Triangle. Freetown Police reported one landing in an open field and saw aliens coming out, going to war with gunfire, leaving one officer dead. We don't know if this story is true or if it was drones in the area firing guns. This is not the first time drones firing guns in the Bridgewater Triangle have killed people. A forest fire is happening at the scene right now, and several fire departments from Tiverton to Mattapoisett are fighting the fire. Fall River Police reported a drone carrying a bomb that crashed on Pleasant Street three weeks ago. The bomb did not detonate, and no injuries were reported. We will keep you posted on what went wrong in the Bridgewater Triangle. Drones carrying guns and bombs have been an issue in the past. Jerry Wickedgood reporting from Channel 6 News, New Bedford."

Back at Fort 1420. "Ladies and gentlemen, did you just watch the news? We might not be alone; we might be fighting the cosmos! Was it drones with weapons, or was a Freetown police officer killed by aliens blowing up a police car and causing a forest fire like an erupting volcano? Freetown Police reported a UFO landing in a field, and aliens departed, causing a war zone! This is why we're here—to find out what's happening in the Bridgewater Triangle. True or false, we are here to find out!" said Dr. Fry.

Later, everyone was in bed sleeping. The doctor went to wake up the ladies, blowing a whistle:

"Come on, ladies, grab your socks, it's 6 a.m."

Then he went to the men's bunk room, blowing his whistle:

"Let go of your cock, grab your socks, it's six o'clock! Everyone has 20 minutes to shit, shower, and shave, and report to the mess hall for breakfast. Get on the bus; we're going paranormal sightseeing today!" said the doctor with a lot of humor.

After breakfast, they boarded the shuttle bus. The doctor was the driver and tour guide. They stopped at the Hockomock Swamp.

"Ladies and gentlemen, this is the most dangerous place in the Bridgewater Triangle. The river outside is the Hockomock Swamp, and a monster lives here. Make sure no windows are open. We will not be getting out here because the air is not safe. If you look out the window, notice a green fog known to be a choking gas; people have been killed visiting here. If you get off this bus, you may not get back in—it's that bad! There are sinkholes, quicksand, unknown swamp water holes, and many more traps here to feed the Swamp Monster. Once you get off this bus, you will not go very far. You're on the road; the toxic gas will choke you and kill you. If you make it off the road gasping for air, you will disappear and be pulled into the swamp as a meal for the Swamp Monster. Nothing happens during the day, but the monster resurfaces when it gets dark. People come here to take pictures and disappear! We will visit this site later when it gets dark. Take pictures, but do not get out of the bus," said Dr. Fry.

Then the bus drove into the Colonial Settlements Indian camp. The front gate was open, and Dr. Fry drove into the camp, only to be stopped by a group of Indians, raising their hands to stop the bus.

"Hey! Where the fuck are you going? How the hell did you get in here?!" said the head Indian with a lot of feathers on his head.

"I saw the gate open, so I thought it was okay to come in here. I have a science group with me investigating the paranormal activity in the Bridgewater Triangle," said the doctor.

"This camp is private property. Turn around and get the fuck out of here!" said the Indians.

The bus turned around and was followed by a golf cart to the exit.

"Ladies and gentlemen, I think we're in the wrong place! Our next stop will be the Freetown-Taunton River possible UFO landing from last night, where a Freetown police officer was killed. I don't think they will let us in there either, but we'll give it a try. Let's go!" said the doctor.

The bus drove through the site, and the science tour saw octagon burn marks and burnt trees around the site. Police and the National Guard were chasing drivers away. Everyone was wearing respirators, and there were signs reading: *Radioactive Area. Deadly Gas! Please keep windows closed and drive away.* Other signs read: *No trespassing. Do not enter. Dangerous area.*

The bus was driving down a dirt road because the main road was blocked off by police. Dr. Fry ignored yellow tape closed-off areas and was chased out by police, later stopped by Freetown and Mass State Police for driving on a closed dirt road where he was not supposed to be.

When he drove out of the danger zone, he was stopped by police.

"May I see your driver's license, insurance, and proof of ID, please?" said a Mass State Police woman.

Dr. Fry handed over documents. The police looked them over and gave them back, plus a $500 violation ticket.

"Sir, how did you get through this government no-go zone with all the roads closed?" said the cop.

"Miss, we're from Bridgewater State University. I am not familiar with this area; I've never been here before. We are a science summer group investigating paranormal activity going through the Bridgewater Triangle. Our mission is to find out what's haunting these areas," said the doctor.

"I realize you may be lost, but you just caused a major disturbance in a restricted area. You're lucky you didn't get shot by the National Guard troops. Read the instructions in this ticket, and you will appear in court. If you say anything about what happened here, you could spend ten years in jail," said the cop.

"Officer, sorry about the mistakes I made, but what happened here, our science group has the right to know. Here are the documents to show what we're doing," said the doctor.

"There was a radioactive drone attack that set a forest fire, and a policeman was trapped in his car during a call to the fire. He did not survive. I am sure you heard that on the news last night," said the Mass State woman cop.

"I heard a possible UFO landed or crashed here!" said the doctor.

"There was no UFO; they were a pack of drones. You need to get out of Freetown and do what you have to do because the danger zone is restricted. Don't come back here!" said the cop.

The doctor drove off.

"Ladies and gentlemen, we were in the wrong places at the wrong time. Let's stop at McDonald's for lunch before we continue our search. Be prepared, ladies and gentlemen; some of our summer science projects are going to get us into trouble. I personally went through those closed-off areas riding through a grass dirt road that does not exist to get to where the UFO or attack drones landed to witness what happened, knowing that I was going to get arrested or shot! You people and I agreed to do these projects for the next three weeks, and it's not going to be easy. We have our lives in our hands until we get back to Bridgewater State. I'd rather get arrested than get shot. Many people have been killed in the Bridgewater Triangle doing what we're doing. Look to the left of the bus— there's a movie being filmed. We're going to a McDonald's in Fall River, then after that, we will go to the Freetown Town Hall to get a release form about what happened in the Hockomock Forest last night. Was it a UFO or drones? I believe something landed there because of all the radioactive signs and

I believe something landed there because of all the radioactive signs and burn marks in the landing site. A drone is not bigger than a semi. Then we will go to the Dighton Rock Indian Reservation Camp for a tour and go thru the museum. Then we go back to

1420 for dinner. Tonight we will visit the Hockomock Swamp again to see if there's paranormal activity. The rest of the evening we will ride through the forest to find any action, before returning to 1420," said Dr. Ray Fry.

After lunch they went to the Freetown Town Hall to get a release form then went to Dighton Rock. The bus pulled up to the gate and met a bunch of Indians.

"Good afternoon. My name is Dr. Ray Fry, and I am here with my science group investigating paranormal activity in the Bridgewater Triangle and we would like a tour of the Dighton Rock. I called two days ago and set up an appointment."

"Yes Dr. Fry. It's $35 and the tour last about four in a half hours," said the head Indian.

"Ladies and gentlemen. Get a hold of yourselves; you're going to see some gory shit here that may make you sick! First we will have a lecture with the native Indians before going into the museum," said the doctor.

"Good afternoon. My name is Canvas Cornotch. Hope your stomach holds up, if not we have vomit bags available. We dissect animals, eat road kill, and drink the blood. We kill, we do animal sacrifices, witchcraft, devil worship, ritual practices. Some human sacrifices. When people die they send their organs here for sacrificing practice, then we drain the blood and eat the heart if hearts are donated. Dead bodies are donated to the Indians to be dissected and fed to the animals. We feed on killing animals, such as deer, cows, wild horses, birds, etc... . If you have a dog or cat you want to get rid of, we will put it to sleep, grill it, and eat it! We are open for animal or human sacrifices in need. There's another Indian reservation, called the 'Colonial Settlements,' here in the Bridgewater Triangle. They're private, don't go there. Many people breaking into their camp never made it out. They kill people for cannibalism and animal road kill. Here we do not kill people, we practice animal mutilations. I am sorry to make you sick, but that's what the Indians do in this camp, we kill and dissect animals. Now let's go to the museum before we see a movie about what we do here at Dighton Rock. Grab some vomit bags because you may need them going thru our gory museum," said the head Indian Canvas Cornotch.

Dr. Fry's group went thru the museum and people were getting sick viewing the gross sightings. A cow cut right in half and pigs eating the cow's guts and pigeons sucking up its blood. A black bear cut up in pieces. The head was chopped off the body and ears were cut off and the eyeballs plucked out and its tail chopped off and rats were feeding on the bear's body parts and giant vultures were eating the bear's guts pulling out of the body.

"The Vultures are huge ladies and gentlemen and they are called Thunder birds with a 16 foot wing span. These birds are big enough to eat you alive!" said the head Indian.

People passing through the museum continued. Seeing a horse head chopped off and blood pouring into a bucket, then the horse was chopped slice by slice to use for horse meat steaks, then deer was cut up the same way showing the Indians grinding it up making hamburger patties. Small animals were chopped up to feed lions, tigers and bears before they were chopped up for meals and drinking the blood for sacrifices. Foxes, raccoons, sea otters, water rats, wild dogs, fisher cats, fish, squirrels, rabbits, mice, rats, snakes, chickens and all kinds of small animals were chopped up; thrown into a meat grinder and a blender to feed the Indians and the blood is used to drink.

The crew from Bridgewater State had enough watching movies about animals being sacrificed and drinking their blood and viewing tortured animals and blood-thirsty hunters.

"I can't take another hour and a half watching this or hearing more lectures," said Dr. Ray Fry. He puked too! He got his sick crew and got out of there!

The science team went back to 1420 to rest and have dinner before going out tonight.

217

"If you put an animal on my plate I'm not eating my dinner!" said one girl in the group.

After dinner the group went for a journey to the Hockomock Swamp hoping to see the swamp monster. When the bus stopped at the Hockomock Swamp they saw these creatures coming out of the swamp and they looked like giant snakes; the snakes looked like the ones from the Stephen King movie, *The Mist*. Then white orbs were flying around the swamp and in the dark woods! One giant snake leaped out of the swamp at the bus locking on one of the windows. Everyone was screaming! A second snake attacked the bus showing its mean mouth with a tongue that latches on the windows like a suction cup, showing its mean sharp teeth threatening to push the bus over but Dr. Fry was able to get out of there!

The crew were screaming. The swarming snakes crawled out of the swamp for an attack in seconds!! The crew had little time to take pictures and get out of there. The bus continued to drive through the dark forest in the Bridgewater Triangle and the white orbs followed them, and some of them were different colors.

Had the bus stayed at the swamp much longer, the snakes would have overtaken the bus wrapping around it like a coil and dragged it into the swamp!

One couple stopped by the swamp for a quiet place to make love a little while later. {I hope they got off what they were doing in the back seat of their car because they are in for a rude awakening! They got out to go for a walk around the swamp, until this huge creature that looks like a prophecy rat, not a snake, called the original swamp monster, spit out its tongue latching onto the girl where she could not get free and pulled her into the swamp as she screamed hysterically and drowned! The boy had a gun and he shot the fucking thing in the head! At the same time, the boy was attacked by the swarming snakes! He shot one snake with his gun and tried to get away from another one, but a giant snake leaped out of the swamp attacking the boy while he kept firing his gun at them until the gun chamber emptied, and the boy was pulled into the swamp for a meal for the swamp monster!}

Back to Dr. Fry driving the bus into the deep dark forest at midnight. He said to his crew, "We saw the swamp monster!"

No they didn't, they saw its siblings! Dr. Fry continued talking with his crew.

"Ladies and gentlemen, these orbs we are seeing could be a number of things from the unknown! Is it evil or is it natural? We don't know, that's why we're here to find out. It could be ball lightning, lightning dragonflies, known as lightning bugs! It could be something from out of space, it could be AI spot watchers or tiny light drones. I would not advise anyone to leave the bus. These lights have been following and surrounding us since we were at the Hockomock Swamp. Take pictures of them. Now we don't see any more activity other than these orb lights. We are going back to 1420, because it's getting late. If these lights follow us back just ignore them and get inside and close the doors and windows because these orbs could be dangerous or evil," said Dr. Fry.

The bus was on its way back to 1420, and the orb lights followed them back to their camp. It started thundering lightning, with hail and heavy rain going back to camp 1420. The orb lights disappeared during the storm.

"Ladies and gentlemen, I think we are going to be okay! I believe these lights are ball lightning because they can form on hot days like today, way ahead of a storm and visible during the evening. If you noticed: when the storm arrived, the lights are gone!" said the doctor.

Then the storm was over and the orb lights came back when the bus arrived at Fort 1420.

"Ladies and gentlemen, let's get off the bus and get inside as quickly as possible, because these lights are back and there are many more of them surrounding the bus. If it is ball lightning, it can burn you, so be careful and get inside as soon as we can," said the doctor.

The lights vanished when people were getting off the bus. A man at the check-in desk greeted everyone, the doctor and the 12 guests.

"Dr. Fry, did you see what you wanted to see?" said the man at the check-in desk at Fort 1420.

"We saw the Hockomock Swamp Monster. Here are some pictures of snake creatures we saw coming out of the swamp, before attacking our bus. We had to get out of there in a hurry!"

"Doctor: You did not see the Hockomock Swamp Monster; you may have seen its siblings! The Hockomock Swamp Monster looks like a giant rat frog! No one has seen the Swamp Monster; if anyone saw it they do not live to tell it! Still today in the Bridgewater Triangle, we do not know if this creature really exists or if it's a true demon of the unknown," said the man at the check-in desk.

"What about these lights like orbs following the bus all night; they're gone now, is it ball lightning?"

"What lights, doctor?"

"You didn't see all those round disk lights surrounding the bus a few minutes ago?"

"No doctor, but you might be seeing something evil. The Bridgewater Triangle is one of the most haunted places in New England. We have ghosts, poltergeists, UFO landings and alien abductions. Witches, Bigfoot monsters, giant thunderbird vultures, big enough to take you away and eat you; human and animal sacrifices and people disappear here in the Bridgewater Triangle. Devil worship, witchcraft, missing people and murders here! We have many shadow people and cult churches to brainwash your mind!" said the man at the desk.

"Dr. Fry, who are you talking to the last 20 minutes?" said one of the girls in the group.

"I was talking to the receptionist at the check-in desk, Sheila."

"There's nobody there, you're having a conversation by yourself. Are you alright doctor?" said Sheila.

Dr. Fry looked and the man at the desk was not there! The man at the desk was a ghost, the doctor was talking to, vanished when Sheila saw him talking to himself. The doctor can see the man at the desk but no one else can.

"He went somewhere, he's not there now!" Dr. Fry said to Sheila, the girl in the group.

3:02am, everyone was sleeping at Fort 1420; suddenly the white and colored orbs were flying around in the building. Sheila woke up and she watched them circle around in the bedroom, she tried to touch them but she couldn't catch them. The orbs disappeared a minute later and she went back to bed.

The ghosts go after the women first before shadow people attack!

4:02am, Sheila woke up again and she saw shadow people, ghosts, and poltergeists walking around in the women's bunk room, and locker rooms walking through walls, coming thru walls, rising up and going through the ceiling, crawling under the beds and walking out closed windows! Then the bunk room door slammed shut, then they all disappeared! The sightings lasted only one min-ute, then they were gone! Sheila was screaming hysterically calling names!

"Paula, Claire, Charlene, Colleen, we have ghosts in here and I can see through them! We have to get out of here!" Sheila cried!

The other four ladies did not see anything and they exited the room before 4:30am.

5:02am nothing strange happened, at 6:02am Let go of your cock, grab your sox, it's six o'clock!. The doctor was calling all the men to get up. The ladies had their stories to tell about the orbs and the ghosts in their room.

The group went to continental breakfast for 6:30am before going out for the day; the doctor said,

"Ladies and gentlemen, today we are going for a boat tour up the Taunton River to the Abington Boat House. We may see paranormal activity on this tour. When we get back here for dinner, we need to find another fort to stay in because of the hauntings of ghosts, poltergeists, and I don't like these orb lights following us. They were inside the women's bunk room. Sheila tried to catch them before they disappeared. Their room was full of ghosts keeping the ladies up all night. We have not been here a week and we are getting our share of paranormal activity! When we got back here last night, I was talking with the check-in host holding a conversation and Sheila said I was talking to myself. I did see a man and he was telling me about the hauntings in the Bridgewater Triangle. When Sheila said I may have been talking to a ghost. When I answered my last words the man who never told me his name was still there! Then when Sheila came by the man I was talking here was gone!" said Dr. Fry.

After breakfast, the crew boarded the shuttle bus and went for their boat tour.

"Good morning, ladies and gentlemen. Welcome aboard The Taunton River Tour. We have three groups with us today. My name is Michael S. Santana. We are going to Abington, the town at the end of the Bridgewater Triangle. We may see some paranormal activity on the way. We have Thunderbird Vultures with a 20-foot wingspan capable of grabbing you for a quick meal, I suggest you keep your seat belts fastened and hold on to any small pets you may have on board. We have Mothman creatures, Bigfoot. The Ooh Ooh owl bird creature, the male is an eight-inch bird with a 12 to 16-foot wingspan and his balls hang about eight inches below its body and when it lands, it goes, "Ooh! Ooh! Ooh! Ooh! Ooh!!!!!" You may see shadow people in the water; an occasional dead body may float by. You may see ghosts, poltergeist shadows and unexplained visions. You may see something that looks like the devil; anaconda snakes. Some of these snakes look like a man's penis with a big head and it spits a white and yellow venom. Anything paranormal you can think of; we have it all here. You may see something and you may not. Just sit back and enjoy the tour," said Michael Santana, the boat tour guide.

The boat was going up the Taunton River but no one saw any paranormal activity going to Abington.

"Ladies and gentlemen, look to the right and you will see the entrance to the 'Colonial Settlements Indian Camp.' Do not go there if you don't want to get eaten. The Indians will kill you and serve you up for a meal! Some of these Indians may be humanoids; that's right, half human and half animal, Bigfoot creatures there and French Alps Yeti's, possible creatures from the Moon or other worlds. Large spacecrafts have been known to land there. You can visit the Dighton Rock Indian camp and they will tell you all about what's here in the Bridgewater Triangle. Look again to the right is called 'The Green Ghost Woods,' location of the Hockomock Swamp, where the swamp monster lives and the pecker snake creatures! The Greenman ghost visits the Green Ghost Woods forest. It appears as a giant green man that illuminates like a glowing statue. Look in the water, there's a dead body, it looks like some animal or creature got a hold of it," said the tour guide, Michael Santana.

Everyone on the boat started screaming when they saw the dead body floating in the river with no head. The tour guide continued with his speech going up the Taunton River and the guests never saw anything paranormal; it was a nice and sunny June day.

The boat pulled into Abington Boat House and the tour boarded shuttles and went into town for the day before returning in the evening.

On the trip back about p.m., they saw nothing paranormal until Sheila got up and a mysterious force knocked her off the boat into the water flowing down the river at a rapid speed and disappeared! Everyone on the boat was screaming and crying!

"Ladies and gentlemen, please keep your seat belts fastened, one woman went overboard, something came out of the river and took her away!" said Michael, the boat tour guide. He called for help, and turned the boat around but Sheila was long gone! They searched for her until a search team came and she couldn't be found.

When the boat tour was over, the Bridgewater State tour went back to the fort.

"Everyone stay on the bus; we're going back to the college. If anyone needs to go to the restroom, go now so we can get out of here! Sheila's gone, and we do not want any more people to disappear!" said Dr. Fry.

The bus left the military fort where the Bridgewater State science team was staying, pulling up to a gate to get out. A guard officer/policeman was at the booth to check people coming in and out of the facility.

The guard said, "Dr. Fry, did you see what you wanted to see?"

"Yes we did, and we lost one of our girls. She was knocked off the Taunton River Boat Tour by some unknown force and disappeared down the river," he said.

"A lot of people go missing when they visit the Bridgewater Triangle!" said the guard.

The tour left the Bridgewater Triangle Science Project and went back to Bridgewater State. The time was 3:02am. The white orbs appeared surrounding the bus until it left the area. The orbs vanished a minute later and they were gone!

The hauntings are located in the following towns around the Bridgewater Triangle: yes, Bridgewater, Abington, Rehoboth, Taunton, Freetown, Dighton, Norton, Easton, Stoughton, and Raynham, and many other places. Tours enter the Bridgewater Triangle all the time.

A religious group was looking for a new church to go to from Brockton, visited: 'Raynham Woods Settlement House.'

"Good afternoon, my name is Pam Golden from Massasoit Tours out of Brockton, Massachusetts, and we are an all-church religious group looking for new churches to visit."

"Welcome to Raynham Woods. My name is Pastor Benjamin F. Lawboski. Come in and I will give you a tour. We are an all-abdominal church. We have all religions here, from the Catholic Church to all heavy Christian worship. We have your church here Pam."

The tour was trapped in a cult. Their bus from Brockton stayed inside a locked gate and the people were brainwashed, trapped into something that sounds good; but it's not good, they're trapped in a devil church in the middle of the Bridgewater Triangle.

Nightfall in the first evening, the Massasoit tour was enjoying the church tour sitting around a campfire eating marshmallows when suddenly the Greenman appeared! The tour was shocked to see something that powerful!

"Ladies and gentlemen, you are seeing a present from the Lord, 'The blessed Father from Heaven. It's not Jesus, it's an angel from above!" said Pastor Lombowski.

{Phrase: They're seeing a present from the devil}. Then white and colored orbs started flying around and the pastor said it was angels coming from Heaven and everyone started praying, then the orbs started burning people and setting their clothes on fire!

What else is here in the Bridgewater Triangle!

SEVENTEEN

THE CONJURING HOUSE

People come to visit the Conjuring House in Harrisville, Rhode Island for years. It is now closed and made into a bed & breakfast. Things don't happen here like before, but for those who visit, they take what was here to their home.

Two ladies who had a condo in Burrillville went out for breakfast at what is now called the Conjuring Inn. They stayed overnight before going home the next day. When the two ladies, Sheila and Robin, got home, strange things began to happen at 103 Douglas Road in Burrillville. It was the Fourth of July weekend.

Robin and Sheila were sitting at the picnic table out in their backyard eating cheese and crackers and drinking a bottle of wine. It was dusk, and suddenly Sheila saw a lady hanging from a rope in a tree. She screamed. Then the apparition disappeared! The time was 9:02 pm.

Sheila cried, "Robin, call police, there's a lady hanging from a tree on our property!"

"What!" she said.

The police arrived at 9:18 pm but found nothing.

"Ladies, there's nothing here. If you see it again, take pictures!" said the police, and they left.

At 10:02 pm, the ladies were watching fireworks from their home. Another couple had their wedding at the Conjuring Inn that day, and the host there said,

"Congratulations to Henry and Heather Hellboy on your wedding day! Where are you going for your honeymoon?"

"Where, we're on our way to the Mohegan Sun Casino in Connecticut," said the newlyweds.

"I hope you win a lot of money!" said the host.

Henry and Heather were on their way, driving down Route 101 in Scituate and going on to Route 6 when suddenly a tank truck struck their car, bursting into flames and killing them! Back at Sheila and Robin's condo, they saw the news on TV about that accident. The time was 11:02 pm.

The two ladies went to bed just before midnight. Robin saw a black figure form in the bedroom, and it went out a window. She screamed! Sheila was in the bathroom washing up.

"Sheila, I think we have a ghost in our house. I saw what looked like a black figure. I could not make out what it was. It walked slowly to the window and vanished!"

"You're kidding! I heard you screaming. I'll bet we might have brought something home from the Conjuring House! We're not going to eat there anymore!" said Robin.

An hour later, Robin and Sheila were still awake lying in bed, and they heard noises in the house. Now they couldn't sleep; an hour later they heard the same spooky noises again at 1:02 and 2:02 am. They got up and went to the kitchen to snack and drink more wine.

Suddenly they saw a black shadow go by, knocking a wine glass on the floor. It broke, and they heard a voice that sounded like someone laughing! The time was 3:02 am.

"Did you just see that!?" said Robin.

"Yes, I did. Let's get out of here. We're sleeping at my mother's house. She lives in Johnston, Rhode Island."

The next day, Sheila and Robin got a priest to bless the condo to get rid of the ghost. The Burrillville Police were searching the area around Sheila and Robin's condo, looking for the lady hanging from a tree, and found nothing.

"Stay away from the Conjuring House, ladies," the police joked!

A family stayed at the Conjuring Inn, and nothing happened while they were staying there. When they went home in Connecticut that night, they heard noises, then glass breaking, then windows and doors started opening and closing, then plates and glasses were flying out of cabinets and breaking everywhere! Then it all stopped, and the family had one big mess to clean up just after midnight!

Other guests got into car accidents leaving the Conjuring Inn. One lady driving hit a young girl late at night. She got out to look who she hit, and nothing was there! The lady hit a ghost. She called the police to report what she hit.

"I hit someone crossing the road, officer, and I couldn't stop! I went looking for her, and she was gone! I ran her over, I looked under my car and in the woods, and I can't find her!" the lady cried.

"Maybe you hit a ghost. There's a lot of paranormal stories told on Maple Street in Harrisville," the cop joked. He searched the area and found no girl.

The girl was shocked. She went over to a friend's house and told her what happened.

"Katrina, the cop told me I may have hit a ghost! I ran right over her, and I could feel my car go thump, thump! I got out to look under my car and around the area where I hit her, and there was nothing! The cop couldn't find the body and let me go!"

"Shirley, what did this girl look like?" said Katrina.

"She looked like someone dressed in the 1800s, I guess, or wearing colonial-style clothes. She looked like she was in her 40s."

"That's weird, Shirley."

The two ladies share a townhouse about a mile away from the Conjuring Inn. That night, around midnight, the ladies were in bed in separate bedrooms. Katrina had a baby sleeping in a crib in her room. She woke up around 3 am. She checked on the baby and saw a black fog rolling along the ceiling. She said to herself,

"What the hell is this crawling over the baby's head!"

She looked at the alarm clock, and the time was 3:02 am. The black fog vanished. Katrina said to herself,

"I need to do some major dusting in this house tomorrow." Then she went to the bathroom and back to bed.

One hour later, Shirley heard a loud scream waking her up. She looked at her alarm clock, and the time was 4:02 am. Then she saw the same lady she hit with her car standing at the foot of her bed. She had black eyes! She screamed hysterically!!! The lady then vanished when Shirley was screaming! Then she went into Katrina's room, crying.

"I just saw the lady I hit standing at the foot of my bed, and she had black eyes! We have a ghost in our house!"

"I saw something too, Shirley. I saw a black fog crawling along the ceiling over the baby's crib. I can't describe what it was. I thought it was dust floating around because this room is very dusty. We need to pray and tell these spirits who we are and that they have to leave. You can sleep with me for the rest of the night. Let's pray together." After the two women prayed, nothing happened after that.

Back at Sheila and Robin's condo, Robin was off to work at 5:02 a.m., and Sheila was home for the day. She got up to have breakfast just after 7 a.m., then she read the newspaper. Then she went in for her shower. The water was not coming on; the time was 9:02 a.m. Then the water came on, and she took a shower one minute later. She washed her hair, and after she rinsed off, she got out of the shower and the shower curtain wrapped around her, and she nearly fell. She struggled to get the shower curtain off of her and was okay.

Then she blow-dried her hair, got dressed, stripped the bed, and threw a load of laundry in the washer. Later she got something to eat for lunch and poured herself a glass of wine. She was hearing whispering noises in the house while she was drinking one glass of wine after another. She called a friend on her cell phone, complaining about the weird noises she was hearing in the house. "You need to slow down on the wine. You're drinking too much!" said her friend on the phone.

Then Sheila grabbed the clothes out of the washer and hung them on the clothesline outside. Later, she went out to get the clothes on the line when suddenly a gust of wind blew a bedsheet off the line and it went up against the house, forming like a ghost. Another bedsheet flew off the line and wrapped around her, knocking her down to the ground as she struggled to get the bedsheet off of her! Finally, she was able to get free.

Then she saw the lady hanging from a tree again, the same lady she saw the other day. She screamed hysterically! People go to the Conjuring Inn to take the ghosts home from there!

EIGHTEEN

A Haunting in Tiverton

There are four vacant houses on Main Road in Tiverton, Rhode Island. They were all haunted. High school kids from Tiverton and gangs from Fall River paid a visit and were constantly being thrown out by police. Four kids from Fall River arrived with a Ouija board. A Tiverton police car was racing down Main Road and the four Fall River boys hid behind a tree.

The boys went into the first haunted house. They went down to the basement and the stairway collapsed, and they all fell on top of each other. The drop was about ten feet. One boy broke his leg, another boy broke his arm, the third boy broke a few ribs, and the fourth boy broke his neck and died! The boy who broke his leg called 911 to get help. Rescuers arrived at the scene to take the injured boys to the hospital. The boy who broke his neck fell backward, hitting his head on a cinder block headfirst, breaking his neck!

"Cory Green, one of the boys who broke his neck, and he's dead!" said a rescue worker. All the boys were taken out on stretchers and lifted up ten feet to get them out; this house had no entrance to get out of the cellar. The boy who broke his neck was airlifted by helicopter and taken to a hospital in Boston.

"Are you boys satisfied? One is dead, and the rest of you are going to the hospital, and you're all arrested for breaking into private property! I hope you learned your lesson!" said Tiverton Police.

Later that evening, the Tiverton Police were still there, and a woman cop showed up to check the properties to make sure no one was in them.

"Officer Vivian Mello, be careful, someone died here tonight," another Tiverton cop said to her. Officer Mello relieved the other officers, and they all drove off. She went into the first haunted house, looking around with her flashlight, and she saw the collapsed staircase and blood on the pavement. Then she heard a voice.

"Get out!" Vivian said.

"Go fuck yourself!" She continued looking around, closing any windows that were open, and she left. She went to the second vacant house, securing the place, and she could feel like someone was behind her following her, and she kept looking behind her.

"Whatever is following me, you need to leave; you do not belong here! Leave!" she said. Then she went to the third house and the windows were wide open, and she shut them. Then she heard a big bang in the basement—a crash, boom, and a humming noise! She went downstairs into the basement and nothing was there! She heard rain, and it started thundering and flashes of lightning outside. She saw tree branches banging against the house, making all kinds of noises.

Then she went to the last vacant haunted house. She saw a white mist rolling around, and she saw two big black rats running through the place. Vivian joked, "Hey Misty, are you a good spirit or evil? You're too white to have black rats running around!" Vivian was having fun with the ghosts in these buildings; she wasn't afraid of anything! Then she was picked up and thrown against a wall, pinned there, then the mysterious force dropped her on the floor; she was scared shitless now!! She got up and ran out of house #4. Then she drove back to the Tiverton Police Station and told officers what happened.

"I believe in ghosts now!" she said.

The next day was Saturday, and a group of Tiverton High School kids paid a visit to the four houses. They went into the first house, looking around. One kid was going to the basement, but there were no stairs and damage below. No hauntings. The kids went to the second house, and the same kid going to the basement got his foot caught because part of the floor gave way. The houses are condemned; if you're not careful, more people are going to get hurt! The kid lost his shoe; it was gone!

Then one kid opened a window. The window slammed shut at a high rate of speed, and the glass broke and went flying everywhere! Two kids were hit with flying glass but were not hurt. Get the fuck out of there before someone does get hurt! The kids left the second house and went into the third vacant house, snooping around. The air was heavy, and one of the kids couldn't breathe; he said,

"David, I have to get out of here. I feel like I'm ready to pass out. I'm going to wait outside!"

"Watch for the police!" said David.

Three kids, four all together, were hanging around looking for spooks! Then the rest of the kids started coughing, choking, and sneezing.

"Let's get out of here!" said David to his two friends. A cop drove by but did not stop. The three boys went into the fourth house. They heard some weird noises, and windows were all open. The wind was blowing dust around in the house, and it was getting thicker and thicker; it was like being in a dust storm! It's not dust from outside, it's something else!

The kids all left and went to Subway to get something to eat. While they were there, police stopped by to check on the properties and left. If the kids had still been there a half hour later, they all would have been caught!

Then the same kids made a return around midnight, with six of them this time. One kid waited outside, watching for the police. He hid out of sight near the haunted houses where he couldn't be seen by police. Five boys with David being the leader toured the other four.

"Where's Ricky?" said one of the boys. "He's outside watching for the cops," said David.

The first house was boarded up earlier so nobody could get in. The five boys went into the second house. All five of them froze in place for ten minutes; they couldn't move, and they were scared shitless, screaming and crying! Then police cars pulled up while the five boys were frozen in place. The watcher, Ricky, saw the police coming and ran away. The police heard screams and cries and caught the five boys in the second house and arrested them! The mysterious force turned them loose when the police came to get them.

Four police cars pulled up, and all five boys were handcuffed and taken to the Tiverton Police Station, and their parents had to come and pick them up.

Late that night, in the wee hours at three in the morning, a couple decided to do some exploring, leaving a bar in Fall River and taking a ride to the haunted houses in Tiverton. Ben was the man, and Bee was a young girl. Ben and Bee went to the first house and found it boarded up. They went to the second house, shining a flashlight, and they saw big rats running.

Bee said, "Ben, let's get out of here. I don't feel like getting bitten by rats!" Then they went to the third house and saw nothing. Then they went to the last house. The front door closed and locked on its own, and they started hearing strange unexplained noises. Ben heard something growling, and it was pretty loud. It sounded like a mad junkyard dog!

Sure enough, it was a police dog, guarding the property to make sure no more stupid kids went there! The dog was a German Shepherd. It leaped for Ben's throat, tore his Adam's apple out, and left him bleeding to death! Then the dog went after Bee as she tried to get away. The dog grabbed her foot, dragging her across the floor, then went for her neck and bit her until she was unconscious, until police arrived. The girl, Bee, was taken to the hospital, and Ben bled to death! The attack happened at 4:02am.

"Headquarters, this is Vivian Mello at the fourth vacant house. I believe Canton got a hold of a man and a young girl. I think the man may be dead, and the girl is moving and needs to go to a hospital. Our dog did a job on them!" "10/4, Vivian. I'll send you help. Headquarters, Captain Bogey over."

Police had to put guard dogs to keep the public the fuck out of these buildings! The vacant haunted houses were later knocked down.

NINETEEN

THE PAINE HOUSE HAUNTING

Coventry, Rhode Island. A couple were checking into the Paine House Bed & Breakfast and museum.

"Good afternoon, my name is Paul Penny, and my girlfriend Panama Stevens. We're looking for a Colonial Home stay weekend. We're from Quincy, Massachusetts."

"Pleased to meet you. Robin Valentino, the host guest manager. Welcome to The Paine House here in Coventry, Rhode Island. The rooms are $189 per evening, all colonial-style rooms with antique furniture. All rooms have central air conditioning. On cool nights, you can open the windows and let the fresh air in. You will feel at home staying here. We have the antique museum across the hall and the dining room and bar next to it. Dinner is served at 5:30pm: old-fashioned fish & chips, $15.95 per person. We are a Bed & Breakfast colonial hotel serving a free breakfast every morning from 6am until 10:30am. Take the elevator just past the dining room to the second floor, and you will be staying in room 18."

Paul and Panama went to their room, and the bellboy brought their luggage. Paul gave him the tip, and Panama started unpacking, hanging clothes and putting them in drawers. She said,

"Paul, the air is thick in here. It's hard to breathe!"

"I feel like that too! I know it's hot outside, but we need to open the windows and shut the air conditioner off."

The air was even getting thicker because it was very humid outside, so Paul shut the windows and turned the AC back on. Panama just hung clothes in the closet, and when she went to the bathroom, she found all the clothes on the floor outside the closet. Her boyfriend Paul saw clothes go flying and spreading all over the floor. He said,

"Panama, what are you doing?"

She came out of the bathroom and saw all the clothes on the floor. She said,

"Oh my God, what's going on here! I just hung these clothes! Did you do this, Paul, trying to be funny?"

"No, I thought you were tossing clothes, being pissed off about something!" he said.

"No, I was in the bathroom taking a shit and washing up!"

Then the drawers opened, and all the clothes flew out, hanging onto a ceiling fan, going all over the bed and on the floor. Paul and Panama were watching the haunting unfold. He said,

"Pack everything up, and we're getting out of here!"

The windows were opening and closing, the ceiling fan was turning on and off, the AC turning on and off, and the room door flung open, leading to the hallway. Then it all stopped a minute later. The time was 4:02pm.

The couple went down to the front desk. Paul said,

"Excuse me, miss, but we have some kind of ghost in our room."

The couple told the clerk what was happening.

"I will give you another room. I only have room 3 available. Put the air conditioner on high because these rooms can get very stuffy!" said Robin Valentino, the clerk receptionist.

The couple went to room 3, then they went to eat supper in

the dining room. Later, they checked out all the antiques in the museum.

Another couple checked into room 18; a late check-in. The carbon dioxide detector started going off at 3:02am, waking the man up but not his wife; she died from carbon dioxide poisoning. The man tried waking her, but there was no response. He called 911, and the rescue took her to Kent County Hospital. The rescue workers said,

"Laura Reed is dead!"

The husband flipped out, throwing things around in the Paine House lobby, breaking chairs, breaking glass, knocking tables over, and tipping furniture over until he was arrested at gunpoint by Coventry Police and removed from the property.

Back to Paul and Panama in room 3. Both of them woke up hearing glass breaking and all the noise! The time was 5:02am. The room was quiet for the rest of the early morning. They went back to sleep.

They got up around 8:30am to have breakfast, then they went to Narragansett for the day, going to the beach and sightseeing. Later, they returned to the Paine House for dinner. Then they went back to the museum to look at more antiques.

Panama was looking at a doll that looked like it was stalking her, eyeballing her. The doll fell off the shelf and landed on her, then it fell on the floor. She picked it up and put it on the shelf where it belonged. The doll's eyes were black. Then she went to look for something else. She saw a dragon growling at her. She walked away, then went back to check the dragon again, and it was quiet.

Then she saw a picture of a woman, and the eyes were moving. Then she went to a birdcage to see all kinds of tropical birds, and they were all acting up, making noises. As soon as Panama walked past them, the birds were quiet. She went back to the birds to get a second look, and the birds started acting up again! When she passed, the birds quieted down again.

Then she saw a glowing apparition of a lady in a blue-green color, standing about 10 feet away, looking at her, eyeballing Panama, then it vanished in front of her eyes. She saw the same lady hanging in a picture, and her eyes were moving. She got a closer look, and the lady came out of the picture in a gust of wind strong enough to knock her down, knocking over a table of antiques and breaking everything. She got up screaming,

"Ahhh!" she said.

"Paul, we have to get out of here; there's a ghost of a mean-looking lady stalking me. I saw her ghost floating in the museum, then I saw her picture of her, and she came out of her picture and attacked me!"

Paul looked at the same picture, and nothing was happening. He studied eye contact with the picture for a few minutes to see if something happened; nothing! Then they left the museum. While they were leaving, they both heard a voice,

"Get out!"

"Paul, if anything happens when we go to bed tonight in our room, we have to leave here," said Panama.

In the middle of the night, around 3am, Panama woke up and saw the same lady she saw attacking her and blowing her down in the museum! She started screaming, waking Paul up. The lady vanished when Panama started screaming, and she said,

"Paul, I just saw the lady from the museum picture standing right there at the foot of the bed! We need to get out of here before we get hurt! Get up, get dressed, and let's go!"

The two of them got up, got dressed, and left the room, running out of the Paine House as fast as they could. They didn't get far because the main gate closed automatically, trapping them in.

"Panama, stay here and don't get out. I have to go back in and get someone to open the gate and let us out!" Paul went inside to get someone to open the gate. He told the receptionist what had happened. The receptionist came out with keys to open the gate, and the gate opened on its own. The receptionist was shocked because that never happens.

Paul got in his car and left. Riding down a dark road, both of them saw the lady from the museum picture, and Paul drove right through the ghostly figure and ran it over! Panama screamed! Paul didn't bother to stop; he just kept going.

"In my forty years of life, I never experienced anything like this. I never believed in ghosts until we stayed here! It was a lifetime experience!" said Paul.

The next morning, at 6:02am, a police car and rescue arrived at the Paine House, and a dead body was being carried out and put in the rescue. Carbon dioxide poisoning at the Paine House in Coventry. I guess the lady from the museum picture is trying to kill everyone! Many guests staying there complained of breathing problems.

TWENTY

HAUNTINGS IN CONNECTICUT STERLING OPERA HOUSE IN DERBY, CONNECTICUT

Derby, Connecticut. September 2026.

The Sterling Opera House is haunted. A show was going on in the theater, and a security guard was hired on his first night.

"The Fall Fashion Opera" was playing, and many people were well dressed, enjoying the show. The show was over at 10:30pm, and the evening custodian came in to sweep and clean the theater. The security guard was turning off lights and closing doors when the custodian finished cleaning. The custodian left at midnight.

The security guard worked the night shift from 11pm until 7am. He made sure the building was locked down after everyone was out. Then he went to the restroom, and while he was on the toilet, he heard a noise. When he was through, he went to the sink to wash his hands. He looked in the mirror, and his eyes were black, and he saw a shadow of the back of his head in the mirror. He washed his face and looked in the mirror again, and everything was normal. He turned away and looked in the mirror a third time; his face and eyes were normal.

Then he went to the men's and women's dressing rooms. The lights were still on. He turned the lights off and checked the rest of the building, then went to the lounge break room to read the newspaper. Minutes later, he heard footsteps. He got up, walking through the building again. The security guard was alone and saw no one during his walkthrough.

He checked the theater, and the lights were on. Suddenly he felt a draft.

"I swear I turned these lights off earlier, maybe I didn't get them all," he said to himself. "Anyone here? Hello!"

He checked the outside doors and turned the fans off in the theater. Then he checked the dressing rooms again because he heard music playing, and all the lights were on.

"Hello! Anyone in here? Hello!" No answers. He called the Derby Police.

"Derby Police. Officer Donald Wells speaking."

"Hi, this is Peter Heater, the security night shift at the Sterling Opera House. I have the building secured, but someone is in here, and I can't find anyone. The lights are turning on and roaming the building."

"Okay, Mr. Heater. I will send an officer over."

"Thank you, officer."

The police arrived and checked the building. No one was there.

"Peter, you might be dealing with a ghost!" said the cop.

"A ghost?"

"Yeah, this opera house is haunted, and there are a lot of ghosts of all kinds in here! Late at night, when everyone is gone, that's when the dead rise from their graves and walk through the opera house like the walking dead! You will see them, mostly shadow people. Early in the night, you will hear noises, footsteps, and see things that are not there. The ghosts will set off alarms all night until daybreak. The police ignore them until we get complaints from the neighbors. Some of the ghosts may knock you down. If I were you, just ignore what's going on here and secure the building before you leave at 7am," said the cop.

"That's strange because I never believed in ghosts, and my supervisor never told me the Sterling Opera House was haunted," said Peter Heater, the security guard.

"Be careful," said the cop, and he left.

Peter turned the lights off again in the men's and women's dressing rooms. Suddenly, he saw a lady dressed in glowing green in the women's dressing room when he turned off the lights. Then the apparition vanished!

"Holy shit!" the security guard said to himself.

He went to the men's restroom to take a piss. While standing over the urinal, he could feel someone breathing on his neck and the back of his head. He quickly turned around, and no one was there!

He finished taking a piss, went to the sink to wash his hands, and saw a shadow figure with red eyes in the mirror standing behind him! He quickly turned around to face the apparition, and nothing was there!

"Jesus Christ! I'm not working here anymore," he said to himself and left the men's room in a hurry.

Then he heard music playing in the theater. He saw people dancing on the stage, and the stage curtains started closing and opening. The theater was packed with people, and opera music played louder and louder. Peter looked at his watch; the time was 3:02am. Then the music stopped, and the stage curtains closed.

Peter saw a young girl walking up the aisle from the stage. He said to her, "There are shows here at three o'clock in the morning!" The young girl vanished right in front of his eyes.

Then he faced the crowd. They were standing and clapping. Suddenly the crowd stopped clapping and stood frozen in place!

The outside doors opened on both sides of the theater. All the people in the theater vanished at the same time, leaving an empty seating area. Suddenly the outside doors slammed shut, and a strong gust of wind blew Peter down. He ran out of the theater as fast as he could!

He called the Derby Police and told them about his ghostly encounter. The police said,

"Enjoy your ghostly job because you will see a lot of them at the Sterling. You might meet Bruce Sterling, who died in 1882, during your travels! The Sterling Opera House is the most haunted place in Connecticut, built over a slaughter burial ground from the 1600s! Good luck working there."

Peter locked the theater and suddenly saw two giant black rats running in the hallway coming at him. One of them leaped off its back legs and went for his throat. The rats vanished. Peter didn't feel a thing, but he was so frightened he ran out the front door! He didn't bother to set the alarm and left his belongings and lunch box in his office. He got in his car and went home. The alarms were going off, and the police came to turn them off!

Peter called his boss.

"Hey, Harry, Peter Heater. Sorry to bother you at 5:30 in the morning. You never told me the Sterling Opera House was haunted when I was hired."

"You never asked me," said his boss.

Peter told his boss what happened.

"I have never been so scared in my life, not even finishing my first night. I thought I was going to die from the strange happenings in that place. I never experienced the things that went on in there. It looked like the walking dead appeared and vanished. I don't know what else is going to happen. I can't work in a place like this. Goodbye!" said Peter.

A new security guard was hired, a woman, meeting the boss in the main office. The boss was packing Peter Heater's belongings in a bag to remove from the office when the young lady came in for an interview for the 11pm to 7am security job.

"Hi, sir. Are you Harry Barry?"

"Yes, ma'am."

"My name is Sue Drapes. I'm here for the security job."

"Yes, please have a seat. Before we have the interview, I just want to tell you the Sterling Opera House is haunted," said Harry, the boss.

"Ha! Ha!!" Sue laughed. "You don't believe in ghosts!"

"Absolutely not, sir!"

"Let's go for a tour, and maybe you'll see one! The Sterling Opera House is the most haunted facility here in Connecticut. A man was just hired yesterday, and he had so many experiences he had to leave. He ran out of here and didn't bother to take his belongings!" said Harry.

They went for a tour of the opera house and saw or heard nothing. Then Harry said,

"Put on your uniform, and you will be in here alone tonight. There's no show and no custodian. Your shift starts tonight at 11pm, and you lock up at 7am if you can make it through the night!"

"Ha! Ha!!" she said.

Sue went into the women's dressing room to change her clothes and put on her security uniform. Suddenly she saw a black poltergeist, and it attacked her, throwing her up against a wall and dropping her on the floor! I don't think she'll be there very long!

STERLING OPERA HOUSE HAUNTINGS

The state of Connecticut is buried over one of the world's largest Indian burial grounds. Moodus, CT.

A family moved into a house located near the Moodus River. Peter Heater, the one-night security guard who quit his job at the Sterling Opera House, moved to Moodus, Connecticut, with his wife Mary and his two children, Sue Heater and his son Beaver Heater. If he thought the Sterling Opera House was haunted, he was in for a rude awakening here in Moodus!

A real estate agent arrived to show the Heaters the home.

Bridgewater Realtors:

"Good afternoon, my name is Carol Cox, and my partner Richard Rich, from Bridgewater Realtors in Bridgewater, Massachusetts."

"Pleased to meet you. My name is Peter Heater, and this is my wife Mary, daughter Sue, and my son Beaver."

"Pleased to meet you. This home is a colonial duplex, and your neighbor is Pam Costa, who lives alone with her dog Max. Come inside. This is the living room with a gas fireplace. Next is the kitchen with all stainless-steel appliances, and a two-sided refrigerator and freezer. Here's the stove with six gas burners and oven below, a built-in microwave above the stove, a fan above the kitchen, and a center cutting table, cook warmer, and drawers around the center cable.

Then you have the main bathroom with a jacuzzi tub and shower, two sinks, and two toilets. This is a big bathroom. You have a family room with a built-in workbench and a flat-screen TV built into the wall, and large picture windows in here and the living room. The next room can be used as a bedroom. Above the fireplace in the living room, you have another built-in flat-screen TV. Let's go upstairs.

The middle room is a bathroom with a sauna. You have the master bedroom on the right with another built-in flat-screen TV on the wall. The room on the other side is another bedroom. You have plenty of closet space in the eaves and walk-in closets. You have another gas fireplace in the master bedroom with the TV on the wall above the fireplace.

Let's go up to the attic. Up here you can make two more rooms;

otherwise, you have plenty of room for storage. The attic is big enough to have a bowling alley. Let's go to the basement. Down here you have a wooden staircase and a good-size basement with an exit going out into the backyard. You have washer and dryer hookups, a sink on two sides. You have a small bath with a sink, toilet, and a walk-in shower. Under the staircase, you have a closet," said Carol Cox, the realtor.

"What does this door lead to? Was this home a former funeral home? It looks like one," Peter joked.

"No, this home was not a funeral home. You have a private workroom, storage, and a wine cellar. It's a pretty big room. You can do a lot in here; you can also use this room for storage or private meetings and computer hookups. Let's go outside and see the backyard and the river. Before we go outside, you have a wood stove down here. You can rent an apartment down here if you like. Outside, you have a built-in picnic table that sits up to 20 people. You have a deck with wooden stairs if you come from the kitchen to the backyard. Near the river, you have a gathering area with a round picnic table, and you can put chairs around it and benches to sit on. You can swim in the river, and the water is very clean. You have a mini private beach to bake in the sun; a great home for kids. The backyard you share with your neighbor Pam Costa and her dog Max. The mortgage is $475,000 for 30 years. The address here is 32 North Street, Moodus, Connecticut. Any questions?" said Carol Cox.

"Yes, was there a fire here at one time?" said Peter.

"Yes, there was, back in the early 1980s. An apartment building burned down on this property."

"Carol, what's that big building all fenced in down the road?" said Mary, Peter's wife.

"The building was the University of Connecticut Hospital. It's closed down now."

"Carol, what was in that hospital?" said Peter.

"I heard it was a mental institution facility, then it was a jail at one time, but it's just a vacant building right now. There's nothing there!"

"Carol, is this house haunted?" said Peter.

"No, not that I know of, but strange things happen here in Moodus. We get mild earthquakes here due to water washing up against limestone. We have a few caves and waterways, brooks, and rivers flowing from the Connecticut River making noises. I don't know if you heard about the Moodus Noises on the news, but that's what we have here."

"Back in the 1970s, there was a theory about a lake monster that terrorized the town of Moodus, coming from out of space. A dragon made out of a rock came out of a meteorite, spraying fire, burning the town down, killing people and animals. The Connecticut Native Indians believed this sea dragon was the devil. When the earthquakes sound, the Indians believed the devil was rising from under the ground. There's a book about the Moodus Noises written by author Richard Rezendes called *Ground of the Devil*. You can buy this book in local bookstores or at the town library. The book has a female dragon-looking devil on the front cover," said Richard Rich, Carol's partner.

"The reason I ask if this place is haunted: I heard crazy stories before about Moodus, Connecticut, but I never believed them. I did hear about the Moodus Noises and the earthquakes here. A few weeks ago, I got a security guard job at the Sterling Opera House in Derby, Connecticut, and I thought I walked into the gates of hell with the walking dead, poltergeist neighbors, and big black rats! I never believed in ghosts until I got that job. I worked the graveyard shift from 11pm until 7am, and I left at 4am, taking all my belongings and getting out before I got dragged into hell because that's what it was like! The reason I'm looking for property here is because I will be working at the East Haddam Opera House starting in two weeks. I hope that place is not haunted," said Peter.

"Well, let's go in and sign the lease, and you can start moving in," said Richard Rich.

A week later, the Heaters moved into the duplex in Moodus, Connecticut.

One morning, around 8:30am, Peter went for a walk down by the river. On his return to the house, he saw a naked lady in her mid-40s to early 50s fingering herself, lying on a bench down by the river on his property. He was suddenly blinded behind a tree. Peter got up closer to get a better look, and no one was there! The naked woman was a ghost and looked like the lady next door, whom the Heaters hadn't met yet.

Later in the day, Peter came out to trim some bushes and saw the same naked lady he saw earlier that morning, lying in the yard in a beach chair. She was wearing a bikini bathing suit. Peter walked up to her and said,

"Hi, my name is Peter Heater. I just moved into the duplex next door with my wife and kids."

"Pleased to meet you. Pam Costa."

"Hey, listen, I would appreciate it if you don't lay around naked because I have kids here!"

"I beg your pardon! I don't lay around naked, so get lost, buddy!"

I guess the Heaters were not going to get along with this neighbor.

At nighttime, Sue woke up and saw a lady standing behind her bed. The time was 11:02pm. She said,

"Excuse me, Pam, but you live next door."

The lady backed up, walking out of the room, and vanished. Sue got up and woke her mom.

"Mom, the lady next door is in our house. I saw her in my bedroom."

"What!" said Mary.

Peter got up and went through the house and into the basement. No one was there. He said,

"Sue, you must be dreaming."

"Dad, it's not a dream. She was in my room!"

"I don't see anyone here. Just go back to bed."

Then Peter went up to check the attic. Nothing.

12:02am, one hour later.

Beaver woke up and saw the lady.

"Excuse me, miss, but you're in the wrong house. What are you doing here in my bedroom!?"

Then she left and vanished.

He got up, waking Peter and Mary.

"Mom, Dad, some lady appeared in my room a minute ago!"

"What did this lady look like?" said Peter.

"She looked like a young girl dressed in colonial clothing, and she looked like she was doing a dance near my bed. Then suddenly she ran out of the room! She looked like a showgirl, like someone in a movie," said Beaver.

Peter was shocked, and so was Mary.

"Beaver, go back to bed, and I will check the house. Make sure you say your prayers."

Then Peter said to his wife Mary,

"I think we might be dealing with a ghost, like the one from the Sterling Opera House, Beaver was describing."

"You're kidding!" she said.

Peter got up to check the house. Then, around 1am, he went back to bed. Two minutes later, he heard a noise in the bathroom. He went to investigate and saw the same young girl he had seen in the Sterling Opera House theater—the one who vanished when Peter asked her about the late-night show.

The girl started undressing, and then she vanished again as Peter watched in shock. The time was 1:02am.

The girl looked like the naked lady he had seen lying on the bench near the river the previous morning. He said to her,

"Lady, you do not belong here. Go back to the Sterling Opera

House, where you belong. I don't work there anymore, and you have to leave me and my family alone!"

Peter said to Mary,

"Mary, the ghost of the girl I saw in the theater at the Sterling Opera House followed me here. Tomorrow morning, we need to call a Catholic priest to get rid of her."

"Oh my God!" she said.

Then Mary heard water running in the downstairs bathroom. She went to investigate and found the bathroom full of steam. The water was filling up the tub. The shower curtain was closed, and she pulled it back.

She saw the same lady haunting the house in the jacuzzi, naked, with her hands between her legs, taking a bath. Mary screamed,

"Ahhh!"

The lady vanished, the water shut off on its own, and the jacuzzi tub emptied itself. The time was 2:02am.

Now the family couldn't sleep because this girl kept haunting them all night until sunrise. The girl jumped in Sue's bed at 3:02am, in Beaver's bed at 4:02am, and in bed with Peter at 5:02am. She had black eyes and vanished again.

Mary was making breakfast when she suddenly saw the lady in colonial clothes run by her and vanish in the kitchen, running through a wall. Mary screamed,

"Ahhh!"

The time was 6:02am. Then the hauntings from this young Sterling Opera House lady stopped.

Peter contacted a Catholic priest to bless their home, going into every room, throwing holy water, and placing crosses in each room.

Later, Peter went next door with his wife Mary to meet the new neighbor. Peter rang the doorbell—ding-dong!

"Who is it?" said Pam next door.

"Hi, it's Peter Heater and my wife Mary."

She opened her door. Peter said,

"This is my wife Mary. I just want to apologize for yesterday's remarks. We have a ghost in our house: a lady who appears in colonial clothing and sometimes appears naked. This lady has been haunting me since I was a security guard at the Sterling Opera House in Derby, Connecticut. She followed me here to Moodus."

"I forgive you, Mr. Heater. I saw the priest coming to your house this morning. Come on in, and I will make you some coffee. I have been living here since the COVID-19 pandemic, and I heard that Moodus is not a very nice town to live in; there's a lot of fear here."

"I don't know if Bridgewater Realtors told you about the history of the hauntings here. We get earthquakes, bad thunderstorms, unusual large birds flying around, and giant river snakes in the Moodus River coming from the Connecticut River. I have seen these mega-evil birds and the river snakes going up and down the river. I have not seen them for the last three years living here. The river snakes could be from the Loch Ness Monster family, coming up from the Connecticut River.

I never believed in ghosts or evil spirits until I moved here from San Diego, California. Back in the early 1800s, a possible comet with a demon-like creature may have lived underground for more than 200 years. When it came above ground, it was a killer machine—humans and animals alike. There's a book called *Ground of the Devil*, written by author Richard Rezendes from Brown University. In this book, a devil-like creature terrorized Moodus, Connecticut, with death and destruction during the 1970s and 1980s. That's only a story, however; the Native Americans believed that the earthquakes here were caused by the devil coming from underground.

There's a lot of witchcraft going on here, and currently we have visits from the Ku Klux Klan, burning crosses and worshiping the devil, trying to bring him above ground! In Richard Rezendes' book, the devil is a female! Whether that's true or not, a lot of strange things have been happening here in Moodus. If you noticed the vacant building with a high-security fence down the road, it used to be a haunted nut house with demonic people and animals in there—the University of Connecticut Psychiatric Hospital. Before that, it was called the Boardman Institute of Mental Health, and before that, it was a sawmill that burned to the ground.

The demon-like, mentally ill patients were poisoned with a snake venom called "The Pink Blob Jelly Orange Sand," a bacteria that killed many people, animals, and anything that was alive, deforming them into creatures and animal-human hybrids! I could tell you stories all day about what happens here. I would advise that you obey the town's rules and beware of your surroundings, because a lot of strange things have happened here! I recommend you get a dog and a cat to keep evil spirits away," said Pam Costa, Peter's neighbor.

"Pam, the real estate agent told us about some of those things that happened here, but he never said anything about the river snakes in the Moodus River. He said the river is safe to swim in."

"Again, the snakes may be gone because I haven't seen them in three or four years," Pam said.

The couple made amends with the next-door neighbor and became friends.

The next evening, the hauntings continued at 32 North Street. Sue saw a black figure with red eyes standing over her in bed when she woke up. The black figure growled like some animal, and she screamed hysterically, running into her mom and dad's room and telling them what she saw. The time was 11:02pm.

One hour later, Beaver woke up and saw a black figure in his room standing behind his bed. It looked like the devil, with red eyes! He grabbed his cell phone to take a picture before the apparition vanished, capturing footage he later showed to Peter, his dad. He woke Mary and said,

"Look at this! It's the same demon I saw in the men's room at the Sterling Opera House while I was washing my hands, before I saw the lady that vanished in the theater."

Now it was another sleepless night at 32 North Street. Sue and Beaver were sleeping with their mom and dad tonight.

Peter looked at the alarm clock. The time was 1:02am. He heard a voice:

"Get out!"

He said, "No! You get out! You do not belong here! Go back to the Sterling Opera House where you belong!"

He heard "Get out" three more times, then saw a black shadow run across the bedroom and vanish.

He said to his wife, "Mary, do you hear these voices telling me to get out? I just saw a black shadow vanish!"

Mary heard nothing or saw nothing. At 2:02am, it was Mary's turn. A mysterious force threw her out of bed onto the floor. She couldn't move, then was free a minute later.

"We need to get out of here and go to a motel before someone gets hurt!" said Peter.

The family left the house and went to a motel out of town. Poltergeists and shadow people from the Sterling Opera House continued to haunt the house at two minutes past every hour until 7am. Sue's bedclothes flew off the bed at 3:02am. In Beaver's room, the bed flipped over at 4:02am. The devil-like poltergeist with red eyes appeared again in Peter and Mary's bedroom, and all their clothes flew out of the closets, falling on the floor at 5:02am. Then dishes flew out of the kitchen cabinets, breaking on the floor, while silverware and knives flew out of drawers, sticking into the walls. The ghosts made a mess of the house at 32 North Street until 7am, when the hauntings finally stopped. The kitchen attack struck at 6:02am.

At 8:30am, the Heater family returned home. The house was a mess.

"Oh my fucking god! Damn devil from hell!" said Peter. Broken glass and plates littered the kitchen floor, knives were sticking in the walls, and a window was cracked.

The Heaters called the real estate agent.

"We have to move. There's a poltergeist haunting this house!" Peter told them.

The family went through the house, cleaning up the mess. Then they went to St. Michael's Church to see a priest.

"We have to do an exorcism to remove what's haunting your house. My name is Father Gordon Wales. I need to hire a powerful friar from Providence College, a paranormal investigation team, and a cardinal from Georgetown University in Washington, D.C., to perform a powerful exorcism to remove the poltergeist in your home. We also have to go to the Sterling Opera House in Derby, Connecticut, but you—Peter—cannot be with us there. The evil spirit is in you, and you attracted it from the Sterling Opera House.

"First, we will do an exorcism here at the church with you and your family. Then I will go back and bless the house again with Sue, Beaver, and Mary—not you. You have to stay somewhere else until the exorcism is over. If you go to the house, the evil poltergeist may return, and it could kill you. Find somewhere to stay for the next two weeks, and then you have to come with us to the Sterling Opera House," said Father Gordon Wales.

After Peter went to stay with relatives in New Haven, the rest of his family returned to the house at 32 North Street with the priest. The hauntings stopped.

Peter stayed at his aunt and uncle's house in New Haven. He told them what happened.

"Uncle Donald, Aunt Jackie, I don't know what got into me on my first night working at the Sterling Opera House. A priest in Moodus, Connecticut, told me I contacted a poltergeist and had to go through an exorcism to get rid of it. He said I should be okay now, as long as I don't go back to my house, because I left it there!"

"Peter, the Sterling Opera House is the evillest place in

Connecticut, and Moodus is possessed by the devil. You need to see a psychiatrist!" said Aunt Jackie.

A psychiatrist in New Haven said, "Good afternoon. My name is Peter Heater. I would like to speak with a psychiatrist."

"See Dr. David in Room 2," said the receptionist.

"Hi, my name is Dr. David Denny."

"Pleased to meet you, Dr. Denny. Sir, the reason I am here is that I have been haunted by a poltergeist devil I somehow contacted while working my first night at the Sterling Opera House in Derby, Connecticut. I left before my shift was over because a big rat attacked me. Somehow it went through me, and I was not hurt. Then a girl in the theater followed me to my new home in Moodus, Connecticut. The demon shadow poltergeist also followed and caused damage in my home, threatening my family, so I had to get a priest to perform an exorcism to remove it! I can't understand how this happened."

"Peter, when you were hired at the Sterling Opera House, did your boss warn you that the theater was haunted?" asked Dr. Denny, the psychiatrist.

"No, he did not."

"Were you aware that the Sterling Opera House was haunted?"

"No, Doctor. I had no clue. I was just looking for a security job there because it was the only opening in New Haven County."

"Peter, here is what happened: You were a target because the place had been vacant for many years. When it reopened and was newly renovated, the spirits were unrestful and went after you. You did the right thing by seeing a priest and getting an exorcism," said the psychiatrist.

About two weeks later, Peter and his family were free from hauntings after the exorcisms were completed. The priests could not handle the exorcism at the Sterling Opera House; it had to be done by ghost hunters and a paranormal investigation team.

Peter got a security job at the East Haddam Opera House, just outside Moodus, working the graveyard shift from 11pm to 7am.

"Good evening. I am looking for Mr. David Green."

"Right here, sir. You must be Mr. Peter Heater."

"Yes, sir. I am here for the new security job."

"Let's take a tour, and I'll show you around. Welcome to the Goodspeed Opera House here in East Haddam, Connecticut, with a view of the Connecticut River. We have the theater, restaurant, and hotel here. There are two shows a month. This month, it's the 'Connecticut Big Dick Opera Play,' playing Thursday through Sunday afternoons. You will be a theater usher during all shows, in addition to your security duties."

"Is this place haunted?" asked Peter.

"Well, at times late at night, you may see shadow people. You might see someone who isn't there, or think people are still present after closing. They will not hurt you—they appear, walk by, and vanish.

"We also have a swinging bridge and a moving boat dock when the river gets rough. People have been thrown off the dock into the water—it's not a safe place to walk during winter months. The swinging bridge can open during strong winds, and cars crossing sometimes get stuck. There have even been reports of cars thrown into the river. You may see something, or you may not. The Goodspeed is a good place to work, but it does go bump in the night once in a while," said David Green.

"You've got my records from the Sterling Opera House in Derby, Connecticut. I didn't last more than five hours there—the hauntings I went through were unbelievable. The ghosts followed me to my home in Moodus, terrorizing my family, and I had to get a priest and a paranormal team to get rid of them. I haven't seen anything in the last couple of weeks," Peter explained.

"Peter, the Sterling Opera House is dangerous—many strange hauntings happened there, and people have even died from falls.

Your home in Moodus has a haunted history with devil-like creatures and deformed animals. Moodus has been quiet for a while, aside from the earthquakes. The Native Americans believe the Moodus noises and earthquakes were caused by the devil coming from underground.

"We have staff here who worked at the Sterling Opera House. Some of the hauntings here are similar, but not as severe. The worst dangers are the swinging bridge and the moving dock. You may see spirits in this building, but they will not bother you," said David Green.

He showed Peter around the building and said, "When you leave, don't forget to reset the alarm after the show. There's a show going on right now. Good luck and have a nice evening."

Peter watched the opera, helping people get to their seats. The theater was not full. After the show, he ushered people to the exits. Once the building was empty, he reset the alarm and closed the theater. The hotel was temporarily closed, with rooms locked. The restaurant and bar were only open during showtime.

Peter walked through the quiet building alone until 7am, checking restrooms, dressing rooms, and turning off lights while locking doors. Looking out a window, he saw several police cars, rescue vehicles, and fire trucks surrounding both sides of the swinging bridge over the Connecticut River.

Then he saw a lady shadow person walking between the bar and restaurant—then she vanished.

"Hello! The building is closed; you have to leave!" Peter shouted. The lady looked real, roaming around, but made no sound and did not answer. When Peter followed her, she vanished. He rechecked the building, and no one was there.

He looked out a window again and saw a girl jump off the moving boat dock ramp into the river. The time was 3:02am.

Meanwhile, the girl and the poltergeist from the Sterling Opera House paid a visit to Pam Costa next door to the Heaters, continuing the hauntings until she eventually had to sell the property and leave.

People reported seeing ghost shadows late at night walking through the Mohegan Sun Casino like the walking dead, vanishing as guests watched in shock. Every day around 3am, the walking dead were seen walking through the casino. Fake wolves would howl for about a minute, and the ghosts would vanish into fog or black mist rolling along the ground. Across Connecticut, ghosts were seen rising from graves, wandering like the walking dead, then disappearing at homes, hotels, schools, churches, and malls.

Back at the East Haddam Goodspeed Opera House, Peter saw strange things during his first night, though nothing as intense as at the Sterling Opera House. Doors opened and closed, and lights flickered or turned on and off in the hallways. He spent the night chasing the Goodspeed hauntings, shutting off lights and locking doors.

Meanwhile, the hauntings continued next door with Pam Costa. After 11pm, her lamp turned on by itself, and the alarm clock rang simultaneously. She shut the alarm off and turned off the lamp.

While her back was turned, a poltergeist devil with red eyes stood behind her bed—but she didn't see it. The lamp turned on again, and she looked at the alarm clock: 12:02am. Suddenly, the hour and minute hands spun wildly before stopping at 12:03am.

"I guess Aunt Catherine died," she said to herself, not thinking about the hauntings next door. She got up to use the bathroom, returned to bed, and saw the clock: 12:10am. She shut the lamp off and went back to sleep.

At 1:02am, the lamp flickered on again. Pam muttered, "Aunt Catherine, I know you may have passed away, but you have to stop turning on lights and ringing my alarm. Let me sleep! Maybe it's a faulty bulb or a bad plug." She shut the lamp off and returned to bed.

The lamp turned on again, waking Pam at 2:02am. Finally, she had enough. She pulled the plug on both the lamp and alarm clock, then went back to bed.

At 3:02am, she woke to hear footsteps and something running. She assumed it was Peter's kids and said to herself, "Peter must be home—why are his kids running around in the middle of the night?" The footsteps and running stopped, and she returned to bed.

Pam Costa could see clearly thanks to the night light near her bed. At 4:02am, she woke up to the sound of running water in the bathroom. When she got up to investigate, she saw a naked lady going into the shower—the same lady who had haunted Peter Heater next door, the one from the Sterling Opera House. The woman looked like Pam's Aunt Catherine. Pam watched in shock as the lady vanished just as she turned around.

Pam called out, "Aunt Catherine, what are you doing!?"

She muttered to herself, "Aunt Catherine, are you trying to give me a heart attack, showing up in my home! I'm not ready to go with you yet! I'm only 44 years old." Pam couldn't sleep anymore, so she went downstairs to watch TV for the rest of the night.

Then a black mist formed into a demonic shadow person with big horns, red eyes, and multiple arms emerging from the mass. The poltergeist grew huge and charged at Pam, passing through her as she screamed hysterically, "Ahhh!"

She was not physically hurt, but the encounter left her terrified. The time was 5:02am. Pam ran out of her house, ringing the doorbell and banging on the door. Mary Heater heard the commotion, looked out a window, and saw Pam acting hysterically. She let her inside.

"Mrs. Heater, your husband's ghosts are in my house!" Pam shouted.

"I'll call the priest," Mary said.

Pam told Mary everything that had happened in her home and

stayed talking until Peter returned from work. By 6:02am, whatever had been happening in Pam's house had subsided. At 7:02am, a priest arrived to bless Pam Costa's duplex. Even after the blessing, Pam still heard noises and saw chairs move and papers fly off a table. She didn't waste any time packing up and moving out. Before a new tenant could move in, the real estate agent arrived with a priest to bless the property.

Peter didn't see any more activity after his first night working at the East Haddam Goodspeed Opera House.

Back at the duplex at 32 North Street, a new couple moved into Pam's former home. While kayaking down the Connecticut River, a giant river snake tipped their kayak over. The couple either drowned or were eaten—no one ever saw the snake. Meanwhile, the Heater kids, Sue and Beaver, continued to enjoy swimming in the river.

One late October night, a police officer patrolling Devil's Hop Yard Park saw something unusual. It was about 8pm, raining, and a group of about twenty people were standing by the waterfall, glowing red as if lit with blood.

"The park's closed. You have to leave!" the officer shouted.

The twenty figures vanished before his eyes. Shocked, he called for backup. A second police car arrived.

"Glenn, did you see the devil on your first night on the job?" asked Officer Jason.

"Not quite. I saw a bunch of people standing by the waterfall. When I went to tell them to leave, they vanished!" Glenn replied.

"Connecticut has a devil creature that has haunted Moodus and East Haddam, living underground and in the Connecticut River. That's why the park is called Devil's Hop Yard State Park. Connecticut is built over Indian burial grounds, and the walking dead rise from graves," Officer Jason explained.

"What is Chapman Falls?" Glenn asked.

"The waterfall is called Chapman Falls. Many people swim

there in the summer and end up disappearing, pulled under the falls into sinkholes, never to be seen again. Walking dead roam this park year-round late at night—likely the victims of Chapman Falls drownings. We see them vanish right in front of us," said Officer Jason.

The same phenomenon occurs at Gunntown Cemetery in Naugatuck, Connecticut. Walking dead roam late at night until police arrived, shining floodlights, and the spirits vanish. Visitors breaking into the cemetery to see the walking dead often get attacked, dragged into the woods, or pushed out, sometimes sustaining injuries. The walking dead can even possess trespassers.

At the New London Ledge Lighthouse, a group of ten Mitchell College students—five men and five women—attempted a dangerous initiation. They brought animals aboard a Noah's Ark replica on a flatbed truck, heading to the lighthouse around 3am. Paul Pauly, from Phi Delta Kappa fraternity, led the group, with Lisa Lester from Beta Phi Pi sorority assisting.

"Welcome aboard Noah's Ark! We're breaking into the lighthouse to sleep there and visit the ghosts. We need to be quick before the police arrive. Kill the alarm and get the animals inside," Paul instructed.

They rowed to the lighthouse, using nets to bring animals aboard. The deer jumped into the water and drowned. Paul smashed a window to silence the alarm. Once inside, a voice boomed:

"Get out!"

"Did anyone say something?" Paul asked nervously.

As the students carried the animals up the 50-foot spiral staircase, it collapsed. They fell, breaking bones, and some died. The animals were injured or killed as well, except for the cats, who survived. The injured cried for help as a figure appeared above them:

"I am Ernie. I hope you learned a lesson breaking into my lighthouse. Get out now or suffer!"

The lighthouse ghost vanished, appearing repeatedly until

police arrived. Paul cracked his head and died; Lisa was impaled on the metal staircase and died. At 6:02am, a thunderstorm struck, lightning hit the Noah's Ark, and it burned to ashes. The Coast Guard saw the burning boat and notified police. By 7:02am, the storm passed, and the ark sank. Police and Coast Guard rescued survivors; some were taken to a morgue.

The Remington Arms Factory in Bridgeport, Connecticut, is another location haunted by the walking dead. Once a steel-melting and glass-making factory, many died from falls, explosions, steam pipe bursts, and fires. One man witnessed a humanoid human-animal creature burning in a furnace; before he could call for help, a flame struck him, killing him instantly. Steam pipes exploded, floors collapsed, and the factory burned to the ground. Unrest spirits rose from the ashes.

Even the funeral-home-turned-office building in Connecticut, the basis for the movie *Haunting in Connecticut*, attracted ghost hunters, churches, and paranormal investigators. The family that once lived there, caring for a sick teenager, reported hauntings and exorcisms before moving out safely. Richard Rezendes, author of *Ground of the Devil*, had nightmares about the devil with black eyes haunting the property.

Now, the house is renovated with offices for doctors and lawyers. "The Kahunas, Bataros, Rasmini's, and Bob Levine—heavy hitters—settle this one. Welcome to the Connecticut House!" said a doctor.

TWENTY ONE

EMILY BRIDGE IN STOW, VERMONT

The Emily Bridge is a wooden haunted structure located on Gold Brook Road in Stow, Vermont. It was late October 2026, about a week before Halloween—a perfect time for a scare.

A group of University of Vermont students arrived at the bridge on a cold, rainy, windy night with thunder and lightning. Although the bridge was closed for repairs, eight students decided to cross it anyway, stepping over the police tape.

As they reached the middle of the bridge, a bright flash of lightning illuminated the structure. The students were horrified to see a woman hanging from a rope at the top of the bridge rafters. The time was 3:02am. The girls screamed, and the group ran back to their cars, calling the police.

"There's a lady hanging from a rope on top of the Emily Gold Brook Covered Bridge!" they reported.

Stow Police arrived to investigate.

"Stay off the bridge, kids, if you want to stay alive. You probably saw the ghost of Emily! Not many people or animals make it across safely—the bridge is old, unstable, and haunted. Many have died trying to cross," the officers warned before leaving.

Ignoring the warnings, the students tried a second attempt. Before they could step onto the bridge, a bolt of lightning struck the metal rafters, lighting up the entire structure. Suddenly, a gust of wind roared across the bridge at an estimated 100 miles per hour, throwing the students backward in all directions. One girl was hurled into a tree, and the others were blown down the road about 100 feet from the bridge entrance. Then the wind abruptly stopped.

The girl in the tree saw Emily swinging from the rope in the wind, then slip onto the bridge and vanish. Terrified, she cried hysterically as her friends helped her down. The students fled back to their cars in the pouring rain and returned to campus, spreading word of what they had seen.

More students later attempted to visit Emily's Bridge at night but were chased off by the police.

Meanwhile, a newlywed couple, Emily and Eric Endicott, were leaving St. Anthony Church in Mattapoisett, Massachusetts, after their wedding. They planned to visit Stow, Vermont, for skiing in the mountains. A family member warned, "Don't go to Emily Bridge—it's haunted!"

Emily laughed it off. "That's nonsense. There's no such thing as ghosts."

After a week at a ski resort, Emily and Eric decided to visit the bridge on their way home. On Sunday afternoon, October 25th, 2026, at around 1pm, the day was sunny and 43 degrees. Ignoring the yellow police tape, they began crossing the bridge on foot. Halfway across, they stopped to take pictures of the waterfall below and the bald eagles soaring overhead.

Suddenly, part of the wooden structure gave way. Both fell 100 feet to their deaths. Eric struck tree branches on the way down and landed in the icy water below, breaking several bones and drowning. Emily hit a large rock, cracking her skull and breaking several bones, dying instantly.

Giant vultures arrived and dragged Emily's body into the wilderness. Their bodies were never recovered. The waterfall and surrounding wildlife washed away all evidence, including the couple's belongings.

Stowe Police arrived and examined their parked car near the bridge. Officer Roberts discovered the car belonged to Eric Endicott and found marijuana and a pistol inside. The trunk contained a wedding dress, clothes, skiing equipment, a bowling ball, and a camping bag. Officer Smiley refused to step onto the bridge to search the brook, leaving Roberts to check the surrounding woods.

The next day, workers arrived at 9am to repair the bridge. That night, Officer Smiley returned around 9pm. Shining his flashlight, he noticed a raccoon approaching the bridge before it scurried away. Then, looking up at the moonlit rafters, he saw the ghost of Emily hanging from the rope. He heard a scream as she slipped onto the bridge and vanished. Smiley hurried back to his car, shaken.

"I saw the ghost with my very own eyes. She hanged herself, fell onto the bridge, and disappeared. I never want to go over there again!" he told Officer Roberts.

A week later, the bodies were still missing. The Endicott's' car was towed to a police auto salvage lot and remained unclaimed.

On Halloween, the Endicott family held a welcome-back party in Mattapoisett—but Emily and Eric never arrived. The family contacted Stowe Police.

"We found their car at Emily Bridge, but the couple is missing. If anything develops, we will let you know," the officers said.

Despite regular surveillance, Officer Roberts saw no ghost activity at the bridge for a week. Then, a car with four University of Vermont students crashed through the police tape and crossed the bridge, only to go over a cliff in the November fog, falling 100 feet onto rocks and bursting into flames. All perished dead, and their bodies were never found.

Even joggers trying to cross during snowstorms experienced strange forces. One man found himself running in place, unable to reach the other side. A gust of wind rolled him into a giant snowball, which he eventually broke free from before returning to his car safely.

The Emily Bridge remained a deadly, haunted landmark—one that warned everyone to stay away, especially after dark.

TWENTY TWO

THE JENNINGS MUSIC BUILDING
IN BENNINGTON, VERMONT

December 2026, around Christmas time, on the Bennington College campus. A school band was practicing Christmas songs in preparation for a concert in the Jennings Music Building auditorium. The building is a mansion with private rooms for band members to sleep before big shows. All the students were gone for Christmas vacation, and the band members and musicians stayed behind. The rooms in Jennings Music Hall were being rented like a hotel. The visitors would experience a rude awakening.

The rooms contained all antique furniture and had a working fireplace in each. During practice:

"Ladies and gentlemen, welcome to the Jennings Music Building on the Bennington College campus. The Vermont Choral Music Orchestra will be playing in the Jennings Hall Auditorium each night starting at the end of the week until December 22nd. My name is John J. Jennings. No, I am not the owner of this building—I am the music instructor for all the shows. After we finish practice, we will be assigned to our rooms, and we will continue practicing here in the music room before playing in the auditorium.

"This is not a dormitory; we are staying in a mansion located on a college campus. This mansion is a private hotel that holds private events. We have a restaurant and dining room, and a lounge with a large fireplace the size of the one in the Stanley Hotel. This mansion looks similar to the Stanley Hotel, but much smaller, and the grounds surrounding it are open fields covered in snow. No, we do not have a maze like the one in *The Shining*—just open snow-covered fields! Any questions?"

"Yes, Mr. Jennings: are there any ghosts here? This building looks like a haunted house!" said one man playing a trombone.

"I don't know. I guess we'll find out pretty soon, staying here for the first night," replied instructor John J. Jennings.

Late in the night, windows were opening and closing, and gas fireplaces started turning on and off. Some rooms were very warm, waking guests at three in the morning, and some were ice-cold. Doors opened and closed on their own, freaking guests out. Footsteps were heard, and guests felt as if someone was watching them, seeing shadow people in the empty halls late at night. Orbs of light flew around the rooms, and voices called, "Get out!" Strange voices were heard in rooms and hallways. Guests also heard instruments playing in the music room.

Instructor John Jennings woke up hearing music at 4 a.m. He got up and went to the music room, where he saw a piano playing by itself, a cello moving wildly, guitars strumming alone, bass, drums banging, and horns and trumpets playing on their own. The lights were blinking on and off, and thousands of orb lights flew around the music room, flashing in all kinds of colors. Then he saw shadow people playing the music—ghosts! John Jennings was terrified.

"In God's name, everything stop!" he shouted. He then turned all the lights off in the music room. Everything went dark, and the music stopped. When he turned the lights back on, the room was quiet. He turned the lights back off, shut the door, and locked it. He returned to bed at 5 a.m.

John would have stories to tell during practice the next day. Many music guests could not sleep due to the hauntings, shadow people sightings, and noises throughout the night. Some rooms were haunted, and some were not. Guests stayed together in the lounge because they were so scared. Orb lights flew around the lobby, and the desk manager, Arron Cole, kept clapping his hands, turning on lights, and making noise to try to make them go away. The time was 6:02 a.m. John slept with the lights on in his room. The hauntings stopped at sunrise.

At 8:30 a.m., all the musicians went to breakfast together and then returned to the practice room. John spoke to his group:

"Ladies and gentlemen, as you know, we have more company than just ourselves here. Last night, I heard music playing in this building and came down to see why you people were playing at 4 a.m. All the instruments were playing by themselves! I can't explain it. Then I saw a bunch of colorful lights, lots of them! At first, I thought something was put in my drink to make me hallucinate, like LSD. I never believed in ghosts before, but I experienced something I can't explain. The lights started flickering, and I saw what looked like spirits playing the music—you could see through them! I was freaking out. Arron Cole at the front desk told me the Jennings Music Building was haunted when I got up this morning. I slept with the lights on in my room. I had to yell at it to stop. I shut the lights off, and the music stopped. I turned the lights back on, then off, and locked the music room.

"We will need to find another place to sleep tonight because we can't stay here before someone gets hurt. Let's start practice until lunch, then find another hotel to stay in. We will continue to play here, but we must exit after dinner, before the hauntings begin when it gets dark."

The orchestra practiced until lunchtime. A black fog formed, crawling along the ceiling, but no one noticed while playing Christmas music. The orchestra stayed at a Holiday Inn in downtown Bennington. They returned to the Jennings Music Building only for dinner, then back to the Holiday Inn. No hauntings occurred there.

All the guests were forced out of the Jennings Music Building due to the hauntings. Desk manager Arron Cole was left alone in the building. Around 4 a.m., he heard noises but was used to them. At 4:02 a.m., he heard music playing in the music room, just like John Jennings had the night before. Arron went into the room, blowing a loud whistle, and the music stopped. He turned off the lights and locked the room.

The next day, the orchestra arrived at 7:30 a.m. for breakfast and practice in preparation for the Christmas show in the auditorium.

Showtime! The auditorium was packed. John Jennings spoke to the audience:

"Good evening, ladies and gentlemen. Welcome to the Jennings Music Building Christmas Music Show. My name is John J. Jennings. No, I don't own this building, thank God! I am the music instructor. Please welcome the Vermont Choral Music Christmas Orchestra. Enjoy the show, and Merry Christmas to everyone!"

The curtain opened, and the orchestra began playing: "Oh Holy Night," followed by "Jingle Bell Rock," "Jingle Bells," "Santa Claus is Coming to Town," "Frosty the Snowman," "Rudolph the Red-Nosed Reindeer," and "The Christmas Song."

Suddenly, a devilish black mist formed above the orchestra, with hands reaching out, grabbing arms. The mist entered the dark auditorium and disappeared. The crowd cheered, thinking it was part of the show.

Then hundreds of white orb lights began flying around the auditorium. The crowd remained unaware of the danger. The orbs started attacking people, setting them on fire. Flames spread across the seating area. The audience screamed and ran for the exits. The auditorium was engulfed in fire.

TWENTY THREE

THE BENNINGTON TRIANGLE

Bennington, Vermont. December 2026.

A car was driving on a dark, winding road, with light snow falling. The car drove for miles down the mountain-like road. The driver almost hit a raccoon the size of a large dog.

"Gary, you almost hit that poor animal," said Eileen.

"Eileen, I wasn't about to slam on my brakes in this slippery weather. We're on a mountain road with no railings. If I stop short, we could go off the road. If something runs in front of me and I can't stop, I'll run it over!"

A few minutes later, after driving about 13 miles, they found a gas station and country store. Gary pulled up to the pump to gas up and get directions while three kids sat in the back seat. Gas was $3.49 a gallon.

"Good evening, sir. I am looking for directions to the ONYX Lodge Ski Resort," said Gary.

The man in the country store, who was deaf and could not speak, showed Gary directions on his phone.

"How far is the ONYX Resort from here?" Gary asked.

The man showed him the distance on his phone again. Gary

paid for gas and some snacks for his three kids, then stormed out of the store, slamming the door. The deaf man waved goodbye. Gary threw chips, candy bars, and water into the back seat. The kids grabbed the snacks like a pack of hyenas attacking a fresh kill.

"The goddamn man in the store is deaf! He showed me directions on his phone, and I still have no idea where I'm going or how far this place is!" Gary exclaimed.

Gary drove another four miles. The weather worsened; it was all woods with nowhere to stop for directions. Rain, sleet, thunder, lightning, and snow battered the car as he drove uphill.

Then, a moose stood in the middle of the road, feeding on a dead animal—likely a raccoon. Gary stopped.

"You've got to be kidding! A moose in the middle of the road! Goddamn it!" he yelled.

The moose was bigger than Gary's car and started moving toward him, defecating and urinating in the road. Gary had to put the car in reverse to avoid being trampled.

"I don't believe this! This moose will not move!" Gary honked seven times, but the animal stayed.

"Gary, why don't we turn around and go home?" said Eileen.

"Eileen, I've driven 40 miles. We should be there soon once this goddamn moose gets out of my way!"

Finally, a snowplow struck the moose, sending it flying into the woods. Gary continued, cleaning the windshield of snow, slush, and moose excrement.

Then he saw a sign: CANADIAN BORDER 5 MILES AWAY.

"Eileen, Mary, Bobby, and Aden! I think we're going to make it! The ONYX Ski Resort is near Canada."

Gary drove through a whiteout, following the winding road. He hit black ice; the car went off the mountain, striking several rocks, burst into flames, and fell into a lake below. Everyone was killed, and the car and bodies were never found—joining other victims of the Bennington Triangle: cars sliding off mountains in snowstorms.

Bodies of drowning victims, like scenes from *What Lies Beneath*, lay on burnt car wrecks at the bottom of lakes. Skiers disappeared at resorts, campers went missing, UFO abductions were reported, Bigfoot creatures and grizzlies attacked camps and homes. Strange noises echoed from Glastenbury Mountain; hikers went missing, attacked by aliens, humanoid creatures, and giant Bigfoot-like monkeys.

Visions of ghosts, poltergeists, shadow people, and orb lights caused forest fires and destroyed homes, camps, and businesses. Vehicles fell off mountains in storms, fog rolled in, and heavy rain and snowstorms made travel dangerous. All of these occurrences happened in the Bennington Triangle.

June 2027, A couple, Jennifer and Joseph, drove down the same road Gary and Eileen had in December. Joseph pulled into the same gas station. The deaf man was gone. The gas was $3.19 a gallon.

Joseph entered the country store to pay. The cashier was a woman with long hair past her knees, huge ears, buck teeth, bulging eyes, and a nose like Pinocchio.

"My name is Vivian," she said.

"Vivian, I'm Joseph from West Bridgewater, Massachusetts. I need directions to the ONYX Hotel. And can you tell me where I am?"

"You're on Native American Lore Road in Bennington, Vermont. Take a left when you leave here and follow the winding road for about 45 miles until you reach Glastenbury. The ONYX Hotel and Resort is not far. You can't get lost—this road goes all the way to Canada. If you see a 'Canadian Border' sign, you've gone too far."

"Thank you, Vivian."

Joseph joked with his wife: "The woman inside that store looks like a humanoid. I wonder if we're in alien country!" Jennifer laughed.

Joseph drove to Glastenbury, stopping at a small breakfast place called *The Egg Depot*. They had pancakes with Vermont maple syrup, scrambled eggs, orange juice, and coffee.

They arrived at the ONYX Hotel and Resort at 3:02 p.m. on a sunny day, 72 degrees.

"Good afternoon, and welcome to the ONYX Hotel. My name is Carolyn Carpenter, the hotel receptionist," said Carolyn.

"Pleasure to meet you. I'm Joseph Frostbite, and this is my wife, Jennifer. We're from West Bridgewater, Massachusetts, checking in. Here's reservation #23 for three nights in the ONYX Suites."

"Okay, welcome. You'll be staying in Suite 1102, overlooking Mount Glastenbury and the lake. Your three-night stay is $960, including continental breakfast from 7:30 a.m. to 11 a.m. Check-in is at 4 p.m., and check-out is 11:30 a.m. on your third day. The bellhop will bring your luggage. Go past the dining room, gift shop, and mini-mall to reach the elevators. Tomorrow we have a ghost tour up the mountain; the bus leaves at 10 a.m. Enjoy your stay."

Their suite was beautiful, with mahogany furniture, leather couches, high lamps, French doors leading to the bedroom with a king-size canopy bed, two sinks, two toilets, a jacuzzi with gold faucets, a living room area, full kitchen, and a patio overlooking Mount Glastenbury.

After dinner, they met another couple, Mindy and Frank Hartford, and went to see a documentary: *The 4 Boy Scouts Abducted by Aliens*. The film described abductions, strange experiments, and alien acupuncture-like procedures. Joseph and Jennifer decided to join the hotel's ghost tour the next morning.

At 10:07 a.m., the ONYX Ghost Tour bus arrived. Tour guide Jwu Curry welcomed them aboard:

"Good morning, ladies and gentlemen! We're going up Mount

Glastenbury to visit ghost sites. Our first stop is the Lore Bridge Lookout. The pool below is deadly; currents sweep victims into hidden caves under the rapids. Hundreds of people have died here. Take pictures, but be careful. You have 15 minutes."

Next, the bus stopped at Lore Cemetery. Curry warned of sinkholes and ghost sightings:

"Visitors have disappeared here. Look closely; you might see a ghost even in the daytime. Next is the Lore Altar and Mary's Park. Shadow people and gray mists are often seen. Several exorcisms have been performed. The Lore Museum of the Dead contains spirits that can possess your soul—say prayers before entering. You have 30 minutes here."

The bus then ascended Glastenbury Mountain, with warnings about haunted walking trails. At the summit, there was a mini-mall, restaurants, and a McDonald's. The bus would return to the hotel at 5 p.m.

Joseph and Jennifer explored the trails, taking photos. They encountered wildlife, including a bear.

"Jennifer, just be still and don't run—the bear will go away!" Joseph whispered.

The bear retreated into the woods. They saw signs pointing back to the summit but kept getting lost. A storm rolled in, bringing thunder, lightning, hail, and heavy rain.

"Grab something to protect your head, Jennifer! We have to keep moving west to reach the bus!" Joseph yelled. They were ten miles from the summit with no cell service. Lightning struck trees, starting fires, forcing them to reroute.

Jennifer screamed hysterically.

"Jennifer, we don't have time to stop! We have ten minutes to reach the bus!"

The bus left at 6:37 p.m., and Frank and Mindy could not find Joseph and Jennifer. The couple spent three days trapped in the forest, hiding from wildlife: bears, moose, vultures, foxes, snakes, coyotes, wolves, and eagles. They had no food but plenty of rainwater.

One day, a large owl attacked, and Joseph killed it with a piece of wood. That night, a brown bear attacked and killed Joseph. Jennifer, trapped among a bear, a moose, and a ground vulture, was killed by the bear. Their bodies were never found.

Meanwhile, a car driver saw a giant ten-foot-tall Bigfoot blocking the road. After waiting 23 minutes, he tried to run it off the road. The Bigfoot scooped up the car, threw it off the mountain, and killed the occupants. Their bodies were never recovered.

A police officer saw a flying saucer while patrolling the Bennington Triangle. His car and lights failed. When he fired his gun, lasers from the UFO burned him alive. A helicopter sightseeing tour encountered a radiation cloud from UFOs, crashed, and burned, killing all aboard. The remains were consumed by animals and buried by Native Americans.

"That's what's here in the Bennington Triangle!"

ABOUT THE AUTHOR

Richard Rezendes worked at Brown University and the East Greenwich, Rhode Island school department before retiring at age of sixty-two. He likes sports, football, basketball, and baseball, in that order. He is a bowler tenpins and currently holds a 220 average. His dream was to one day publish a book, and he has since published nine—*Ground of the Devil: Book One, Ground of the Devil: Book Two, Ground of the Devil: Book Three, The Revelation of Emma Grace, A Haunting in Mattapoisett, Hell Under the United States, Windy Outbreaks, A Little Bit of Everything,* and *Hauntings in New England.*

www.richardrezendes.com
rezendes_richard@yahoo.com